RETURN OF THE SCOT

The Scots of Honor Series

ELIZA KNIGHT

ABOUT THE BOOK

Scarred by the brutal ravages of war, Lorne Gordon, Duke of Sutherland, returns to the Highlands to discover that his clan thought him long dead. His greedy half-brother has assumed his title, sold his family seat and disappeared with the fortune. Once he engineers the return of his title, he must convince the new estate owner to reverse the wholly legal sale with the promise that his half-brother, and the funds, will be found. However, that goal seems impossible when Lorne discovers the buyer is none other than his ex-betrothed's sister.

After several humiliating attempts at securing a husband, Jaime Andrewson gives up on marriage and throws herself into her father's business. She burns with vengeance towards the entire Sutherland family after their chieftain caused her sister's fall from grace. Although she'd thought the man who betrayed her sister was dead, acquiring his property had been her main goal since taking over her father's company. But with Lorne Gordon alive, vengeance is all the sweeter, for she desires only to watch him suffer.

Despite Lorne's fury, he has to find a way to convince her to return what is rightfully his—even if he has to go so far as to marry her. Though out of practice with the arts of flirtation, there is one thing he does not lack—determination. With his pockets empty and a snarl on his lips, Lorne is determined to win her trust and her hand. When unexpected family secrets on both sides are exposed, Lorne realizes that wooing Jaime will be a bigger challenge than any of the other battles he's ever fought, but it is one he refuses to lose.

MORE BOOKS BY ELIZA KNIGHT

Scots of Honor

Return of the Scot
The Scot is Hers
Taming the Scot

Prince Charlie's Rebels

The Highlander Who Stole Christmas
Pretty in Plaid

Prince Charlie's Angels

The Rebel Wears Plaid
Truly Madly Plaid
You've Got Plaid

The Sutherland Legacy

The Highlander's Gift

The Highlander's Quest
The Highlander's Stolen Bride
The Highlander's Hellion
The Highlander's Secret Vow
The Highlander's Enchantment

The Stolen Bride Series

The Highlander's Temptation
The Highlander's Reward
The Highlander's Conquest
The Highlander's Lady
The Highlander's Warrior Bride
The Highlander's Triumph
The Highlander's Sin
Wild Highland Mistletoe (a Stolen Bride winter novella)
The Highlander's Charm (a Stolen Bride novella)
A Kilted Christmas Wish – a contemporary Holiday spin-off
The Highlander's Surrender
The Highlander's Dare

The Conquered Bride Series

Conquered by the Highlander
Seduced by the Laird
Taken by the Highlander (a Conquered bride novella)
Claimed by the Warrior
Stolen by the Laird
Protected by the Laird (a Conquered bride novella)
Guarded by the Warrior

The MacDougall Legacy Series

Laird of Shadows

Laird of Twilight
Laird of Darkness

Pirates of Britannia: Devils of the Deep

Savage of the Sea
The Sea Devil
A Pirate's Bounty

THE THISTLES AND ROSES SERIES

Promise of a Knight
Eternally Bound
Breath from the Sea

The Highland Bound Series (Erotic time-travel)

Behind the Plaid
Bared to the Laird
Dark Side of the Laird
Highlander's Touch
Highlander Undone
Highlander Unraveled

Touchstone Series

Highland Steam
Highland Brawn
Highland Tryst
Highland Heat

Wicked Women

Her Desperate Gamble
Seducing the Sheriff
Kiss Me, Cowboy

HISTORICAL FICTION

Releasing Early 2022
The Mayfair Bookshop

Releasing 2023
The Other Astaire

Tales From the Tudor Court

My Lady Viper
Prisoner of the Queen

Ancient Historical Fiction

A Day of Fire: a novel of Pompeii
A Year of Ravens: a novel of Boudica's Rebellion

French Revolution

Ribbons of Scarlet: a novel of the French Revolution

June 2021

Cover Design by Dar Albert

Edited by Erica Monroe

August 1816
Scottish Highlands

Despite exhaustion racking his body in aching shudders, Lorne Gordon, Duke of Sutherland and Chief of the Sutherlands, forced his spine to straighten as he sat in the saddle. A bone-deep weariness left him in desperate need of a respite he was certain not to receive. But he could not miss a single familiar tree or boulder as his mind sifted through years of growth to uncover what he'd once known.

Dawn had come and gone over three thousand times since Lorne had stepped foot in his own country. Nearly a third of those days, he'd wondered if he'd ever see home again. While the road from London had been long, the journey from France felt like a lifetime.

Thick layers of dust coated his skin and clothes. No doubt

anyone that saw him would mistake him for a lowly beggar, rather than the powerful man he'd once been.

To say the last two years had been a living hell would be an understatement. Every day had been torment, and if Lorne never had to think of those harrowing moments again, he'd be a happy man. Unfortunately, every time he shut his eyes, night terrors consumed him, disallowing him the freedom to forget.

And neither would the War Office, who sought to press charges against someone, anyone, for Lorne's unlawful imprisonment abroad after the Peninsular War. The War Office had kept him for days, questioning him until he was hoarse, more concerned with their enemies than with his welfare, which he understood. This was the way of things with war, but he'd wanted to get the hell out of there.

Lorne crested another hill, drawing in a deep lungful of crisp Highland air and letting it out in a long whoosh, driving some of his angst away with it. Beneath him, his mount shuddered, as tired as him. They'd ridden hard the last few days once they'd reached the Highlands.

His journey home had been a little longer because of his refusal to trade out his mount, but he couldn't imagine parting with the animal. The horse had been given to him by the War Office a scant week ago, but…it had been so long since he'd had any sort of connection with anyone—human or beast alike—that he couldn't let the animal go. The steed was the first personal possession he'd had in nigh unto two years.

If they weren't so close to home, if he weren't so desperate for familiar walls and people, he would have set up camp and resumed again in the morning. But the turrets of his magnificent Dunrobin Castle came into view, beckoning him to make the last couple of miles home.

Home.

Finally.

Lorne dismounted, coming to his knees upon the grass he'd tramped as a child. He pressed his palms flat to the ground. Softer, warmer than he remembered. The sweet scents of heather and grass. He touched the soft strands of the meadow, threading his fingers through it, and bent to kiss the earth with grasses tickling his lips, breathing in the clean scent of the Highlands. As his eyes closed against the sting, emotions welled in his chest.

No gunpowder residue or the stench of blood. No dank, stale air. No death. This was his place. His heaven.

He could have stretched out flat, sunk into this earth and thanked every deity known to man for being here again. For he'd not thought it possible. Not when he was chained to a wall...or strapped to a chair while they...Lorne shuddered. For as long as he lived, France would be synonymous with the devil.

He cleared his throat and pushed back onto his aching feet. The boots he wore were much too tight. Lorne was not a small man, and none of the extra boots at the War Office had come close to his size.

As much as he wanted to continue to enjoy this moment, it was time to finish his journey. Time to close the gap of time that had passed since he'd left nearly eight years before.

Giving his horse a break from carrying his weight, Lorne walked the rest of the way, until he came to the gate at the head of the long road leading toward the castle. He touched the cool wrought iron metal with his gilded crest in the middle, still disbelieving that he'd made it. The castle turrets rose high in the sky, and even from here, he could make out the fleur-de-lis and carved knights in the stone.

"Lo, there!" the gatekeeper called.

Lorne jerked his gaze up, forcing himself not to cower at the sharp surprise of the man's shout. A head poked out from the top of the tower gate.

Then a curse escaped the man's lips as he tossed off his feathered woolen cap, revealing ginger hair and thrust himself over the parapet so hard Lorne feared he'd dive right off. "Your Grace! Is it ye? Do my eyes deceive me?" The guard made the sign of the cross.

Lorne could have cried at hearing the familiar voice of his childhood friend, to have recognized a much beloved face. "Mungo, 'tis I. Open the gate for me."

Mungo let out a lengthy tirade of mumbled Gaelic Lorne couldn't discern, but the gate did open, and kilt-clad clansmen rushed through beside Mungo, their swords clinking against their boot spurs, each of them muttering prayers and crossing themselves.

"How is this possible?" Mungo said, reaching out to touch him and then yanking back as though he might be burned. "We were told ye were dead."

Having been warned of this in London, Lorne was not surprised at the news. He gripped his old friend on the shoulder and squeezed, a smile stretching wide across his face. "I assure ye I'm verra much alive and in need of a bath, a bed and a hot meal."

"Aye, Your Grace." Mungo glanced at the other men, and a silent message passed between them. "Come, we'll get ye settled." He signaled for the gates to close and called up for another man to take watch as they led Lorne down the road.

One of them tried to take the reins from Lorne, but he held them tight, barely suppressing a growl. At the man's startled expression, Lorne laughed it off and reluctantly let go. He was home. His men could be trusted.

Mungo let out a tirade of queries, which Lorne barely answered. Instead, he picked up his speed, questioning what the men would think if he tore off his boots and ran inside. But he didn't want his homecoming to be any more awkward than it already would be, so he remained walking at a steady pace and ignored the increasing pinches in his toes.

As people came out to see who walked with Mungo, a whisper like the buzz of bees passed over the wind. Mungo waved away anyone who came near, thank goodness, and the men rushed ahead to open the wide, arched door. When they entered the castle, hurried footsteps sounded in the corridor from the left and then Mrs. Blair, not looking a day older than when he'd left, burst into the entryway. His housekeeper took one glance of him, blanched as white as a sheet and then dropped in a heavy faint to the floor.

"Blimey!" Lorne jerked forward to check on her. White wisps of hair framed her face, and on closer look, the lines beside her eyes and mouth had deepened.

"'Tis like she saw a ghost," Mungo jested beside him.

Lorne gave him a wry glance and lifted his housekeeper into his arms. "Carry her to the drawing room," he said to the two men who'd accompanied them.

"There is something ye should know, my laird." Mungo avoided his gaze, watching the men take the woman from Lorne's arms, having to share the weight, where he had strength enough yet to hold her himself.

"Aye?"

Mungo looked as though he'd eaten a pot of spoiled mutton. "As I mentioned afore, the clan, they thought ye were dead."

Lorne ignored the painful prick in his heart. He removed his cap, sat down on the stairs and started to pluck at his boot laces—to hell with waiting for his chamber.

"Lord Gille, he assumed the role as duke and chief."

"Naturally," Lorne said tightly, tugging off one boot and biting his cheek to keep from moaning at the uncomfortable restriction being removed. He glanced around the grand entrance to the castle, searching out his half-brother Gille and not seeing him. 'Haps he was visiting a crofter or working in the fields as Lorne had often done.

"Well, he..." But Mungo didn't continue. He pinched his cap and twirled it round and round while his gaze landed anywhere but on Lorne.

Mungo's gaze shifted warily to the place above Lorne's head. Forgetting his other boot, Lorne followed Mungo's line of vision to the place behind him. He gaped at the empty spot on the wall where the sword of his ancestor, who had fought beside William Wallace and Robert the Bruce, used to hang. The artifact had been there so long that there was still an outline of its placement, a faint shadow shouting of something being amiss. "Out with it, Mungo." His voice shook.

"The castle...Gille...he took it, and—" Mungo sounded as if he were suffering an apoplectic fit.

Lorne suppressed the urge to smack the words out of Mungo's mouth and instead tore off his second boot.

Finally, his old mate spoke, "He sold the castle. And the property surrounding it."

Lorne snorted and plucked off his sock, wriggling his toes, reddened from the tightness of his boots. "That is a cruel jest, Mungo. If ye're attempting to make me laugh, ye might want to try a little harder."

Mungo stopped twirling the hat. "I assure ye, Your Grace, I am no' jesting, and it is the verra last thing I want to tell ye upon your homecoming, but it had to be done before ye settled in."

Lorne felt his throat close up tight as the truth of what Mungo was saying sunk in. Gille had sold the castle? Sold his land? The very stairs he was sitting on right at that moment were not his own?

It was an effort to speak, and when he did, his voice came out sounding strangled, far-off. "Where is Gille?"

"We do no' know."

"How long has he been gone?" Lorne stood, tossing his hose aside and placing his hands on his hips, so he didn't grab Mungo by his shirt.

"A few weeks now. Since the sale."

"Has anyone attempted to locate him?"

Mungo shook his head. "Nay, Your Grace, as we thought he'd abandoned us…"

Lorne nodded, speechless. The castle, the lands—all of which had been in his family for generations dating back to Scotland's first kings—were no longer his. No longer a Sutherland holding. He was the bloody Duke of Sutherland and didn't have a castle?

Was he a pauper now, too? What other reason could Gille have had to sell the property than for want of money? A vein pulsed in his temple as he wondered about the fate of his other properties and the fortune he'd left behind. Lorne closed his eyes to breathe in deep. This was not the homecoming he'd expected, not by half.

But at least he was in his home country. As bad as this news was, it didn't compare to the hell of France. And he had the freedom to undo what his idiot half-brother had wrecked.

"We'll fix this." Lorne gritted his teeth. "I'll fix this. Send for my solicitor in Edinburgh. Immediately."

"Aye, Your Grace. Right away."

"And ready a bath in my chamber. Or is that also no longer mine? Dear God, is the new owner here?"

Mungo thankfully shook his head.

"We'll make up another room for ye right away for your bath and then prepare your chamber for tonight." Mrs. Brody, roused from her faint, came toward him. She'd been the castle's housekeeper for as long as he could remember, ever since he was a bairn. Since Lorne was motherless, Mrs. Brody had stepped in to clean up his scrapes. She touched his cheek, squinting as she stared into his eyes. "Is it really ye?"

"Aye." He smiled softly, feeling emotion tighten his throat.

She nodded, pressed her lips together, and blinked away the tears that had gathered in her eyes. "Welcome home, Your Grace. We're all happy to have ye back."

Lorne cleared his throat, standing tall and glancing at the people he loved most, there in support of him. "Thank ye, Mrs. Brody. Mungo. Everyone. Ye've no idea how much I've longed for this moment. Albeit under different circumstances." He let out a short laugh, trying to lighten the mood.

"As have we all. Lassies," Mrs. Brody clapped her hands, "a bath for the master and a hot meal." She glanced behind him. "And dredge up some of his old clothes that Gille had sent to the attics."

Gille had his things removed? Of course, he had. Gille had thought him dead. That still didn't explain what possessed his brother to abandon their heritage. Nor did it explain what had happened while Lorne had been gone.

Shortly, he would get to the bottom of this predicament. As the people around him moved in swarms, the exhaustion he'd felt on the road swooped in tenfold, and he gripped the wall to keep from swaying.

Mrs. Brody ushered him up the stairs and into a guest chamber. He could only assume that Gille had taken his room —well, the new master now, he supposed. And just as well. He couldn't blame his half-brother for believing him dead, for assuming the title and taking what he thought was rightfully his.

But he did blame him for selling their birthright. For absconding with the ancient sword that belonged to Lorne.

Gille had always been jealous of him. Once in a fit of rage, he'd mentioned that he no longer wanted to be in Lorne's shadow. The comment had confused Lorne, for he'd always considered his brother to be his close confidante, despite there being five years between them.

8

When Lorne was a wee lad, his mother passed from a fever and his father had remarried a bonny lass—Catharine. She'd been sweet and kind to him, and Lorne had loved her. But she'd died soon after birthing Gille, and their father never remarried, often lamenting that two wives gone in half a decade only meant a third would also be sent to an early grave.

Lorne walked to the window and glanced out over the back garden and the sea beyond. The beach where he'd played with his brother, taught him to swim. To skip rocks. Despite their having different mothers, Lorne had always considered Gille to be his full brother. Loved him as such.

"Thank ye, Mrs. Brody."

"Och, but there is no need to thank me, Your Grace."

Lorne glanced over his shoulder at the older woman, who fretted with the corner of the bedspread.

"I thank ye all the same."

She opened her mouth and closed it several times before saying, "Well, 'tis my duty, that's all. I'm just grateful ye're alive and have returned."

Lorne grinned and turned back toward the garden and the lush maze he and his brother had raced through countless times. The same maze where he'd first kissed a lass... Beside it was a graveyard full of beloved animals. Gille had begged their father to bury his favorite dog there, right beside the warhorse their father had taken into battle. The memories made his heart twinge. When at one time it had been the three of them against the world, now he was the only one left standing in this castle that was no longer his.

Where the hell are ye, Gille?

It was hard to imagine that this was what Gille wanted. That he could be so filled with hurt and anger, he would want to leave it all behind.

When their da died in a hunting accident three years

prior to Lorne leaving for France, he'd asked Gille to work with him on maintaining their holdings. To be a part of the clans' daily processes, the judgments. But Gille wanted nothing to do with any of it.

Instead, his brother became quite adept at racking up gambling debts and had a string of scorned lovers, along with their angry fathers, knocking down Lorne's door. Lorne had done his best to keep them all appeased. Paid off debts. Got his brother out of many a scrape.

Lorne finally had to draw a line, hoped that taking Gille in hand would bring the man to some sense. But his plan backfired. When a local lord had come to claim the coin Gille lost at Edinburgh's gambling tables, Lorne had denied the payment, and his brother had been arrested. Lorne could still hear him shouting, "I'll never forgive ye for this. Ye've betrayed me. A curse on ye! Ye're no brother of mine!"

Lorne had ignored the words of an angry lad. But perhaps he should have listened. He hoped his actions would have taught his wayward brother a lesson, that he would return to Dunrobin a new man, a matured young lord. That was not the case, it seemed.

Was this Gille's revenge—getting rid of what he knew Lorne loved?

A bevy of servants carried in a large tub, then poured bucket upon bucket of steaming water inside. Mungo remained behind to assist in his bath, but Lorne sent him away. He wasn't ready yet to reveal the scars on his body from his suffering. Over the weeks, the bruises had faded. His tormentors had been kind in leaving him with all his fingers, toes and teeth, but they'd not been so kind in other ways.

Lorne tossed off his clothes and climbed into the tub. He leaned his head back on the rim. The last time he had a warm bath might have been the last time he was home—two years shy of a decade, when it had felt as if his world was falling apart. The very reason he'd accepted his commission overseas. A time he preferred not to remember.

A soft knock interrupted his darkening thoughts. Mungo entered, carrying a tray of food that smelled as though it had come straight from the king's finest chef. He set the food on the table, then handed Lorne a cup smelling of spirits.

"Nay, thank ye," Lorne said, pushing the liquor away, even as he sank deeper into the water to keep his scars hidden.

"Drink. It'll make hearing the truth no' sting as much."

Lorne didn't have the energy to argue. He downed the dram in one swallow. "What else do ye have to say, Mungo?"

"As I mentioned, Gille sold the castle." Mungo moved to the far wall, leaning against the stones outlining the window.

"My hearing is just fine." Lorne massaged his temples.

"He has also absconded with the funds, my laird."

Lorne gritted his teeth, having surmised as much. "Has he sold my other holdings as well?"

"I'm no' certain, but your solicitor will be able to tell ye more. I've already sent a man to summon him."

"Who owns my castle?" Lorne bit out, imagining some pompous windbag coming in and desecrating the place that had been in his family for generations.

"J. Andrewson, my laird."

Andrewson. Lorne tried to hide how startled he was at hearing the name, but water sloshed over the side of the tub. It fell into the grooves between the wooden planks of the floor in long, wet lines. Was his past coming back to haunt him—or was it just a coincidence?

"That is a common name, is it no'?" Lorne asked hopefully.

"Aye, Your Grace. I've a cousin in Edinburgh by that name."

"No' J?" Lorne asked, half-jesting.

"No relation, I swear it."

So, it was possible it did not belong to that family of which he did not want to think about, the one he'd separated himself from, though he hated the coincidence of it.

"When does Mr. Andrewson take residence?"

"He has no' said, sir. But he did mention we could stay in the meantime."

Lorne jerked forward, hands on the rim of the tub, as he met Mungo's gaze. "Does that mean there is an expiration date on everyone's occupancy? That I am at his mercy, accepting charity from a stranger?"

"There were no specifics." Mungo glanced toward his boots. "But some of the clan have already found work with relations, and others are making preparations. The clan is worried, my laird. I'd no' wanted to tell ye this so soon after ye've returned, but I did no' think it could wait."

"Ye're right. I will write to Mr. Andrewson straight away. Fetch me paper, ink and quill."

"Aye, Your Grace."

Mungo headed for the door, but Lorne stopped him. "I will fix this."

"I have no doubt."

"Tell everyone no' to...worry."

"I will. We trust ye. And know that ye have only to ask anything of us, and we'll see it done."

As soon as Mungo was gone, Lorne dried off and dressed. He'd not worn a plaid in years, and the feel of being unrestricted on his legs was a welcome comfort to the tight breeches he'd worn when confined. The shirt, however, was snug nearly everywhere and made up for the comfort of his kilt exponentially.

Mungo came back with the writing implements as Lorne was finishing up his food and downing a mug of ale.

"Do we have a new cook?"

"Nay, Your Grace."

"Huh," he mused. "Well, send my compliments."

"Aye, I will. Will there be anything else?"

"Join me." He indicated the empty chair opposite him. "There's plenty here for us both."

Mungo looked as if he was about to hesitate. "Master Gille did no'…"

"I am no' my brother, and whatever heinous acts he wrought on ye, on anyone else, can no' have erased how I treated ye in the past. I might be a duke, but that does no' mean I'm no' one of ye. Ye're my oldest friend, Mungo. Sit. Drink. Tell me what I have missed, besides my…" He couldn't quite bring himself to mutter the word "brother" anymore. Not when Gille had done just about the worst thing Lorne could think of. "Besides the most recent shift of ownership, which I will soon rectify."

While Mungo spoke about the thriving crops, the new pier on their beach giving them access to the North Sea and the marriages and deaths that Lorne had missed, he imagined the many ways in which he'd surprise his half-brother. The dangerous smile he'd flash at Gille. The way he'd like to take his sgian dubh from his long sock and use it to peel back the skin from Gille's arms slowly. How he'd flick the flesh to rabid dogs if any were near.

When his bloodlust seemed mostly quenched, then he imagined what he'd say to Mr. Andrewson to convince him that reversing the sale without the funds readily available to compensate him would be in the man's best interest. That part proved harder to imagine than the many ways he would torture Gille for his treachery.

"Then we discovered the sword gone," Mungo said, and Lorne realized he'd missed what the man had been talking about.

"Why would he take it?"

"We all thought to put at his new residence."

But Lorne didn't believe it. Nay, his brother wanted to make sure his betrayal hit Lorne hard. Selling the family seat was a knife to the throat, but stealing the family relic was twisting that knife. But that didn't make sense because, at the time, as far as everyone knew, Lorne was dead.

Lorne gritted his teeth. He'd left one hell only to fall into another.

2

One week later
Edinburgh, Scotland

J aime leapt to her feet at the sound of a knock at the door, followed by her butler entering the drawing room.

"Miss Andrewson, pardon my interruption."

"Aye, MacInnes?" She wiped at her lips to make certain she didn't have any stray crumbs.

"There is a gentleman here to see ye, my lady. He has asked me to give ye this." He held out a silver tray with a crisp white envelope on it, addressed to "Sir Jaime Andrewson."

Sir? She rolled her eyes. It wouldn't be the first time some ignoramus thought her to be a man.

"He does no' know I'm a woman?"

"Nay, miss, and given he did no', I have yet to correct him."

Thank heavens for small favors. "What would I do without ye?"

MacInnes nodded, his lips twitching into the only grin he'd give her. The man had been with her family since she was a lass, and she looked up to him as though he were an uncle rather than her servant.

She took the envelope, running her thumb over what looked like a hastily scrawled script.

"Shall I wait for your reply?"

Jaime hesitated. "He is downstairs?"

"Aye. "

"Please wait, then." Breaking the unstamped seal, Jaime pulled out a card that said "Lorne Gordon, Duke of Sutherland."

"Impossible." Jaime swayed on her feet, grabbing the back of a chair to steady herself. She lifted her gaze to MacInnes. "Did ye recognize him? Or is it an imposter?"

MacInnes nodded. "'Tis the former Duke of Sutherland. Well, the rightful duke, I suppose."

"How?"

"A miracle?" MacInnes kept his face blank of any expression.

"There is no such thing as miracles. Men do no' die and come back to life, MacInnes. He was never dead. The entire thing has been a great farce played on all of England and Scotland, which I would no' put past him, given his propensity for falsehoods."

MacInnes did not answer but patiently waited as she resumed her pacing, the card crumpled in her fist.

He was supposed to be dead.

Jaime stared down at the letter in her trembling hand, trying not to toss it into the fire.

How in Hades could a dead man be paying her a call?

Why now? Dead for two years, and just as she was about

to complete what she'd been working toward, he'd decided to show his face.

Oh, dear heavens—had her sister run into him? Jaime had gifted her sister and nephew Dunrobin Castle a week or so ago, and they'd left right away, though she still held the deed in a locked drawer in her office. Had poor Shanna been subjected to a specter? Was that why her sister had failed to report on the castle in the Highlands? She'd sworn to write Jaime as soon as they arrived. That had been days ago.

Jaime paced her drawing room, certain she would wear a path into the beautiful silk Persian rug in light blue, gold and rose medallions.

Lorne Gordon, the Duke of Sutherland—former duke—alive? No. His title had been given to his half-brother upon his death. She'd read all about it in The Edinburgh Advertiser. The only Duke of Sutherland was Gille Gordon.

There had been some kind of mistake. Lorne was supposed to be dead. She scoffed.

This was a cruel trick. A scam from someone jealous of her. Someone who wanted her out of the way, perhaps to sabotage all she'd worked for these past years. MacInnes was getting older; his eyes must have deceived him.

Without a doubt, purchasing the Highland castle had been about revenge. Revenge against a dead man who'd scorned her family. She'd felt satisfaction in holding the deed to his home. Despite her motivation, the move had brought about something else—her plans to build a great port in the north to expand the Andrewson shipping company.

So why did she feel so awful right now?

Wasn't revenge supposed to feel better than this? It was supposed to leave a gleaming satisfaction that rippled through the veins and a permanent smile on the face of the victor.

Scowling, Jaime marched over to her teacup and sipped.

Drat, it had gone cold. She set her teacup down and stared out the window overlooking the city of Edinburgh. The day was overcast, but she could still see a parade of noble ladies taking constitutionals in Charlotte's Square. Aye, perhaps it would have been better for Jaime to have her residence near the Port of Leith, closer to her father's—nay her—shipping company.

But why should she not be in the center of high society? New Town was all the rage for those who thought themselves too good for everyone else. And Jaime took a perverse pleasure in snubbing her nose at those of the Scottish ton. How dare they tell her she did not belong? Now, here she was in a house sought after by many, she being the highest bidder.

Her walls were papered in robin's egg blue silk with silver-trimmed flowers in a deep rose, and the crystal chandeliers sparkled when they caught the light. The furniture was the most fashionable, and the walls were covered with artwork that she'd slowly acquired since she'd learned the value of a fine piece as a girl of thirteen. Her cook was the finest in Scotland, her servants discreet, and her butler served as a faithful bodyguard.

And yet, profound loneliness still filled her.

With Shanna and Gordie no longer here, and her parents passing years ago, the house was very quiet. Jaime herself had never married. Not for lack of her mother and father trying to attach her to a man. But she always had a troublesome time with the opposite sex. Her mother's attempts at seeing her married at the appropriate age were humiliating, at best. With a sharp tongue, a desire to be independent and a mind for business, Jaime was not a prime catch for men looking for a fashionably docile wife.

When her father passed away, leaving her in control of Andrewson Shipping Company, Jaime threw herself enthusiastically into the business.

And now, appreciating the freedom she had, Jaime had chosen not to marry, even if there had been more interest from the rougher sex after her sudden influx of wealth and her assumption of power over the shipping company.

If they didn't want her before, why should she give them the time of day now? It wasn't as if her personality had changed. They weren't worth her time. Marriage and children would not be her legacy; instead, her contribution to society would be the company, which she would one day leave to her nephew, Gordie.

After wearing another side of her rug down to the weave, a lemon tart beckoned, and Jaime forced herself to sit a moment and take a delicate bite if only to absorb herself in a moment of deliciousness. Frowning, she set it back on the plate, the usual clashing flavors of sweet with sour dull on her tongue.

Maybe revenge would have felt better if the man she was seeking her vengeance on had not suddenly come back to life —as though he were haunting her for having managed to purchase his birthright.

Hopefully, her sister kept the castle gates locked if and when the duke decided to return to his holding.

Jaime would not be bullied into parting with the property. That had to be the only reason he was here. All of the papers were in order. According to the War Office, Lorne Gordon had died. He'd made certain they thought so, and in his irresponsible absence, his brother had been desperate enough to sell the castle. According to Gille, Lorne had run the family's funds and properties into the ground. There had been no other choice but to sell to save the other properties and the clan from starvation and utter ruin.

"Miss, I can send him away if ye wish."

"Aye." She paused, then shook her head. "Nay. If ye send him away, he will only come back."

MacInnes gave a curt nod.

To hell with the duke. No one would tell her what to do. Not even a duke come back from the dead. Jaime was a free woman. A wealthy woman. And she could do whatever she pleased. Including buying a castle and its surrounding lands. Which she'd done.

Lorne Gordon could not waltz into her drawing room and demand she return it. And she wouldn't, even if he offered double the money. Because buying his castle had not been about money or the ownership of a grand estate. It had been about something much deeper. Besides running the family company, one other thing had filled Jaime's days the past nine years—a burning vengeance toward the Sutherland clan.

Perhaps there was a silver lining to the duke's return— this would make her vengeance all the sweeter, for she desired only to watch him suffer.

Jaime moved toward the window and stared down at the street below. A carriage waited outside her house, black and shiny with the duke's gilded crest on the side. All of New Town would be talking about his visit before high tea could be cleared. "Send him up, please."

She waited nervously, listening to the sound of footsteps beyond the door, and when they came, she was still shocked to see the tall, brooding figure of Lorne Gordon filling the doorway.

Lorne Gordon, living and breathing—seeming to suck all of the air from the room.

He looked taller than she remembered from a decade ago. Broader. Most definitely broader and with an air of danger about him that elicited a rush in her blood. He was elegantly dressed in a kilt of green and blue, a white muslin shirt, crisp cravat, green waistcoat and tailcoat to match. Cream-colored wool socks came up to his knees, and his feet were clad in polished leather shoes. Compared to the merchants, sailors and businessmen she dealt with daily, this man cut a distracting and—dare she even think it—dashing figure. Heat flooded her face, and her belly welcomed a swarm of bees to zoom about, making Jaime feel as if she were crawling out of her skin.

Dark hair swept over his brow. While she normally preferred a man that was cleaner cut, neat and tidy, the instant attraction she found to his wild look had her mouth going dry in both shock and dismay. Murky gray eyes, the color of aged steel, locked onto her face and widened with surprise. Elegantly arched brows rose, and a frown creased the corners of his full lips.

How was it possible she was still standing when her knees felt so weak? Oh, bother, she couldn't care! She could not allow wayward thoughts or idiotic physical impulses to sway her decision to see him suffer.

Lorne glanced at MacInnes when her butler spoke.

"Miss Andrewson, allow me to present His Grace, the Duke of Sutherland."

"Thank ye, MacInnes. Would ye care for some tea, Your Grace?" she asked.

Lorne stared at her, speechless it would appear, and to be honest, she wasn't certain how she was finding the strength to inquire about his interest in a drink. Without waiting for him to respond—which from the looks of it, he might never—she said to her butler, "Tea, please."

"Right away, miss." MacInnes bowed to the duke, backed from the room and shut the door quietly.

Lorne cleared his throat, shifting on his feet as he worried the bottom of his waistcoat.

"Miss Andrewson, have we met before?"

Jaime was proud of herself for not blanching at his question. The ridiculousness and preposterousness of his query made her want to scream. Instead, she folded her hands in front of her and met his gaze head-on, refusing to be cowed as any other woman might have been in the presence of a duke.

"We have." She did not elaborate.

Firm lips pressed together as he nodded, crossing into the room some more but still looking quite out of place. Uncomfortable, even, in his skin.

"Please have a seat." She swept her hand toward the finely brocaded silver-and-yellow wingback chairs.

He looked as though he would hesitate but then stepped cautiously forward and sat. Dear heavens... The man filled what she'd thought was a large chair, making it appear as though it were made for a toddler. Pretending she wasn't so affected by his presence, Jaime took the chair opposite him, perching on the edge of it and miraculously keeping her hands from trembling.

"What can I do for ye, Your Grace?"

He narrowed his eyes, obviously not one for having to voice his desires. "I'm certain ye know."

She gave a dainty shrug, flicked at an invisible piece of lint on her skirt. "Why do ye no' tell me?"

His sudden shift forward had her narrowing her eyes. Was he trying to make her feel uncomfortable? Scared even? Clearly, he didn't know who he was dealing with.

"Ye know verra well what I've come for."

Jaime's heart did a little skip, and suddenly, she found the silk walls of the room a bit too constrictive. What she wouldn't have given to blow the roof off her townhouse and feel the cool air wash over her skin.

"I'm afraid if what ye've come for is the deed to your castle, I can no' oblige ye." Fabulous! Her voice did not waver at all. Soon, she'd be rid of this man—and the twisting in her belly.

Lorne's teeth pulled back in a momentary snarl before

softening into a smile. The man had amazing control of his temper; she would give him that.

"What do ye want, Miss Andrewson?"

"What I want, I already possess."

"What else do ye want?"

As if she'd divulge that to a virtual stranger and one she loathed to boot. She smoothed a hand over the skirts of her pale blue gown. "I can no' be bought."

"Everyone has a price."

"I do no'."

"We shall see." Suddenly he stood, towering over her.

Jaime craned her neck, marveling at the way his eyes pierced through her, but as quickly, he walked toward her window to look down below. There was a tension in his shoulders she found unnerving and alluring all at once. The urge to massage the rigidity away was intense.

Guilt riddled her. This was a man she hated. A man who had done her family wrong. Brought shame upon them. How could she possibly look at him with anything but disgust?

MacInnes reappeared with a second tray of tea, a serving lass behind him removing the set she'd been sipping before her unwanted guest arrived.

"Thank ye, MacInnes," Jaime said, nodding when he gave her a look that asked if she was all right. Turning back to the rogue by the window, she asked, "Would ye care for some tea, Your Grace, or perhaps ye'd like to crawl back into whatever grave ye climbed out of?"

Her voice sounded jovial, welcoming, the opposite of how she truly felt. She hated this man. Had hated him for quite some time. If she had a vial of poison, she would likely pour it into his tea before serving it to make certain he died and stayed dead this time.

Lorne turned around, his expression blank as he eyed her and the cup of tea she held out.

"I did no' come for tea, Miss Andrewson. I came for my castle, and ye well know it. Return the deed, reverse the sale, and I'll be on my way."

Jaime stood frozen, afraid the trembling in her hands would translate into the tinkling of the cup against the saucer. Quickly, she set the service down, folded her hands in front of her and fixed a stare on him not unlike what she used for the shipyard men. The true Duke of Sutherland was leaking out of his cleverly disguised ruse. While she'd not had much interaction with him nearly a decade before, she'd heard enough, knew enough, to ascertain exactly what type of person he was.

"I see being dead has done nothing for your manners or incredibly selfish nature, Your Grace. But might I remind ye that ye're standing in my house, and I am no' one of your servants, nor a subject suffocated by feudal codes. I am a successful businesswoman, one who has had the forethought and money to purchase your property. I am no' interested in selling it back to ye. I am no' interested in negotiating. What I am interested in is ye taking your leave." Jaime drew in a deep breath through her nose and slowly let it out as the man standing before transformed from one of complete confidence and scorn to utter shock.

The moments ticked by as they stared at one another. Sweat started to accumulate on her spine. Oh, she couldn't stand it any longer. If he didn't speak, she was going to leap out of her skin.

Jaime went to the bell pull, her hand upon the rope, when his voice, filled with misery, stopped her.

"Miss Andrewson, please."

3

L orne was not a beggar.

Never in his life had he pleaded with anyone.

Not even when he'd been held prisoner. He hadn't entreated his captors for mercy. Lorne was a warrior. Bashing his head against anyone who came near, fighting until they knocked him out. Rebelling until the day he escaped.

So, what in the bloody hell was he thinking, beseeching the harpy standing a few feet from him?

Momentarily stunned by his request, by her beauty, Lorne couldn't form a single sentence. She stared at him with wide brown eyes, the color of freshly turned peat. Even though her chestnut hair was pulled into a tight bun at her nape, he could see the subtle threads of auburn and gold, practically feel the softness. There was not a trace of the lass she'd been when he'd known her sister. If he had to guess, he would have said she was not the same person. That someone was playing a trick on him, but the way she pursed her lips at him right then, the unforgiving line of her mouth—he'd seen that same look in her father.

When last he'd seen her, Jaime had been a dowdy lass

25

headed for spinsterhood. And not because she wasn't particularly attractive, but for her venomous tongue, which seemed to pull a veil over everyone's eyes. He'd heard rumors, listened to her sister complain about it. But now to be on the receiving end—to know exactly what she thought about him as each word sliced into his gut.

The woman stood rigid, hands fisted at her sides, looking as stiff and stalwart as any warrior, save for the pretty light blue gown, the womanly curves. Ballocks…

In all her goddess-like glory, she glowered down her nose at him. A lovely package filled with animosity. Despite the circumstances, Lorne was intrigued by her and unbidden sparks of desire lashed within him. Which only made him feel more disgusted. He'd had entanglements with this family before. What he wanted was Dunrobin back, and he wasn't going anywhere until she returned it to him.

Before the silence stretched on too long, Lorne cleared his throat and turned fully to face her, touching his fingers to a cool button on his waistcoat to ground himself.

"Miss Andrewson," he started again, then stopped when she raised a perfectly arched brow and gave him such a look that if he'd been a lesser man, he might have backed toward her window, opened it up and flung himself out. The way to gain her attention and cooperation was not by telling her what to do. The only reason she'd turned around was that in a moment of weakness, he'd called out to her like some feckless fool.

Before he could continue, Jaime interrupted him. "I am unwilling to return the property, Sutherland. I understand that ye might have some attachment to it, but this was a business decision. The way Dunrobin Castle is situated upon the North Sea allows me access, and I have plans to build a private port there to expand my company."

Some attachment to it…as if a favorite trinket or pair of

boots. Good God, she tried his patience. And yet, he had to try and warm her up to him, gain her trust.

He fiddled with his button again, taking a step closer to her. "There are other properties. Better ones, even. Some with docks already built. I can help ye find the right one." In all his training, Lorne had become quite accustomed to reading body language, and the way she was pinching her fingers together was a telling sign that she was nervous—that she might not have been telling him the whole truth. Suddenly, he was speaking before thinking. "Did my brother put the castle up for sale, or did ye approach him?"

She stiffened, perhaps not expecting his bold question. "Why does that matter?"

Lorne shrugged, feigning indifference.

Her gaze shifted from his. "I do no' recall."

He moved closer, impressed that she didn't back away from him but held her ground. There was a defiance in her eyes that lashed out and struck him in the chest.

"Why did ye want to buy my castle, Miss Andrewson? Tell me the truth."

Anger flashed across her face, a ripple in cream. "How dare ye come into my house and accuse me of being a thief and a liar."

"I never accused ye of being a thief."

"Ye might as well have." Her hands were flying around as she spoke, and he dared not get any nearer in case he came into contact with one of them.

"I am simply trying to understand what has happened. And I think ye're hiding the truth from me."

"I am a businesswoman. I want to expand my business. That does no' make me a liar. But ye, Your Grace," she said the latter in a disgusted hiss and poked him in the chest, "ye're a hypocrite."

"What?"

"All this talk of thieving and lying when the only one in the room who's done any of the latter is ye."

"I'm no' a thief, nor am I a liar. What basis have ye to make such an accusation?"

Jaime snorted as though he'd told her the most hilarious of jokes. "Let me introduce ye to the elephant in the room, Sutherland. The reason ye're no' my brother-in-law at this very moment."

Och, but he could have bloody guessed that there was more to her choice in buying his castle than a load of ships. The cunning wee wench. Lorne ground his teeth, fisted his hands and took a step back as anger filled him; the need to roar out the injustice of what she implied.

There was no way he'd continue to take the blame for what happened between him and Jaime's sister. Nine years ago, before he'd accepted his commission in his regiment, Lorne had been betrothed to her. Shanna was an heiress and lovely to boot, with auburn hair and eyes very similar to her sister's. Eyes that stared at him right now with such fury, he nearly retreated another step back.

The way she looked at him, the stubborn set of her jaw, Lorne knew that nothing he could say would change how she felt about him. Not even if he told her the truth about what had happened the night of his and Shanna's engagement ball. The night he'd found her fumbling in the darkened library with a lover. As soon as he'd made himself known, the man had run, leaping out the window—his identity a mystery to this day. And Shanna, sobbing like a bairn, had begged Lorne to look past her indiscretion. Told him it was a mistake, that she'd been coerced. What a fool he was to have believed her. To have kept the secret, to save his pride in making him a cuckold, to have saved both their families the humiliation.

His hands clenched at his sides. What lies Shanna must have told...

When she'd tried to move their wedding date sooner, his suspicions of her being pregnant grew. Lorne broke off their engagement, appalled that she would think him such an idiot. And then more appalled at himself because he had been for trusting to begin with. Shanna must have told her family the bairn was his. That he'd soiled her and then left her to her fate.

The same sourness that filled his belly whenever he thought of Shanna filled him now. How could Jaime think her sister deserved any sort of retribution? That he was at fault?

Because she didn't know.

"Ye do no' know what ye're talking about." Lorne shook his head, thrust his fingers through his hair. "Ye're a fool."

A flicker of uncertainty showed in her eyes. But he was too much of a gentleman to correct her. Too proud to air his humiliation before a lass he barely knew.

And bloody hell, if she believed him a monster, despite the truth of what had happened, there was no way he would garner her favor by proving her right with his temper.

Lorne gritted his teeth and swallowed his fury, determined not to offend her and risk never regaining his family's castle.

Despite Lorne's frustration, he had to find a way to convince Jaime to return what was rightfully his. But right now, he needed a bloody drink.

"This is no' over, Miss Andrewson." Lorne brushed past her.

The best thing to do right now was to walk away, which fought against every intuition in his body to stay and battle it out. To prove to her that she was in the wrong, that he deserved for her to listen, to understand, to give him back his bloody castle. He needed a plan.

His hesitation lasted a fraction of a second before he was through the door. MacInnes, like all butlers, seemed to have a sixth sense to those within residence and was by the door with Lorne's hat and greatcoat.

"Good day, Your Grace."

Lorne nodded curtly before walking out into the crisp Edinburgh air.

His coachman waited beside the carriage, rushing to open the door for Lorne. "Where to, Your Grace?"

"St. Andrew's Square." Perhaps at the New Club, he'd find comfort in a glass of whisky.

The sensation of dozens of eyes on him left him feeling out of sorts as he climbed into his carriage. No doubt everyone in Scotland would know he'd visited Jaime upon his return from the dead.

And they would all be drawing the wrong conclusions.

His coachman meandered around the Charlotte's Square circle until he was back on George's Street. The road was filled with other carriages, people walking and merchants touting their wares. What should have been a short preamble down the road turned into nearly half an hour. At last, they rounded onto St. David's Street at St. Andrew's Square and pulled up in front of New Club.

The building looked as inconspicuous as the others. People wandered the square, casting him glances, eyes riveted to the crest on his carriage. The buzz of their hurried whispers increased with each of his steps toward the front of the club.

Ignoring them all, he entered the establishment. The dimly lit building smelled of cigar smoke and men's aftershave, a little overwhelming after coming from the outside. Lorne had never had much interest in cigars, and if he was going to smell a man's aftershave, it was going to be his own.

"Your Grace." The footman kept his gaze level, not blinking at the fact that Lorne had not been there in nearly ten years and had also been pronounced dead.

Lorne handed the footman his hat and coat and then sauntered toward the rear of the room where his old friends used to take up residence. There were many new faces and several not-so-new. A few clad in casual buckskin breeches, others in more fancy wear he'd seen the dandies of London sporting. Only a few of the gentleman wore kilts, which made him the odd man out. Much had changed since he'd been there last.

Some of those who recognized him stopped speaking to their companions right away to stare, mouths agape. Those with a connection to the War Office gave him respectful nods.

Lorne wasn't in the mood to chat. He simply nodded and passed by everyone to seek out a quiet corner in which to think, plan and imbibe a drink.

"Sutherland?"

Lorne halted, surprised to hear a very familiar voice. Lord Alec Hay, the Earl of Errol, who also happened to serve with him overseas, emerged from the shadows where it looked as though he'd been sitting alone—in Lorne's favorite spot.

"Errol." Lorne drew in a deep breath through his nose. He wanted to grasp the man up in his arms, glad to see that he was alive, after thinking that he'd died on Lorne's watch. The man had a scar slicing from his temple down over his cheek and toward his chin. Not long after he'd sustained the injury, Lorne had been...taken. "God, 'tis good to see ye're alive."

Alec clapped him on the shoulder. "Likewise. Where the hell have ye been?"

"Purgatory, and I'm no' going back."

Alec seemed to understand that he had no wish to speak on the topic. And as he'd suffered in the war alongside him, perhaps he was the closest thing Lorne could find to a person who could recognize the desire to leave the past where it lay.

"Sit with me." Alec didn't wait for Lorne's answer but

headed toward the corner he'd staked out, snapping his fingers at a passing footman. "Bring me the bottle." Slumping into his chair, Alec shook his head in disbelief. "I heard ye escaped, and I could no' believe it. What are ye doing in Edinburgh?"

Lorne groaned at the question, flashes of a hellion running rampant. He was relieved when the footman returned with a fresh bottle of whisky and an extra glass for him, allowing him a moment to think before answering.

"Can I interest ye in anything to eat, Your Grace?"

"Aye, the house special." He prayed the food was as good as it had been the last time he'd been there. The last decent meal he had before he'd left for the nearly five-day ride to Edinburgh was in the Highlands.

"Aye, Your Grace. And for ye, my lord?" The footman turned to Alec.

"I'll have the same." Alec uncorked the whisky and poured two healthy portions, sliding one of the glasses toward Lorne. "To your return."

Lorne lifted his glass and consumed the whisky in one burning swallow.

Alec seemed on edge, setting down his glass and continuously darting his gaze about the room.

"Are ye all right?" The way the man was acting had Lorne wanting to leap out of his skin.

"Aye." He cleared his throat, laughed off his awkwardness and poured a second helping of whisky. "Have ye got a place to stay in town?"

Lorne had not thought about that before. Aye, he'd had a house in town—one in London, too—but Gille could have sold off those properties as well.

"I've got a meeting with my solicitor in an hour." He scanned the dim room, frowning at the surreptitious glances he was getting from men playing cards or at the bar having a drink.

"Is this about Gille?"

Lorne let out his breath. "So ye heard?"

"Most of Scotland heard..." Alec sat forward, his fingers steepled. "Perhaps your solicitor will be able to make the sale contract null and void. After all, there are clauses for if a man is presumed dead and his property is sold."

"That is my hope."

Alec shrugged and sat back again. "Then again, ye could always marry the lass and take what is yours."

Lorne's frown deepened. Marry her? Not on his life. Well, that wasn't exactly true. If the only option left was to marry the lass, then he might consider it. But before he chose to toss himself into the dark depths of hell once more, he'd see what his solicitor could do for him.

"I'd rather no'."

Alec drummed his fingers on the glass, his heel tapping on the floor. The man was more anxious than Lorne, which seemed impossible given Lorne had been the one imprisoned.

"Are ye certain all is well with ye?" Lorne asked. "Ye seem...out of sorts."

Alec grunted. "My mother. She wants me to marry. I've been dodging blushing bonnets and their mothers for weeks. Last week, however, a persistent papa sought me out here. I'm trying to lay low."

"And ye'd see me wed first?" Lorne chuckled. "Hypocrite."

Alec grinned. "'Tis a bit hypocritical of me, aye. Miss Andrewson is a beauty, though, and turned down every man in Edinburgh and even some from abroad. Rich as Croesus, too."

"Even if she were a legendary Greek royal, I'm no' interested in marrying the chit." There was an edge of bitterness to his tone.

Alec chuckled. "Got under your skin, eh?"

"A little." He hated to admit that.

"She has that effect on most people. Bristly like a thistle."

That was one way to describe her.

Though perhaps there was some merit to what Alec was saying. A little flirtation could go a long way in disarming a person. Just look at how he'd trusted his ex-fiancé. While he was out of practice with the arts of flirtation, there was one thing Lorne did not lack—determination.

All he had to do was win her trust, and if she fell in love with him along the way, what difference did it make? As soon as he had the deed to his castle back in his hands, he'd say goodbye to the vindictive wee wench, rich and beautiful or nay.

Wooing Jaime was likely going to be a bigger challenge than any of the other battles he'd ever fought—but one in which he refused to lose.

⁂

JAIME STOOD THERE SO LONG GLARING LEMONS THAT THE wallpaper could have begun to peel. Her—a fool? How naïve did that pompous duke think she was? Did he honestly believe that she wouldn't have noticed her sister had born a bastard? That the man Shanna was supposed to marry abandoned her to such a fate?

Perhaps the lying rogue had presumed her sister would run away or that her family would accept what fate dealt her. Maybe he was even idiotic enough to believe that society wouldn't shun Shanna for what he'd done. That some other man would come along and marry her, take care of her. Take care of the consequences of the duke's indiscretion...

Fury rolled through her veins like molten lava. For years now, she'd had to protect her sister from the pain of that loss.

The pain of what people said about her in public. The ridicule of those who thought themselves better. The disappointment of their parents.

All Jaime wanted was for her sister to be happy—and to make Lorne Gordon pay for what he'd done. Even when he'd been pronounced dead, she'd not given up that vendetta. Jaime had taken his legacy and given it to those who rightfully deserved it. Duke or nay, he couldn't walk back into the world and demand that everything be righted to the way he'd left it.

Jaime wouldn't—couldn't—allow it.

Who in all of Christendom did that man think he was? Waltzing into her drawing room as though he owned the place, as though he could tell her what to do, and then to retreat with a threat so boldly and arrogantly on his tongue.

Not over, indeed.

Well, he was wrong. Dead wrong. Anything between them was most decidedly over.

And yet that incredulous, almost pitying expression he'd lobbed at her. Those words that burned inside her head— "Ye're a fool."

No, she wasn't. She was anything but a fool. Didn't the fact that she'd tripled the size of her father's shipping company prove that?

Jaime left the drawing room and marched into her study, sifting through the papers on top of the desk in search of the bill of sale for Dunrobin Castle. The solicitor, Mr. Corbett, who had drawn up the papers for Gille Gordon, had made her skin crawl in the way only a charlatan could, and she hoped her intuition that he was a bad egg wasn't right. Her lawyer had been in London, so she'd had to go with someone else she didn't readily know.

There were laws to protect men at war from losing their property when they were gone. Laws to make certain if their property was sold that it was quickly returned to them.

If that were the case, Lorne could have his solicitor drawing up legal demands at this very moment. To take her to court and make certain she returned the castle. Then her sister would be tossed out. Poor Gordie without a home. Without his legacy.

She sifted through the language, not finding what she was looking for and praying it was because she had an unpracticed eye with real estate law.

If only she had a way to get into contact with Gille, but after he'd sold her the castle, she'd not asked him for a forwarding address. She supposed if she sent an investigator to look for him, he would be easy to locate, but better yet, she'd best have a visit with her own solicitor.

"MacInnes," she said, stepping into the hallway. "Send word to Mr. MacDonald that I shall be arriving at his office directly and then have my carriage brought around."

"Aye, miss."

There was no way she was going to let her sister suffer more at the hands of Lorne Gordon.

4

The sun split through the blinds in Lorne's bedchamber at Sutherland Gate, his Edinburgh townhouse, searing itself into his eyes like a blade. He sat up in bed, rubbing his face, and reached for the glass of water on his nightstand, laid out by the very same man who'd opened the blinds. Mungo stood there before the light, arms over his chest, assessing Lorne with what could only be described as impertinence. Blast the man for being his oldest friend, or he'd have ordered him out on his arse.

"Are ye trying to kill me?" Lorne asked, his voice thick from too much whisky the night before. He wasn't used to drinking, and even the few cups he'd had felt as if he'd drowned himself in an entire distillery tub.

"Nay, Your Grace. But when ye stumbled in last night, ye did request I wake ye early for your appointment with your solicitor." Mungo stood near the door, looking a wee bit too gleeful.

Lorne should have stopped after the second whisky with Alec, but alas, he'd missed his friend. They'd both been celebrating and commiserating at the same time. And the hoyden, J. Andrewson, was never far from his mind, nor the out-of-place vengeance she'd targeted him with.

The insane prospect his friend had presented came spiking back into his head, along with the vow not to drink so much again. If he couldn't get Dunrobin back by legal means, then he ought to marry the hellion and take it. Absurd.

"Where is my valet?" Lorne slid his legs over the side of the bed, glad he'd recuperated briefly at Dunrobin before embarking on his journey to Edinburgh. The blisters on his feet had healed, as had all the aches and pains. Hearty and delicious meals made by his cook made him feel more like himself. Now that he wasn't so weak, he was ready to start exercising again as well.

"I imagine Paul is sleeping as ye told him to take the day to himself, seeing as how he'd been serving your brother all these years, and ye wished him a day of rest." Was there a hint of mocking in Mungo's voice?

Lorne grunted. "And that's why ye're here?"

Mungo shrugged. "No' exactly. Ye're a grown man, and I figure ye can dress yourself."

"I can." Lorne stumbled toward his dressing room to splash water on his face.

"I'll see that the dining room has breakfast placed out."

"I do no' need anything special."

"I'll be sure to tell your cook that."

Lorne dressed quickly in breeches, shirt and coat, forgoing the kilt he wished he were wearing in favor of more businesslike attire for this morning's task. He wolfed down eggs, toast and bacon, slugged back two cups of black coffee, and then called for his horse.

"No carriage?" Mungo asked.

"No." Edinburgh hadn't changed much; most things were still in the same place. And if he got lost, he'd toss a coin and be pointed in the right direction. At least he hoped so.

Besides, he didn't want his new mount to think he'd abandoned him, especially when he'd yet to christen the steed with a name.

Lorne mounted the sleek black Friesian, rubbing a hand down his neck. "What shall I call ye? George?"

The horse snorted and shook his head.

"Ah, so ye understand me. What about Andrewson, then?"

The horse nodded and Lorne chuckled. Seemed only fitting that he should name the beast he rode after the family that had screwed him over six ways to Sunday.

"Well, Andrewson, my faithful mount, to my solicitor's office, then. And I vow never to mistreat ye the way I wish to treat your namesake."

They rode through the city already coming to life with merchants and the like, until they arrived at the low brick building that housed the best solicitors in Scotland, and likely England, too.

"Mr. Lindsey's been expecting ye, Your Grace," the solicitor's clerk said, standing to bow. "Right this way."

Lorne entered his longtime solicitor's office, where papers lined Lindsey's desk and books were floor to ceiling. The window had its curtains pulled back, the sun shining in to light the dust motes in the air.

Lindsey stood, coming around the desk to shake his hand. "My God, Your Grace, I did no' believe the news when I heard, but here ye are in the flesh."

"Aye, and without my castle."

Lindsey frowned, nodding, and then pushing his spectacles up his nose from where they'd slid. "That was a sad business."

"Can we undo it? And what other damage has my brother caused?"

"Well, the young lord did no' use my services for the sale of Dunrobin. Had a rather unreputable man go about the paperwork, but it was a legal sale as far as such things go. With evidence of your body buried, they were able to pass the probate quite quickly." Lindsey moved around his desk, and the contents of Lorne's stomach started to curdle as he took a seat.

"How bad?" Lorne plucked a peppermint from a bowl on his solicitor's desk and popped it into his mouth, willing his sour belly to calm.

Lindsey tapped a pile of papers on his desk with one finger and opened a large volume sitting beside them with the other. "Ye're in luck, Your Grace, because the law protects men at war. I just need to get the letters of administration of probate canceled, have Lord Gille return the bill of sale and funds, and all will be well."

Lorne ground his teeth. "The lad has absconded with the funds and, from what I understand, a large part of my fortune."

Lindsey's brow furrowed. "I had hoped it was no' true."

"Me too." Lorne crunched the peppermint into dust.

Lindsey sifted through some other papers and then pulled out another volume, opening it and sliding his finger about mid-way down a page. "All right, well, he's no' absconded with it all. Given the probate, Lord Gille was no' able to garner control of the funds held in trust in the Bank of Scotland. Ye're still a verra wealthy man, Your Grace, with several other properties still within the family name—your name. Ye could use your money to pay J. Andrewson back until ye locate Gille, but it will require ye to either sell several of your other properties or deplete half the trust."

Half the trust… Ballocks. Though the trust was vast, the idea of parting with half his fortune for a property that should have already been his stung more than a little. "How the hell did she come up with the funds to purchase my castle, to begin with?"

Lindsey blew out a long breath, shaking his head. "I can no' say, as I was no' involved, but the Andrewson name has grown exponentially in Scotland since ye've been gone. They've got a hand in the imports and exports of nearly every good coming in and out."

In other words, Jaime Andrewson was almost one of the most powerful people in the city—besides himself.

"I do no' want to give up half my fortune or be rid of my properties." He'd only just returned. Lorne wanted everything back to the way it was before. "I want my sapskull brother to return what he stole."

"Then ye need to find Gille."

Bloody hell. Lorne nodded curtly, unable to speak for fear of the vulgar words that might escape.

"In the meantime, I can start the paperwork. Perhaps approach Miss Andrewson about a reversal on your behalf."

Lorne shook his head. "Do no' say anything to her as yet." He was fairly certain that it would take a miracle to convince Jaime to return what was rightfully his. Not when she'd been so damn eager to seize it. The more he thought about it, the more he wondered if it had been Gille's idea to sell in the first place. What if she'd approached him with an offer his greedy mind couldn't refuse?

Knowing that Lorne would likely be unable to convince the chit to return what was his and that if he did find his brother, the idiot could more than likely have gambled away the funds, there was only one other option—Alec's idea. Even if the last thing he wanted to do was marry the lass, it was something he should at least consider.

She was so prickly that she'd never go for it. Especially given he was out of practice with the arts of flirtation, though he doubted even Robert Burns could crack the ice around Jaime Andrewson's heart. But there was one thing Lorne didn't lack—determination. Without the deed to Dunrobin

Castle and with a grimace on his lips, Lorne was resolute in his decision to win her trust, and if necessary, her hand. Wooing Jaime would be a bigger challenge than any of the other battles he'd ever fought—but one which he refused to lose.

Lorne would work both angles: locating his brother and getting the money back and convincing Jaime to wed him. One or the other had to work.

"Is there anything else I can help ye with, sir?"

"Aye. I want ye to hire men to find Gille. I'll be working my damndest to discover him myself, but I've been gone a long time and lost touch with my brother years ago. I've no idea what he's been up to, and I have to find out. I want my money back, or what's left of it."

"Already on it, Your Grace. I made inquiries last night."

"Excellent."

"We'll get everything straightened away. And ye just say the word when ye're ready for me to contact Miss Andrewson."

Lorne stood. "And any information ye have on the Andrewson family and shipping company, I'd like that as well."

"I also thought ye might." Lindsey handed him a file. "This is a copy for ye."

Lorne took the thick file, glancing inside for a brief moment, seeing Shanna's name blaring on the first record, and he slammed it shut. "Thank ye."

"I'll be in touch, Your Grace."

Lorne returned to Sutherland Gate and marched straight into his study. The room was clean and looked the same as it had the last time he'd been in town. Gille might not have even touched this room, though he knew his half-brother must have. How could he have run the estates and satisfied his duties as duke and a member of Parliament if he'd not?

Throwing the file onto the desk, Lorne opened the draw-ers, finding the pack of cigars where he'd left it. That was a clue as much as anything else that Gille had not been in the study; else, he would have pilfered every last one of them.

Lifting one of the cigars, he twirled it around in his fingers, feeling the smooth paper, smelling the pungent tobacco. It had been over eight years since he'd had a cigar, having declined one offered in the club last night. These were not a luxury afforded a soldier fighting in the Peninsular War, nor a prisoner. And after the whisky he'd had, he knew a puff would have tossed him right over the edge.

Still holding the cigar, Lorne walked to the window that faced the street, taking in the sights of women walking arm in arm and servants scurrying about their duties, shopping or running other various errands. A stray dog darted in and out of the crowd, slinking behind a house down the lane. He leaned against the frame, watching as everyone went past, none of them the wiser for what it was like to sit in the bleak darkness with only the company of other miserable souls. To not be free to walk the street. To smoke a bloody cigar.

Lorne didn't want to think about those dark moments. He wanted to put it past him. To move on. Lord knew he had enough to worry about, dealing with his brother right now. The last thing he needed was to sit there and commiserate about the suffering he'd been through. He had problems to solve. Big problems.

With a groan, he turned away and went to his desk, replacing the cigar and sitting down in the creaking, old leather chair that had belonged to his father, and if he remembered correctly, his grandfather as well.

The Andrewson folder that Lindsey had given him was the only thing on his desk. He should look through it because if he were going to convince Jaime to either give him back his castle or marry him, he'd best know everything there was to know about her and her family.

Which meant he'd be finding out what happened to Shanna since he'd been gone. Lorne grimaced. He didn't give a shite what had happened to that conniving wench. But he did feel sorry for the child she'd ended up bringing into the world. Poor whelp. And for the backlash that must have come down heavily on Jaime. Was Shanna's indiscretion the reason she'd yet to marry at the age of four-and-twenty?

Instead of flipping through the folder then, Lorne opened his study door and summoned his housekeeper. "Coffee, please, and keep it coming."

If he was about to fall into the past, then he needed to stay awake for the journey.

JAIME PINCHED THE CUFF OF HER SLEEVE, THE ONLY SIGN that she was extremely vexed. Over an hour she'd spent in Mr. MacDonald's office, and no matter how many minutes ticked by and solutions hashed, she was still not hearing the answer she wanted.

"My sister can no' be expected to vacate the home I gave her." It was probably the eighth time she'd said it.

Mr. MacDonald let out a long-suffering sigh that made her irritated with herself as much as he was losing his patience. "I understand your position, Miss Andrewson, but the fact remains, the Duke of Sutherland is alive, and his property was sold without his consent and is therefore not a legal sale."

That truth smarted. If he'd handed her a sack full of banknotes yesterday, she would have had to give him the deed and somehow tell her sister that she'd failed. Poor Gordie's birthright stolen from him all over again. As if it wasn't bad enough that the lad was the duke's unclaimed child, and Shanna should have been married to him.

That castle was Shanna's home, but even saying that to Mr. MacDonald had not helped the situation. And only served to deepen the pitying look he gave her. A regard she'd seen all too often in society.

"There are plenty of other castles for sale, Miss Andrewson. I would be happy to look into drawing up a legal deed of sale for any others that ye might desire."

"I wanted that one." God, she hated how she was starting to sound like a petulant child.

"I understand." And his expression said as much, but what he understood and what she implied seemed to be two different things.

"So what do I do now? Wait for the duke to grace my threshold once more?"

Mr. MacDonald nodded. "Or ye could seek him out yourself with the deed. He must, of course, return the money ye paid for it."

That would be an easy enough task. The Gordons were filthy rich.

Jaime resisted the urge to let out the frustrated screech tickling the back of her throat. The past few weeks, Shanna and Gordie had finally been able to live the life they deserved. Now she was going to have to take it away. Of course, she'd buy them another residence, but the gossips would love this debacle. As it was, this morning's society papers had been all about the duke's return, and the miracle it was, and how wonderful, blah-blah-blah.

Was she the only one who'd burned the sheets in her hearth?

His return was the worst news.

There was no way about it.

"Miss..." Mr. MacDonald hedged. "While I'd love to

continue conversing with ye, I do have another client waiting."

Jaime snapped her attention away from the papers floating through her mind and back to her solicitor. "Of course. I'll be in touch as soon as the duke asks for the deed to Dunrobin back. I do no' plan to seek him out."

"I will be at your service when the time comes."

Jaime stalked from the offices of MacDonald & Sons and stepped outside into a day that was decidedly too cheery for the season and her mood.

A child ran up to her then, waving one of the society papers in his hand. "Buy the *Lady Edinburgh*, miss, the Duke of Sutherland's back."

She wanted to turn away, to snub the duke in any way she could, but the poor lad only made money when he sold his papers, and she didn't want to be the cause of him missing a meal. So she reached into her reticule and handed him a coin, taking the dreadful paper.

The headline made her nauseous. "Return of the Scot! A Duke Back from the Dead—Heads Will Roll."

Oh, how she wished it were his head that was going to roll, not his poor brother. Jaime didn't read further but walked briskly to her carriage, climbing the step laid out by her groom and sliding onto the plush, purple velvet seat.

"My office, please," she said before shutting the door and staring down at the society paper.

The Duke of Sutherland has returned to Scottish shores after nearly a decade absent and two years thought dead. If he is standing here in the flesh, who is buried in the family plot? A better question might be, how could anyone have confused the strapping Duke of Sutherland with the poor sap six feet under?

"Och," Jaime groaned. Whoever had written this wasn't

informed by Gille as she'd been of the conditions of the duke's remains.

Except they weren't his, were they?

She'd not known Gille well as he was much younger than Lorne, but when they'd discussed arrangements for the sale of Dunrobin, he'd been pleasant and kind. Sorrowful, even.

That was the one reason she'd been able to overlook his choice of solicitor. A little tickle started at the back of her head, and she pushed it away. She refused to believe that their transaction had been anything other than legitimate. Gille believed his brother dead, as did everyone else.

"Oh!" Jaime gripped the seat as the carriage made a hasty stop.

"Sorry, miss! Just a tramp who jumped in the road without paying attention." Her groom shouted at whoever it was and then continued.

The men in his regiment had seen Lorne die. They'd taken on heavy cannon fire that obliterated much of their battlefield and their men. A body was recovered, Lorne's ornamented coat slung over his chest. With his face unrecognizable, the men believed it to be their colonel, and he was pronounced dead.

Without a body, it could have taken years, a decade or more, for the title and all that went with it to be granted to Gille, but there had been a body...

Did Gille know that his brother had returned, and if he did, why had he not come to make amends right now? Obviously, Lorne had not seen his brother, or he wouldn't have visited her demanding the deed.

Jaime's head was spinning as she made her way through Edinburgh's streets and pounding by the time she arrived at her office in Leith.

Inside the small office attached to her warehouse, Jaime's clerk, Emilia, was busy with her head over the desk, scratching endless numbers into the columns of their books and pushing her spectacles back up the bridge of her nose from where they kept sliding.

"Good morning, Miss Andrewson," Emilia said, insisting after all this time to address her formally. Jaime had made certain to hire a female to work with her daily for a number of reasons. One, she didn't want to hear anyone balk about the impropriety of a woman sequestered alone in a room with a man all day, even if their primary job was running numbers while she oversaw the rest of the company. Most importantly, however, was that Jaime felt that women needed to be empowered by other women, and so she made a point to do so.

Women on the ships, however, was not a task she'd met yet. The dockhands and sailors were all too wary of a woman on board, and she needed them to stick around, or else her empire would crumble. As it was, she was certain there were plenty of them who had to cross themselves whenever she did an inspection.

"Emilia, I trust all has been smooth this morning."

"Smooth for the books and docks, aye. Not so smooth for..." Her eyes lifted from the ledger she was writing in to study Jaime. "Perhaps the Andrewsons."

"I do no' know what ye're talking about."

Emilia smiled and went back to work. Normally, Jaime would engage her in conversation over a sentence so cryptic. Force out of her whatever it was she was thinking. But not this morning, for Jaime knew exactly what her clerk was implying, and she had no interest in talking about the duke any more than she already had today.

Instead, she sat at her desk and began going through her morning correspondence. While her company was vast, she'd always made it a part of her day to directly reply to all queries. It gave their business a more personal touch and made their clients feel as if they were each cherished and important, which, in turn, kept them loyal. It was one of the ways she'd been able to grow the company, and she was proud of it. Since she'd taken over, Andrewson Shipping had become the principal shipping company for luxury imports from other European countries and Asia.

But hours later as she continued to mull over the manifestos and ledgers, for the first time since she'd taken over her father's company, she was not fully engaged. Her attention was continuously pulled away by a certain very tall, very handsome, very aggravating duke.

How dare he be handsome to boot? That wasn't fair at all.

"Are ye all right, Miss Andrewson?" Emilia said from her desk across the room. "If ye frown any more, the milk in my tea's going to curdle."

Jaime tried to smile but it felt so brittle, and the way Emilia winced, she was certain it looked as she felt—more like baring her teeth.

"Apologies." Jaime stood and stretched. "I'm going to walk the docks a minute and hope that settles me."

Emilia leaned back in her chair, setting her pencil down. "This is about the duke."

Jaime stopped in her tracks and whipped her head toward her clerk. "What makes ye think so?" Was she so obvious?

Emilia shrugged. "Everyone is talking about him."

"I've no' said a word."

Emilia's gaze strayed toward her desk where the crumpled *Lady Edinburgh* edition sat in a ball, the victim of her irritation a few minutes ago. She raised an eyebrow in Jaime's direction.

That was a direct challenge, and at some point, Jaime was going to have to deal with her clerk's impertinence. For now, she pursed her lips and folded her arms over her chest. "I said I'm no' talking about him."

"Do ye want to?"

"No." Jaime raised her chin.

"All right." Emilia dropped the topic without argument, which was also very much like her. "Do ye want me to walk with ye?"

"I'll be fine. I'm going to check on the repairs for the Shanna."

"They should be coming right along. Our men did well on the high seas, escaping the pirates."

Jaime frowned, recalling the Shanna captain's rendition of the attack. They'd been lucky to have seen the ship coming and cautious not to engage. Though they'd taken some damage from cannons, they'd been able to use the wind in their sails to escape. "They are thieves, no' pirates. Do no' glorify them."

Emilia grunted. "If ye say so."

"I'm sorry, Emilia. I slept little last night, and if ye must know, and ye might already as it was in the papers, the duke did visit me yesterday, and I'm quite put out by it."

Already mouths were flapping about what the duke might have been doing there. Looking for Shanna, coming to claim his child, perhaps seducing another of the Andrewson sisters. It was the latter that had got to Jaime the most. As if she would allow herself to be seduced by anyone, let alone the duke.

She scoffed once more, much to Emilia's attempt at concealed glee.

"No' a word," Jaime warned.

Emilia pressed her lips together and winked. Jaime wrenched open the door to her office and walked straight into a brick wall. Nay, not a brick wall, but a man.

And not just any man. Her hands were splayed on the hard abdomen of the Duke of Sutherland.

5

L orne had raised his hand to rap on the office door when it burst open, and a bundle of woman smacked into his frame. He stood rigid, peering down into the surprised face of Miss Jaime Andrewson.

His first instinct was to frown and advise her it was best to look where she was going, but he was fairly certain such a reaction would garner him the opposite of what he needed, which was her cooperation.

"Pardon me, Miss Andrewson." He tried on a smile, surprised when pink tinted her cheeks, and she looked flustered.

Jaime leapt backward as though she'd stuck her hands in a vat of broken glass and shook her head up at him. "I did no' know ye were there," she muttered.

A pretty woman, tall with dark hair in a bun atop her head, rushed forward. "Your Grace, what a surprise."

He cocked his head at her, not used to being addressed in such an informal manner, even with his title presented before

.

"Your Grace, my clerk, Miss Emilia Baker."

Emilia curtsied, then looked behind her as if searching the office for something.

"What do ye want?" Jaime asked, avoiding all pleasantries and skipping right to the matter.

Ordinarily, her brisk attitude might offend him, but he was starting to enjoy her sour nature, if only because it was part of the game—he was going to turn her sour lemons into sweet lemonade.

"I brought ye scones."

"Scones?" Jaime narrowed her brows at him.

Lorne held up a box of scones from his favorite bakery. "They are quite delicious, and I assure ye, no' poisoned."

Jaime rolled her eyes and passed the box to her clerk. "Poisoning me would no' get ye what ye want."

"Oh, currants." Emilia had opened the box and was taking in a deep breath, licking her lips.

"Ye'll find a pot of cream inside as well." Lorne nodded toward the box and then smiled down at Jaime. "Someone appreciates my gift."

"I want nothing from ye, except for ye to return to the grave."

He gave an exaggerated wince, and for a split second, she looked as if she regretted her words.

"Och, that's painful, J." He liked watching the way her eyes widened at his use of her pseudonym, and he ignored the fact that she wished him dead. He had to remain on course if this was going to work.

"Leave," she said, then added, "please, Your Grace."

Lorne chuckled. "I've no intention of leaving just yet."

"If no' to deliver scones, then what?"

Now to deliver the speech he'd prepared on his ride over to the wharf. "I was curious, if I may confess, about your company."

"My company?" Jaime cocked her head to the side.

"Andrewson Shipping?" Lorne spread out his hands, indicating their surroundings.

She pinched her lips closed, opened them, and then pressed them closed again.

When she still said nothing, he continued, "I thought ye might give me a tour of the docks."

"Why would I do that?"

Heavens, but this was not going at all the way he'd planned. "Is this how ye treat all of your clients?"

She crossed her arms over her chest and tapped her foot. "Ye're no' a client."

"But I might be."

"And what would ye export?"

"Well, ye must know Sutherland wool has been coveted around the world for the last six hundred years."

She didn't flinch, which meant she was well aware, and it was likely one of the reasons she'd wanted to get her hands on Dunrobin. And it was lucky for him that a decade ago, he'd moved the majority of the flock and fleece company to his holding in Dornoch. Something she might not have anticipated when she'd purchased his family seat.

"Why would ye use Andrewson?"

"I've heard ye're the best."

"Flattery will get ye nowhere."

"Is it flattery or a fact?" Hooking a thumb in his coat pocket, he leaned against the frame, blocking her exit but giving her room to retreat backward.

"Fact."

He grinned, and she grimaced in turn.

"Miss Andrewson, I could escort the duke around the docks if ye wish," her clerk said.

Jaime looked ready to agree, but her words contradicted his observation. "I'll do it. Mind, it will be quick. Come on, Your Grace."

She shooed him, and Lorne wondered if she would put her hands on him to shove him forward—thought about waiting long enough to see if she would. But the pained expression on her face was enough to have him moving. Why did she hate him so much?

Sure he'd broken off the engagement with her sister, resulting in humiliation for all parties, but the deep-seated hatred within her seemed to go way beyond that. Perhaps one day, she'd find out the truth about Shanna. He could blurt it out right now, but he was certain she wouldn't trust his word over her sister.

"This way." Jaime marched forward.

He followed, watching the way her shoulders squared, and as much as she tried to be militant in her departure, there was an enticing sway to her hips that he could not ignore.

That gentle rocking drew his eye to her arse in the soft green gown she wore with a plaid bodice. A working gown, but it didn't matter if it wasn't made to entice—for it was her, and not the fabric, which drew his attention. And that was a problem. Lorne hurried to walk beside her.

Jaime glanced over at him, that same pained and pinched expression she wore every time he was around her—well, today and yesterday. It was starting to grow on him.

"What do ye really want, Sutherland?" she asked. "Ye're no' a delivery lad. And I'm no' fool enough to believe ye would use my shipping company for your exports, breaking off a long-standing partnership with your current export company, especially given our present circumstances."

They rounded the corner, and the docks came into view. Massive ships rocked in the quay, their high masks stabbing at the sky and their sails tied down tight. Men teemed, carrying crates and barrels. Hammering, chiseling. Busy with all that kept her company running. The salty scent of the wharf was stronger as a breeze blew in off the water.

Lorne glanced sideways at Jaime, watching her expression soften as she took in the docks, her ships, her employees. There was pride in her face, a satisfaction that he could understand. And it made him long to be back at Dunrobin, to be back in the fields with his crofters. To be right there in the thick of everything that made the lands thrive. He might have been born a duke, but he was no stranger to work, and he'd never been one to shun the working men who made his entire existence possible. Nay, he leapt right in there with them.

In fact, he wouldn't have minded right then and there, rolling up his sleeves and—

A shout came from their side as two men worked to carry a precarious crate and wavered on their feet, slanting sideways as if they were going to fall. The box started to tip.

Lorne dove into action, picking up the leaning side until the men were steady on their feet. It'd been an age since he'd worked his muscles, and though he strained, his body remembered what it was made for, and he held onto the weight, waiting until they were ready for him to release it.

"Good God, what is in this?" he asked, the weight of the crate all centered on that one side rather than evenly distributed. Probably had happened in the way they lifted it and was the fault of whoever had done the packing.

"None of your concern," Jaime quipped, waving over another dockhand to take Lorne's place.

"Thank ye, Your Grace," the men speaking the words their mistress did not seem able to utter.

Lorne nodded and stepped out of their way as they continued on the path toward the ship, struggling as they went.

"I should help them," he said.

"They'll manage." But as she said it, the three of them

wavered again, only this time they were amidst their men, who hurried forward to help them settle the awkward haul.

Lorne raised a brow at her, but she ignored him. Why was she being so stubborn?

"Listen, Your Grace," Jaime said, turning to face him fully, though she stared at his forehead rather than meeting his eyes. She ran her tongue over her lower lip, and he watched its quick glide, trying not to be mesmerized. "I spoke with my solicitor this morning. He informed me that ye have the right to reverse the sale and return the funds to me for the deed. But I warn ye that I'll fight it."

She looked so resolute that he almost didn't have the heart to tell her that she didn't have a choice. "Ye're verra stubborn," he said softly.

"I am determined. There is a difference."

"I recognize and admire that, for I'm the same way. But I have to ask, why?"

Jaime's chin lifted, her mouth clamped as tightly closed as an oyster. He waited a few moments, but she didn't answer him, and he guessed at this rate she wouldn't.

"J, ye'd be the last man on the battlefield, fighting against enemies quickly closing in. Except too late, ye'd find out the ones ye were fighting against weren't your enemies and that ye'd been stabbing a comrade in the back."

With those words and his irritation slowly boiling over, Lorne turned on his heel. This morning had not worked out the way he'd planned at all. Perhaps it would behoove him to pay her off and accept the loss. He'd find his brother eventually and squeeze out of the sapskull whatever remained from the sale.

Mouth agape, Jaime watched the duke stride away, his shoulders broad and square, confidence oozing from every limb.

What could he possibly mean that she'd stabbed a comrade in the back? As if they were friends. As if they should have been fighting a common enemy. He was not her comrade. He was mad. Touched in the head.

But as she checked on her various ships and cargo, her mind kept drifting back to what Lorne had said. There had been real anger in his words and flashing in his soulful gray eyes. No. Not soulful. The man didn't have a soul because he had sold it to the devil.

Jaime instead rearranged her way of thinking and chalked up his reaction to being frustrated that she wouldn't agree to give him back his precious castle.

The more she thought of it, the more her mind, however, took wild turns. What if that weren't the only reason he was so irate? Maybe it was because he already knew that Shanna was living in the castle. He'd not mentioned her when he came to her house the day before, but if his first stop after London had been Dunrobin, then surely, he would have run into her sister.

Shanna, who had still not sent Jaime word.

The messenger that Jaime had sent north should be returning in the next few days, and then she could rest easy that her sister was all right.

Or she could ask Lorne if he'd seen her and settle her mind now that Shanna hadn't been set upon by highway thieves.

A prickle of nerves made her antsy on her feet. Maybe before returning to her house in Charlotte Square, she should first go to the duke's residence and ask him.

But would he even give her an answer after their latest encounter—probably not. She'd been rude to him since she'd set eyes on him the day before, and just as rude this morning. He owed her nothing, and from the interactions they'd been having, she wouldn't be surprised if he would only give her the information she sought for a price.

A price she wasn't willing to pay.

Under normal circumstances.

But it wasn't like Shanna not to send word, especially when Gordie was involved. And with such an extravagant gift given to her by Jaime. Well, that wasn't exactly true. Jaime's sister had always been spoiled and not necessarily thankful when she thought she was owed something simply for being who she was.

And in this case, Shanna would feel that way about Dunrobin. Which was probably why she'd not said thank you to Jaime, but she'd been appreciative in her way. Shanna had been through a lot over the last decade. It wasn't easy to be shunned from society and bear the fruit of a man's transgression.

Father nearly had a heart attack when he'd found out—only a heavy dose of laudanum and twenty-four hours of sleep had ceased his shouting. Mother tried to get Shanna to have the child discreetly and give it away, but her sister had refused. In the end, the late Viscount and Viscountess Whittleburn, their parents, had shunned Shanna and her unborn child. She'd been sent away from the houses they occupied, allowed only to remain on a remote Irish property they owned, well away from both London and Edinburgh courts. Few servants had been there, and Shanna had been cut out of the will when their parents passed. It was only Jaime's kindness that had kept Shanna from the poorhouse. And her child from starvation.

Shanna had been disowned and essentially alone until their parents died not a year apart, her father from a heart condition, and her mother seemingly following in his footsteps. Jaime had immediately welcomed Shanna home and rejected the whispers of the women in high society. Though her father's title and the family home had been passed on to her uncle, the shipping company had remained in Jaime's hands, and she vowed to do right by her sister.

Jaime bid her dockworkers farewell and headed back to her office to let Emilia know that she would be leaving for the day. Though the argument had slung itself back and forth in her mind, she'd finally settled on going to speak with the duke. To alleviate her nerves as far as Shanna's whereabouts. It wouldn't hurt. Nothing ventured, nothing gained. It was the same motto she used in her business. And she wasn't about to let his overbearingness get in her way.

A short time later, Jaime sat in her carriage, staring out the window at the vast brick manse before her. The wrought iron gates with gilded spires. The Sutherland crest gleaned in the sun that peaked through the clouds.

The duke's house was every bit as grand as she remembered. She'd not been there since the night of the engagement ball, when she'd been on the cusp of her sixteenth birthday.

Out the window of the carriage, she spied her groom shifting on his feet. Already, he'd tried to open the carriage door once, and she'd slammed it back shut. She wasn't ready. But would she ever be?

Likely not.

Her fingers sweated in her gloves, and from all the work she'd been doing, she must look a mess. Wisps of her hair had come loose from her bun and were tickling her cheeks, no matter how many times she swiped them away. And now she'd sat there long enough that her carriage had drawn the eye of every passerby, as well as those who stared out their townhome windows watching every move on the street, especially where the duke was concerned.

She could see what the papers would say now: Sister of Spurned Fiancée Stalks Duke.

With an unladylike snort of disgust at herself, Jaime pushed open the door and stepped down on the walk, surprised that her legs didn't tremble with nerves. A stray dog weaved between her and her groom, looking pitiful, and nearly skin and bones.

"Poor hound. Put him up with ye, and we'll see he's taken care of. I will no' be long," she told her coachman. Jaime had always had a soft spot for strays.

The iron knocker in the shape of a unicorn was heavy in her hand, but she didn't yet let it fall. She was well aware she'd gone against the grain once more by not sending a calling card ahead. By not being issued an invitation. And even worse, by not arriving with a chaperone. All of which she didn't care about. The duke had now shown up uninvited at her home and her place of work, so why shouldn't she do the same? The papers were already wagging their tongues. What was one more bit of gossip?

That thought cemented in her mind, Jaime let the knocker drop, hearing it thunder through the cavern of the inside of his house.

A moment later, a man the duke's age answered, examining her as if she were a rare species that he'd never encountered before. Dressed in a kilt and tails, he must be the butler.

"Can I help ye?" he asked.

"I'm here to see His Grace."

The man narrowed his eyes. "Is he expecting ye?"

Jaime hesitated, shifting on her feet, aware of the eyes at her back. She wanted to lie but gave him the true answer. "No, but he'll see me all the same."

The man's eyebrows shot to his hairline, and he opened the door wider, stepping out of her way and sweeping his hand in a gesture for her to enter. Well, that was unexpected. She had truly expected him to slam the door in her face. Dukes did not take orders from mere lassies.

"I'll just let him know ye're here." The man sauntered off, leaving Jaime to stand in the grand foyer's center, glare at the winding marble stairs to the upper floor. Polished wood floors covered in expensive rugs. Oil portraits of dukes and duchesses, ranging back hundreds of years. Overhead, a vast chandelier held two dozen candles, their wax dripping down the sides. The pure opulence and wealth in that entryway gave way to irritation. By taking the seat of his dukedom at Dunrobin, she'd still not robbed him. The man was rich beyond reason.

"Miss Andrewson." Lorne's voice was soft, coming from somewhere in the shadows behind the stairs.

He stepped out, rolling the sleeves that were halfway up his forearms back down in a gesture of propriety, but she couldn't stop looking at the strength rippling along his exposed flesh in that brief moment. Dear heavens. There was a little flutter in her belly that she chalked up to nerves and nothing, absolutely nothing, else.

Jaime cleared her throat, aware she should curtsy and not wanting to do it anyway. "Your Grace." She settled on a slight bend of her neck.

Lorne gave her a once over, his expression leaving his thoughts a mystery. "To what do I owe the pleasure of your visit?"

Pleasure? He was mad if he thought this visit was pleasant at all. His eyes danced as he came to stand a mere foot away from her. Aye, he appeared amused at her intrusion rather than irritated at seeing her again.

"I had a question for ye." Jaime tried to keep her voice confident. She laced her gloved fingers in front of her.

He didn't make a move to lead her into his drawing room

or study but instead crossed his arms over his supremely muscled chest and stared down at her. How had he maintained his strength when he was "dead?"

"Where were ye?" This was not the question she'd come to ask and had nothing to do with her sister, but curiosity had gotten the better of her. She let her gaze rove over his figure.

"Imprisoned." The word was curt, and all the merriment that had been in his eyes before she'd asked evaporated.

He did not expound on the explanation, and she was too embarrassed at her forwardness to press. Her bringing it up had caused his mood to so swiftly change, leaving her with more questions. And worse—sympathy. The man must have been through purgatory. But why should she care?

"Is that the reason ye came?"

Jaime shook her head. "Nay, no' at all." She was getting flustered and hated that he was able to take away her wit so easily. Well, she might as well blurt the reason before he kicked her out on her ear. "Ye were at Dunrobin before ye came to Edinburgh, were ye no'?"

He crossed his arms over his chest and stared down at her. "What's it any business of yours?"

Well, this wasn't going well at all. "I take that as an 'aye.'"

Lorne shrugged, moving from ire to indifference. "I choose no' to say."

"Why?"

"Many reasons."

Was one of those reasons Shanna, and the other Gordie? Well, she wasn't leaving here without an answer. Jaime squared her shoulders and pressed on. "If ye did happen to be there, and for whatever reason, ye choose no' to tell me, I would hope that ye would at least alleviate some worry I'm having."

Lorne let out a derisive grunt. "Ye, worried? I thought ye a hard arse."

Jaime was able to clamp her jaw before her mouth fell open. She supposed she deserved that. No one had ever spoken to her so bluntly before. A true lady would have been offended. Might even take him to task for using vulgar language in front of her, but Jaime found she rather liked his use of uncouth tongue, for it showed he thought her more an equal than most men might have considered her.

Still, Jaime found herself pinching her cuff. "My sister was supposed to be in residence, and yet I've no' had any word from her. Did ye happen to notice if she was there?"

Lorne narrowed his brow at her. "If I was at Dunrobin, and I'm no' saying I was, mind, I would no' have seen your sister."

"By choice?"

"Or by Fate."

"So she was no' there." Och, but she hated to play mind games.

Lorne threw his hands up in the air. "I think I've made that clear."

"In no' so many words."

"For fear of your retribution upon the staff."

"My retribution?" Jaime was taken aback by that. What was he insinuating about her?

"Aye, they were told, all of them, to find employment and housing elsewhere. Quite cold of ye."

"I said no such thing."

"Alas, they all have, or plan to, follow your instructions."

Jaime frowned. "So let me see if I understand correctly, Your Grace. My sister was no' in residence, and the staff have been told vacate the premises?"

"Aye, dismissed." Lorne made a sharp cutting motion in the air that reminded Jaime of heads rolling with the swift chop of an axe.

Jaime tried to swallow around the lump in her throat, but

it only felt like it was getting bigger, and it was harder to breathe.

"Thank ye," she managed to whisper, backing up toward the door. Her shoe caught, and she lost her balance, falling backward, bracing for the tumble.

But it never came. Instead, she landed in the arms of the duke, his gray eyes boring a hole right through hers.

She felt weightless in his arms and all the more lightheaded.

"I've already borne the tricks of one Andrewson female, and I'll no' abide by tricks of another," he growled, righting her. "Ye'd best leave. Mungo."

The man who'd answered the door appeared as if from nowhere, opened the door, and the Duke of Sutherland lifted her and deposited her on the doorstep before shutting the door in her face.

❧ 6 ❧

"**D**o no' look at me like that," Lorne said to Mungo, whose expression gave away everything he wasn't saying.

And then Mungo went ahead and said it anyway. "I do no' think ye're going to get what ye want that way."

Lorne growled, knowing that the man was correct. If anything, now the chit would probably try to contrive a dozen other ways to steal what was his. But when she'd fallen and he'd been obliged to catch her, feeling the warmth of her lush body against his own—his suspicions were raised as to what her intentions were. Shanna would have fallen on purpose, so he had to hold her. So she could entice him with her female curves. What was to say that Jaime wasn't doing the same? And oh, how he'd enjoyed it. Which only sparked his irritation all the more.

Mungo held up his hands. "I'm no' an expert in ladies, but from what I've heard, they are no' pleased when dismissed in such a...rude manner."

Lorne jabbed his finger at the door. "That's no lady."

"But she is, Your Grace. The daughter of a viscount is a

lady indeed. And she's one ye need on board if ye're to get Dunrobin back. Might I remind ye that it is no' simply the castle at stake, but everyone's position as well?"

"I do no' need her on board. Nor do I need the reminder. I take care of those who depend on me. When I left, I told them all to stay put and that I'd take care of it. They have my word, as do ye, Mungo. I'll have Lindsey draw up the papers and take funds from the trust. Dunrobin will be mine once more, and I'll no' need to deal with that hellion ever again."

"She's getting under your skin."

Lord, was she ever. He wanted her under his skin, over his skin. Bloody hell...

"Everything is getting under my skin." Lorne clenched his fists at his sides. "I want to go home, and here I am groveling at the feet of a woman who wishes me dead for deeds I am not complicit in."

"Perhaps ye should tell her the truth." Why did Mungo have to sound so rational? It only served to sour Lorne's mood.

"She'll never believe me."

"Maybe she will. She's different than her sister."

But was she? Lorne stared at the closed door, wondering if she was where he'd left her on the other side. It was easier to believe that Shanna and Jaime were two peas in a pod. Even if there were at least a dozen glaring reasons that they were not the same at all. He was going to ignore those reasons, for there was one major fact he couldn't ignore—she still "owned" his castle.

His muscles were tight, and a maddening buzz volleyed through his veins. Years of pent-up energy funneled violently through his limbs. From experience, he knew the only way to get rid of it was to let out his aggression.

"Is the gymnasium prepared?" he asked.

"Aye, Your Grace."

"And the invitations sent?"

"Aye. They should be arriving shortly."

"Good. See that they are brought up."

Lorne made his way to the gymnasium he'd had installed a decade ago when as a much younger man, he'd needed to let out some steam. He was very much looking forward to his friends and cousin joining him, as well. Like old times when they used to get together and beat the hell out of each other. They'd all met at Eton as young lads whose fathers seemed to believe the only education for a lord was in an English institution. On to Oxford they'd gone, and even abroad for their tours. But he'd not seen any of them since he'd been back, except Alec.

The gymnasium was furnished with a boxing ring, a fencing planchet—a beam several feet off the ground they would balance on—to keep them on their toes. Another section for increasing strength was outfitted with various dumbbells, not a very popular form of exercise for gentlemen, but which Lorne loved.

He rolled his sleeves to his elbows and loosened the neck of his shirt. He always warmed his body up with a jog around the room's perimeter before he started to exercise and was mid-stride when his cousin Malcolm Gordon, Earl of Dunlyon, strode into the room. Malcolm was as tall as Lorne, and given he'd lost some of his bulk while imprisoned, they were now matched in that area as well.

"My God, ye do no' look half-dead at all." Malcolm grinned as he strode forward.

Lorne chuckled. "I feel better every day. If ye'd seen me a couple of weeks ago, I'd have been in different shape."

They embraced, both of them clapping each other hard on the back. This was yet another thing he'd missed when he'd been locked up. Companionship from people who knew him to the deep marrow of his bones.

"'Tis good to see ye, cousin," Lorne said.

"And ye. We missed ye here and in London."

"Trust me, I'd have rather been here."

Malcolm nodded with a frown. He didn't ask about Lorne's imprisonment, to which he was grateful. Malcolm knew him well enough that he understood when Lorne was ready, he'd spill.

"How's Gille taking it?"

Lorne scrubbed a hand through his hair. "I have no' seen him. In fact, I have no idea where he is."

"No?" Malcolm frowned. "The lad is much the same, albeit more reckless. I'm surprised he's waited this long to come to ye."

"When was the last time ye saw him?"

"Months." Malcolm shook his head. "But I was no' surprised because I did no' agree with what he did, and I made my feelings plain. Which, of course, Gille took a little too personally."

"I asked my solicitor to hire detectives to look for him. But I've no' heard back yet."

"Why no' let me take care of finding him?" Malcolm said. "I'll be more discreet, and being we're blood, I have more of a vested interest."

Malcolm had always been good at finding people and information. Though he was a member of the House of Lords, he was also well respected in the War Office for his talents.

Lorne nodded, squeezing Malcolm's shoulder. "All right. I should have thought of that before. I'd appreciate it."

"It'd be my pleasure to gift ye with your brother," Malcolm chuckled. "All of us were stunned when he sold Dunrobin. What could the lad want with the money?"

"I still can no' believe it happened." Lorne shook his head.

"And I do no' think it was about the money, so much as being rid of me completely."

"Easily reversible, aye?"

"Easier said than done." Lorne let out a long breath, not wanting to explain further. And luckily, he didn't have to as Alec Hay and Captain Euan Irvine, whom he'd not seen since the battlefield, arrived.

"Ye haunted me in my dreams, Sutherland. God, I'm glad to see ye're alive," Euan said.

Lorne embraced his friend, the lot of them chatting about old times as they prepared.

"What's first?" Alec asked, nodding toward the equipment.

"Your choice." Lorne held out his arms. "It's been a bloody long time since we were all here together."

"I think I'll take on Malcolm in the ring," Alec said with a grin that suggested he'd been waiting a long time to settle a score.

"Ye just want to see if I can still maintain my balance on the planche," Lorne accused with a chuckle.

Alec let out a loud laugh. "Ye said it, but we're all thinking it."

"I may impress ye yet," Lorne boasted.

"Never happened before," Malcolm teased.

The men ribbed each other about the first time they'd gotten into a round of fisticuffs as youths over a game of rugby. After they'd been broken apart and made to suffer the same punishment of peeling potatoes for a week in the kitchens, they'd been the best of friends.

With their slim foils and masks in hand, Lorne and Euan climbed the short ladders to the planche, the very same wooden beam they'd balanced on years before as they fenced. It felt good to be with his friends again, working not only his body but also his mind. The beam was sturdy beneath his feet, and he tested the bottom of his shoes on the wood, testing the slide and catch of his soles.

"Are ye ready?" Euan asked.

"Aye. Blast, but it's been a long time."

"Too long," Euan agreed.

They tied on their wire mesh fencing masks.

"Thank God ye're covering up your ugly mug. I could no' stand to look at ye another minute," Euan jested.

"Ye might need some extra padding, as ye know I'll be giving your arse a sound beating," Lorne quipped with a mock salute.

Euan grinned, saluting back, and then took up the proper stance, one leg forward and the other behind, bearing most of his weight on the rear leg. Lorne did the same. He was surprised at how easy it was to remember what to do despite him being untried for so long.

Euan's foil pressed forward. "En garde, my friend."

"Fence," Lorne said with a grin he hoped Euan could see behind the mask.

They advanced, each of them being cautious for a moment to get their bearings and balance. Lorne attacked first, but Euan was quick to parry. Back and forth they went, each of them seeming to melt into a time when they'd done this on the regular. Lorne feinted right, then attacked left, throwing Euan off-balance. His opponent leapt and retreated out of range, wobbling slightly on the planche as he worked to regain his balance. Lorne wasn't ready for their bout to end and backed up a step to allow his friend a moment to recuperate.

Behind Euan's mask, his grin grew wider. "Ye should have kept attacking, knocked me off."

"Maybe I like the challenge of ye angry," Lorne retorted.

Euan laughed and attacked in a pounce that Lorne wasn't sure he'd be ready for, and yet he was. Lorne parried with a flick, bending Euan's blade enough he had to back up, off-balance once more.

"Did ye fence wherever ye were?" Euan asked.

"Something like that," Lorne said. A flash of his time in prison, where he'd been made to fight with the others for their captors' pleasure, took him out of the moment. It had never been as civilized as this and never as safe.

A bitter taste swept into his mouth, and he retreated, taking a deep breath. But Euan hadn't noticed his sudden change in mood and continued to attack forward. Lorne was slow to recover, and the top of Euan's foil stabbed against his chest, off-setting his equilibrium, and he stepped off the planche, his right foot catching air. He tumbled to the mat below with an "Oof."

Euan jumped down beside him, pulling his mask up to stare at Lorne with a frown. "What just happened?"

"Ye won." Lorne held up his hand, and Euan pulled him to his feet.

"It's no' winning when your opponent gives up."

Lorne lifted his mask, wiping the sweat slicking his brow on his sleeve. "I did no' give up. I was...distracted."

Euan nodded, intelligent eyes studying him. "Perhaps ye'd prefer the ring then. Maybe get some of those distractions out of your head."

"We'll get to that." Lorne pulled the mask over his face, shuttering his eyes from his friend, feeling too exposed. "That was just a warmup."

They climbed the ladders to the planche again, and when Lorne put up his sword this time, he was determined to win.

JAIME PACED HER DRAWING ROOM, MAKING CERTAIN TO DO so in a different place than she had been before so as not to wear the rug out in one spot.

MacInnes waited patiently by the door as she tried to sort through the thoughts tumbling through her head. But she couldn't seem to get a handle on a single one. Since she'd arrived home after the duke had so unceremoniously dumped her on his front stoop, she'd had one caller after another. Everyone wanted to be on the inside of the drama festering between herself and Lorne.

Oh, how she wanted to box his ears for him thinking she'd tripped and fallen on purpose. That she'd wanted him to catch her so she could somehow seduce him with her clumsiness. Of all the absurd things she'd heard... But it had been a wonder to have his bulk pressed so close to hers. To feel the heat and strength of him. The way his eyes had blazed into hers. She'd be lying if she didn't admit feeling in her belly, and the buzzing of bees in her head. Blast it!

MacInnes checked his pocket watch, a subtle reminder that she had callers waiting.

To deny them entry would be to fan the flames and allow their comments to run wild and out of control. She'd never be able to get a handle on it then. But to let them in would be to plaster a smile on her face that she didn't feel. To speak with people she loathed and to play their stupid society games, which she hated. One of the reasons she'd moved her office permanently to Edinburgh, instead of remaining in London as her father preferred, was because it was more informal in town here.

Not that it didn't have its share of stiffness. Edinburgh was like a finger of London if London were the hand. The royal family still held residences down the street from her and often came to make their roundabouts.

Which meant so did the rest of Scottish and English society alike.

"Miss..." MacInnes hedged.

Jaime whirled to face her faithful butler. What would she do without his patience and guidance? "All right, fine, MacInnes. Tell Lady Giselle she can come up and leave the rest of the cards with me. I'll think about my replies later."

Her butler nodded and left the room. If she had to get this over with, fine, but she wasn't going to entertain more than one person today. And she was going to make certain it was a person she at least used to enjoy the company of.

Lady Giselle Hepburn, the Earl of Bothwell's daughter, swept into the room in vivacious yellow silk skirts and a gauzy emerald-green sash beneath her bosom. Her golden hair was twisted into a fashionable style, with several curls framing her face. Giselle was lovely as ever, a hint of a smile on her lips, her gaze cautious. It had been so long since they'd seen each other.

"Oh, Jaime, I'm so glad ye let me up." Giselle came forward, pulling her in for an embrace. At twenty-one, a few years Jaime's junior, Giselle still had a whole wide world in front of her, though she didn't appear in any hurry to take it. Jaime, however, at twenty-four, was basically on the shelf, a placement that suited her fine.

Giselle had come out for her season three years after Jaime, but they'd still found each other to be good company, even if the Countess of Bothwell had warned her daughter to stay away for fear of Jaime ruining Giselle's chances at a match. Through the swift intervention of the countess, they'd lost touch when Jaime's parents had both passed, and she was no longer attending husband-hunting society functions. The blasted affairs were so obvious. Why not simply line the eligible males up on one side and the females on the other and have an auction? Pretending they were all civilized by dancing, laughing and drinking punch when they were being paraded and prodded was offensive to both parties.

"You look beautiful, as always," Jaime said, kissing the air beside her old friend's cheek. It wasn't until this moment that she realized how much she'd missed having a friend. But she didn't want to get her hopes up. Giselle had not come around in the last two years and had only now decided to show her face. Her visit could not be genuine. "Shall I ring for tea?"

Please say no.

"Aye, please."

With a tight smile, Jaime rang the bell alerting MacInnes of her request and then took a seat on one of her silk chairs facing Giselle, who'd opted to sit on the settee. The younger lady fixed her skirts so they wouldn't wrinkle and then looked up at Jaime with a beaming smile that confused her in its sincerity.

"How have ye been?" Jaime asked, smoothing down her own skirts to occupy her hands.

"Oh, the usual." Giselle waved her hand in the air with an eye roll. "Mother is disappointed I've no' yet found a wealthy lord to wed. But who can blame me with the choices we've got?"

"Fair enough. And does your mother know ye're here?"

Giselle's eyes widened slightly. "No."

So the countess still looked down her nose at Jaime. "She will now."

"And my ears will blister from her ranting, no doubt." Giselle shifted in her seat, opened her mouth and closed it again. It was clear she had a question that she was not asking, and Jaime had a good idea what it was.

"Ye came here to ask me about the Duke of Sutherland." It was a statement rather than a query, and the way Giselle blinked rapidly, Jaime knew she'd been right. She let out a long sigh. She wasn't surprised and shouldn't be disappointed. But she was.

"I'm sorry, Jaime. I know ye've likely been hounded by everyone else."

"I have." As well as the rumors in the papers.

"I was worried about ye. I remember what happened with Shanna, and well, are ye all right?"

Jaime was taken aback. She'd not expected that Giselle's concern would be for her rather than what was happening.

"I'm fine. How do ye mean?"

Giselle had stopped the rapid blinking, the smile gone from her face, and she appeared to be concerned and interested. But not for gossip—as a friend. "Well, I know it must have been a surprise and brought up a lot of things I'm certain ye would have much rather kept buried."

Like the duke himself. Her pride was still smarting from the way he'd set her out on his stoop and then slammed the door in her face. There'd been a crowd of people outside his gates, pretending they weren't there on purpose to see what happened. Walking down the path to her carriage had felt like a walk of shame, with every pair of eyes on hers, trying to figure out exactly what had happened. They were left to their conclusions, which undoubtedly painted her in a most unflattering light. She could see the scandal sheets now: cartoons of her painted on her arse, skirts billowing up around her head outside the duke's residence.

"Well, yes. But I will no' blame the duke for not remaining dead." Jaime said it as a jest, but it came out sounding a lot more bitter than she had planned.

Giselle's smile faltered, and her expression of concern deepened. "Does Shanna know he's back?"

"I'm no' certain. She's at Dunrobin." Or that was where Jaime hoped she was. According to Lorne, her sister had not been there, and her messenger had yet to return. Where are ye, Shanna? "If she does no' yet know, she will soon." The emotion in her voice betrayed the stoic appearance she was trying to portray.

"Oh, Jaime. I'm so sorry. What a mess."

Rather than comforting her, the pity in her friend's voice made Jaime angry. She didn't want anyone's sympathy. Not now. Not ever. It only reminded her of the various ways the duke had humiliated her and her entire family. And when she'd thought him, and the disgrace he brought, finally buried —now everything was rising from the grave to swirl around her in a choking cloud of ash.

"Is that all, then?" Jaime said, finding some of the hardness that had cracked a moment ago and pasting it back in place. "I do no' have time for frivolous visits. I've a company to run."

Giselle appeared taken aback and hurt, and Jaime was instantly full of regret, but she couldn't stop the deluge she'd started. So, she stood, just as MacInnes brought in their tea.

Her old friend, however, remained seated and offered the older butler a gentle smile. "Thank ye, MacInnes. I hope ye've been well."

"Verra well, my lady." MacInnes set the tea service down on the carved mahogany table and bowed. Cook's currant scones looked decadent and smelled heavenly. Oh, she'd lied to Lorne about not wanting scones. She loved them.

When MacInnes left, Giselle turned her unwavering gaze on Jaime. "I know we've grown apart these past few years, but no' for my lack of trying. Why do ye keep shutting me out?"

"Me, shut ye out?" Jaime didn't try to hide her exasperation. "Your mother made it plain that we were no longer to be friends, and ye did no' argue."

Giselle stiffened and reached forward, pouring out the tea when Jaime failed to do so. She placed in the milk and sugar, remembering exactly how Jaime liked it. How could her friend act so calm in the face of Jaime's discomfort?

"I take your silence as agreement."

Giselle carefully stirred her tea and then lifted the cup to sip. "My mother is...difficult. And I did argue. Quite a lot. I even sent ye letters. But ye did no' reply. And I took it upon myself this time to show up. My mother will have my head over it later. Enough people are milling about outside taking notes, it will likely be in the evening paper."

"I never got any letters." Jaime narrowed her eyes. "Ye need no' lie."

"I'm no' lying. I sent dozens." Giselle's face flamed with color, and she set her cup down. "My God, do ye think my mother could have stolen my letters?"

Jaime shrugged. "I wouldn't put it past her."

"And all this time, I thought ye were shutting me out."

"I'd never shut out a friend, Giselle." Jaime sipped her tea to keep herself from groaning. "And now that we've reconnected, your mother will be certain to keep ye under lock and key."

"No doubt."

"I wish they would leave me alone. Ye might have gotten away with coming if they weren't obsessed over me."

"This will pass when the next bit of scandal sweeps the ton by storm."

Jaime was skeptical. With the duke in town and their issues unresolved, it seemed as if it would be quite some time before anyone had their fill of the Andrewson and Sutherland drama. "Ye risk much by coming here. What about your prospects? Will they back away?"

Giselle waved away the warning. "I'll wed when I find a man who is worthy of my attention. Thus far, they've all been sadly lacking."

"Are ye no' worried your mother will force the issue?" Especially now.

Giselle smiled ruefully. "The countess is no' the only stubborn woman in the Hepburn household. Enough about me, Jaime. I came to talk about ye."

And back to this again. Jaime set down her tea, stood and

went to the window. "Looks as though the street is clearing out." It wasn't. But she was ready to be finished talking about herself.

"Please, do no' shut me out. I'm worried."

Jaime let out a long sigh and turned back to where Giselle perched on the settee. She'd so missed having a friend to confide in, and here was one right in front of her. A dear one who used to hold all her secrets. Perhaps now was a good time to open herself up and let her worries out. She had to talk to someone. Her insides were so coiled into knots, she was afraid she'd wake up twisted. "I am too. I have no' heard from Shanna, and she's about to become destitute again."

"Is that why ye went to see the duke and he ye?" Giselle edged cautiously to stand beside Jaime.

"Partly, aye. He also wants his castle back."

"That was quite a coup." Giselle grinned, obviously having taken pleasure in reading about the sale.

Jaime frowned. "An illegal one, it would seem."

Giselle peeked out the window. "What really happened all those years ago—between the duke and your sister?"

Jaime had only been sixteen when her sister was defiled and betrayed by the duke, and Giselle only thirteen, understanding even less. Their parents hadn't shared much, and as young lasses do when denied the confidences of older debutantes and society ladies, they made up whatever came to mind from the bits and pieces they'd heard. The stories Jaime had heard, repeated by Giselle, were outrageous, and if she'd been in a better mood, quite hilarious. One such rumor had been that the duke had decided to run off with a traveling circus, and another that Shanna had discovered him in flagrante delicto with not one but three ladies from the theater. Of course, none of these came close to the truth.

"Plain and simple. They were engaged to wed, and he convinced her that his promise of marriage alone was enough for them to consummate their union. But as soon as she was with child, he left her. End of story."

Giselle wrinkled her brow. "That is odd, is it no'?"

"It is the worst kind of betrayal."

"But do ye no' think it strange? Why would he propose to her, spoil her and dump her? He's a duke, after all, and a member of Parliament. A war hero. Why would he risk so much of his reputation to get into her skirts when he could have had any woman in Scotland and England—or in the rest of the world, for that matter?"

Jaime pursed her lips. No one had ever put so succinctly into words the very thought she'd had more than once.

But she came back to the same conclusion each time. "I have to trust my sister's word."

Giselle nodded. "Aye, for why would she lie?"

Another question Jaime had asked herself and come up empty. "There is no doubt that she had a child. Gordie is proof of that. And I think he looks the spitting image of the duke."

"Oh, my. Then he is most certainly the father."

"Aye." There was no doubting it. Yet, the prickling questions that had been gnawing at Jaime for years never seemed to rest.

They returned to the couch, each of them picking up a scone to nibble.

"Have ye ever thought—never mind." Giselle gave a little laugh, putting a spot of clotted cream on her scone.

"Thought what?"

"I was going to suggest asking the duke for his version, but it would be quite improper. Or perhaps ye already have."

"No, I have no', but I've thought about it. And it's as improper as me showing up on his doorstep." Lot of good that had done her. It seemed when the two of them were together, all they did was split hairs, rather than move forward with what either of them wanted accomplished.

"I had heard about that. And given he tossed ye out for all to see, perhaps he owes it to ye to answer your questions."

"The man does no' believe he owes me anything. He is demanding I return the deed to the castle and has yet to reimburse me for the sale."

"That's odd. Does he truly want it back?"

"I have no doubt." Jaime lifted the teapot to refill their cups.

"Hmm." Giselle sipped from her replenished cup. "Men are so strange."

"They truly are." And maddeningly insufferable, especially the Duke of Sutherland. She glanced toward the door of the drawing room, half-expecting to see him barrel through it with more of his nonsense. Lord, she wouldn't mind if he did, so she could give him another piece of her mind.

"Another reason I'm willing to put off another season without an engagement. Much to Mama's disappointment."

"I never want to marry," Jaime agreed. Her stomach tightened at the thought, and she decided to change the subject. "Do tell me who made your dress. It is divine."

Giselle smoothed a hand over the silken frock. "Oh, aye, Madame Yolande. She's newly come to Edinburgh from Paris."

"I will have to set up an appointment with her."

"Ye should, and soon. She is filling up fast."

The conversation moved through various fashions and other town gossip, with Jaime certain not to mention the duke again, even if he were all she could think about. The man was consuming her every waking contemplation, taking up residence in her head where he didn't belong and was certainly not welcome.

7

He'd been avoiding her for days now. Consumed with the search for his brother, his accounts, regaining his strength, and of course, the simple act of avoiding her because she drove him mad. Even as maddening as she was, he would choose the torment of her brooding stare and cantankerous tongue over being imprisoned. Hell, he'd bear it for a lifetime.

That was something one learned when they'd been in hell, that there were monsters a lot darker, and troubles a lot harsher, complications grimmer. And so, that was how when he woke up each morning since returning from the continent —he was a survivor and would keep on keeping on.

Over breakfast, he'd sifted through the stack of newspapers and broadsheets brought in by Mungo. He ignored the cartoons of him and Jaime yanking back and forth a small castle that he supposed was Dunrobin. Rubbish. The papers had been filled with rumors about his return and their subsequent visits. Even going so far as to suggest that perhaps he'd come back to ravish Jaime in the same way her sister had accused him of nearly a decade before.

It was all drivel, of course. A bunch of nonsense from writers who couldn't find a fact beyond the tip of their nose and likely didn't get that much right.

However, upon entering his club to locate Malcolm and inquire if anything had been found about Gille, his eye was drawn to five men hunched over a betting book. They were talking rather rambunctiously and laughing, and Lorne could swear he heard them say "Andrewson."

What the devil?

He wedged his way between the men, none of them yet noticing that it was him seeing what was written in the book: Bets on Duke Seducing Another Andrewson.

Lorne could not believe what he was seeing—and then the words blurred, and all he saw was red. Men were betting on how long it would take before he ruined Jaime? The bloody bastards.

"Who created this ridiculous shite?" he demanded, letting his anger show.

The men leapt back, the book dropping as no one wanted to claim ownership. He might have been gone from Scotland for a long time, but they all knew he would beat them bloody in a fight, and Lord, was he wishing one of them would instigate it.

But no one answered. Lorne lifted the book from the floor, turning to the page and reading a few of the names aloud. "MacIntyre, Ross, Blair. The lot of ye bastards."

He ripped the pages from the book and tossed the rest of it at a club footman, who was all too happy grasp the scraps.

"Ye're all a bunch of bloody fools. Return the bets placed. This is a dead gamble." He stormed out of the club, angry that men he'd thought friends were betting behind his back. And grateful at the same time that he'd not seen his dearest mates on the list.

He hopped atop his mount and took off through the streets, narrowly avoiding a cart full of cabbage. Shortly, he found himself near the docks in Leith, watching Jaime talk with her men. Obscured by the dockhands busily working, he was content to watch and learn.

She was so lovely and serious. What he wouldn't give to see a crack in that stony exterior, to see her smile. The lass was so different from her sister. Shanna had been all laughs and gossip. He'd found her irritating, but the match had been good, and her dowry had included a parcel of land in Ireland that he knew would work very well for sheep farming. At the time, he'd been of the mind to ignore the parts of her that irked him, only because brides were meant to carry on a man's legacy. To produce heirs. Once they had the requisite heir and a spare, he'd leave her to her frivolous tendencies, and he could move on with his life. They need not be friends. That was what his mates were for.

The moment she'd betrayed him with the one thing he'd desired out of a marriage—heirs—he'd ended things. In that heated moment, he'd also decided he wasn't going even to attempt to find another bride—that he'd let the title and lands fall to his brother. Soon after, he'd been called to the front lines. And all he'd longed for while fighting a battle, and lying awake in a cold cell, had been to wish that someone back home were praying for him, thinking of him. That there would be a pair of warm arms to welcome him home.

And all this time, they'd thought him dead.

But—there had been at least one person thinking of him. Jaime. Even if her thoughts had veered toward revenge and hatred. Much as she wished him dead now, he'd still take it. Better to be thought of in that light than forgotten altogether.

Lorne approached her as she turned away from one of her

men and sauntered head down back toward her office with a ledger book.

"Miss Andrewson."

She jerked her gaze up, faltering in her steps, obviously surprised to see him. Quick to recover her footing, she demanded, "What are ye doing here?" She slammed her ledger book shut and stopped her forward progression.

"Thought ye'd gotten rid of me?" Lorne dismounted and looped his horse's reins around the horse-tie pillar.

With whitened knuckles, she clutched the ledger to her chest like a shield. "Well, when ye put me out on your stoop, it was quite clear ye were rid of me."

"True. And I apologize for such a rude gesture. I was... frustrated." He offered her a smile that she did not return.

Jaime's brows narrowed, and if possible, her knuckles grew whiter. If she clutched that ledger book any harder, she'd shred it. "Did ye just apologize, Your Grace?"

A tingle rose along the back of Lorne's neck, the same one he got when ready to box or fence—the sign of an imminent challenge. And there were no immediate indications of danger; it was merely his instinctual reaction to the firebrand before him. "Aye."

"And so easily." Oh, he was in trouble, for her voice had taken on the smooth, silken tones of a viper about to strike.

Lorne's smile faltered. "What are ye getting at?"

Jaime shrugged and seemed to file away whatever information she'd gleaned from his reaction. "Nothing. What do ye want?"

Lorne studied her, taking in the splotch of ink on her forehead—a smear really, no doubt from rubbing her brow with a stained finger. Without hesitation, and perhaps hoping to shock her, he tugged his handkerchief from his pocket and pressed it to her skin, wiping away the smudge.

She gasped, jumping out of reach, and then touched her forehead, bestowing upon herself another ink splotch. "What are ye doing?"

At least she'd been forced to drop her shield of the ledger book, and he hoped that meant she'd ditch the other armor she'd erected.

"Ye had ink on your face, and now ye've just added some more. I was trying to help."

"Oh my goodness." Flustered, she wiped at it again, only making the spot bigger until he had to stop her.

Lorne grabbed her hand, turning her palm upright. "Look at your fingers. They're covered in ink, and now your entire forehead is dyed black."

Jaime looked stricken, so he handed her the handkerchief.

"I do no' think this will help ye now. Ye need a good scrubbing, I wager."

She let out a frustrated growl and charged back toward her office. "I'm no' a street urchin."

"I'd never mistake ye for one." Lorne followed behind, allowing her a moment to get ahead of him to compose herself. Though he shouldn't have, for once more, he was forced to watch her retreat, which was not a hardship. But he'd regret it later when the enticing swing of her hips haunted his dreams.

Emilia sat at her desk, glancing up when he came in, then leaping to her feet as recognition hit. "Oh, Your Grace." She made an awkward curtsy. "Can I get ye some tea?"

"No, thank ye. And ye need not curtsy every time I come in," he said softly. "I'm no' the king, and ye are no' my servant."

Jaime came back into the room, her face clean, but her cheeks flushed. "Ye're still here." The woman couldn't have sounded any more disappointed.

He grinned. "I am. I came to apologize, if ye recall."

"Ye already did that. So be about your way. I am busy, and ye are distracting me."

Good. He wanted to distract her.

She stared at him expectantly, and he found himself at a loss for words. Jaime seemed to be the one woman in all the world who didn't find him attractive or interesting. More like a nuisance, a fly she wanted to squash, and he found himself drawn to her because of it. And he shouldn't be. He had to focus on his goal—getting his castle back, either by negotiation or marriage, but neither of these things seemed to be working. Mostly because he'd yet to try to negotiate beyond demanding she return it. And secondly, because a marriage between them was supposed to be a business transaction, yet he felt more and more unbusinesslike every time he saw her.

"Can we speak in private?" he asked.

Jaime glanced at her clerk, who tried to make herself seem busy. "Anything ye have to say to me can be said before my witness."

"Your witness?" Lorne raised a brow at her choice of words as if he were about to do her harm.

"Aye. We are at legal odds, are we no'?"

"Ah, well, that is true. But what I have to say has nothing to do with that. I've no intention to cause ye harm. I assure ye, this is a quite personal matter."

Jaime's mouth formed a little O before she clamped it shut. "In that case, I must insist that whatever it is ye want to say to me, ye say in front of my clerk. I do have a reputation to keep."

Lorne tensed. Had she already heard the rumors of the gentlemen's bet? "As ye wish. I came to tell ye that there is a wager going around town of a rather delicate nature, involving both of us. And I did no' want ye to find out about it before I had a chance to tell ye that I have no intention of doing what they say and that I have put an end to the bookmaking."

"What is it they are wagering?" She narrowed her brows at him, and once more, that ledger book came up like a shield.

"That I will…" How exactly could he put this in a delicate way? Och, the hell with it. Jaime Andrewson was no gentle miss, and she wouldn't appreciate his gentler insinuations. "Seduce ye."

Jaime laughed, the ledger falling as her head tilted back, and she seemed to roar with every part of her. She tossed the book onto her desk so she could wipe the tears from her eyes. Lorne wasn't certain if he should be offended or not. He thought it was likely he should be.

"It takes two in a seduction, Your Grace." All the laughter left her, that serious, no-nonsense expression back. Lord, but she would make a great governess, keeping all the little hellions in line. "The seducer and the seduced. And ye can trust that I have no intention of being seduced by ye. I plan to stay as far away from ye as I can. Ye've said what ye came to say, now leave."

But Lorne wasn't going to be deterred, as much as she had insulted him just now. He rather found it charming. "In that case, I suppose ye do no' want this invitation." He pulled the envelope from his coat pocket that he'd decided to deliver this morning personally.

"What is it for?" She put her hands behind her back as if that would somehow force herself not to reach for it.

"I'm hosting a ball." Of all the godawful things he could have surmised in his scheme to gain her favor.

Jaime screwed up her face, peering up at him, as shocked as he felt when he'd agreed to host one—though it had been a wager gone wrong in the ring with Alec Hay. More wagers…

However, the more Lorne thought about it, the more the idea had grown on him. A ball to show everyone he was well and hearty; a ball to show he was still wealthy despite his missing brother and the woman before him stealing his birthright. A ball to stop all the gossips from guessing about him and to truly see what he was about. And now, of course, a place for the two of them to be seen together and show that he was not seducing her.

"Why are ye inviting me?" She refused to take the offered envelope, folding her hands in front of her hips to keep them still.

Her question was valid, and the answers he'd run through his mind this morning while Mungo gave him a shave mostly made sense to him. Mostly.

"I thought perhaps if people were to see us avoiding each other at the ball, the rumors of my supposed seduction would temper down." This, of course, was not the original idea, as he'd not even known about the wager until after the invitations had been written. But what she didn't know couldn't sway her.

"So this is for your reputation, then, Your Grace. Clever of ye to disguise it as protecting mine."

Lorne was taken aback. "This is no disguise. I care no' so much for mine, but for yours."

"So because ye've already ruined one Andrewson lass, ye hope to save the next one?" She let out a snort that would make a lesser man's ballocks fall to the floor.

Lorne, however, only grew irritated. He'd reached out to her repeatedly, yet she continued to jab him with a metaphorical stick. "The only one who ruined your sister was herself." He thrust the envelope toward Jaime. "Come or do no', I couldn't care less."

Jaime reached for the envelope, taking it with a crisp snatch, more out of instinct than wanting what he offered, he suspected. "I will no' attend. Consider that my response, Your Grace."

Lorne let out a short, bitter laugh. "One day, Jaime, perhaps no' until ye're old and gray, ye'll realize the mistake ye made when ye considered me your enemy."

Lorne nodded to Emilia. "Good day, Miss Butler." Then he turned for the door, but Jaime halted his steps with her words.

"Ye've got to stop leaving me with cryptic messages. I rather tire of our verbal sparring, and I suspect ye must as well. Out with it, Lorne."

But he wasn't ready to do her any favors. Without even turning around to address her, he said, "If we are no' to be friends, then ye may address me as 'Your Grace.'"

Jaime, ignoring his snobbish retort, said, "How can we be friends with all that's passed between us?"

Lorne did look at her over his shoulder then, raising a single brow. "There has been no exchange between us, Miss Andrewson. My past dealings with your family did no' concern ye. And the shady dealings ye had with my brother did no' concern me as both of ye assumed, or rather greedily hoped, that I remained dead. I have come to make amends for whatever transgressions ye took so personally, and yet ye persist in forcing the issue of animosity between us. I see no further need to continue. From now on, ye will address my solicitor with any of your concerns."

Jaime looked stricken, and the guilt he felt at hurting her feelings stung inside his chest. But why should he care? She'd been nothing but rude, wishing him dead every time he'd seen her. Snatching his apology and stomping on it with the heel of her boot until his words held no meaning.

This was not the welcome home he'd wanted. And at his ball in a few days, he'd set the record straight where she was concerned.

THE CRISP WHITE ENVELOPE ON HER DRESSING TABLE taunted Jaime.

She'd set it there after coming home from the wharf, watched it from the corner of her eye as she'd undressed and brushed her hair. It appeared to glimmer in the candlelight as she took her bath, and now from the chair where she'd curled up to read a book, the invitation beckoned her.

"Fine, I'll read it," she said to no one. Slamming her book closed—a gothic romance novel she couldn't get enough of and read six times—she marched toward her dressing table and broke the duke's seal on the back.

In fine, delicate scroll, she was cordially invited to the duke's homecoming ball. Of course, even if she wanted to go, she couldn't, for she hadn't a gown appropriate to wear to such an occasion. All the fancy frocks she possessed were so old she'd be laughed out of the imposing house before she was even announced. And she certainly wouldn't show up in one of her day dresses or her working dresses.

But there was Madame Yolande that Giselle had recommended and whom Jaime had an appointment with in the morning to make her a few new day dresses. Perhaps she could convince the modiste to fashion a new ball gown too.

Och, but nay. That was preposterous. Jaime wasn't going to attend the duke's stupid homecoming ball. Especially not after what the duke had said in her office. She was only to address Lorne as "Your Grace" and only to correspond with him through his solicitor. That meant she couldn't go to his ball. Wouldn't be welcome in his home. If she did show up, she wouldn't be surprised if he passed his punch to his butler and hauled her out of there like a sack of potatoes and, this time, tossed her rather than placed her on his front stoop.

Except when he'd departed earlier in the day, he'd not

snatched the invitation back after she accepted it. He'd left it with her as he stalked out of her office as if he owned the place. Head held high, broad shoulders exuding power. He'd made her feel small in the one place she felt large.

Was the wager he'd mentioned true? Were the men of Edinburgh gambling on her virtue, believing that Lorne would ruin her? Such a gamble was as much an insult to her as it was to Lorne. For he'd been nothing but a gentleman—albeit a cantankerous one—since he'd been back. Did they respect him so little?

She couldn't blame Lorne for his frustration with her. She'd been rude to him every chance she got, quite on purpose. A decision she would repeat if given a chance. Apologies and niceties meant nothing in the grand scheme of what he'd done to her sister.

But still, she did feel slightly guilty for having told him more than once she wished him back in the grave. That part wasn't true. She'd never really wished him dead, even if she did wish him to be punished. The guilt wiggled a little deeper, too, for not once had she inquired as to how he was after being imprisoned for two long years or how he'd managed to escape. Or maybe he'd been let go. She'd know if she'd bothered to ask.

Jaime bit her lip, folding the invitation. Rather unfairly, shame pulsed in her chest. But why did she feel this way? Lorne's troubles were not hers. The man had ruined her sister's life.

The only one who ruined your sister was herself.

Lorne's words came back to haunt her. He'd blamed her sister for her circumstances, of course. The man wasn't willing to take responsibility for his actions. Jaime marched toward the hearth, prepared to throw the invitation into the flames, when her conversation with Giselle flashed in her mind.

Despite his humiliating her in her office, Jaime still had way too many questions that needed answers. And if she weren't going to be allowed to ask him to his face without permission from his solicitor, perhaps attending his ball was the last chance she'd get to settle the uncertainties that plagued her mind.

With her decision made to acquire a ballgown and attend the ridiculous fete, Jaime tossed and turned throughout the night until it was time for her appointment with the modiste. There was a slight drizzle, and she entered the shop damp from having to cross the street, as the number of carriages in the way had not allowed her coachman to deposit her out front. She didn't have time to wait or she'd risk losing her appointment.

Madame Yolande, however, was waiting for her, all kind smiles and interested eyes.

"Apologies for my state," Jaime said.

"You are lovely, mademoiselle. Please, do come in."

For a price, Madame Yolande was willing to make the ball gown in blue gossamer silk, studded with crystals. She assured Jaime the dress would make her look like a fae princess and draw all eyes. Which was not what Jaime wanted, and she'd argued the point. But Madame Yolande tsked and tutted and would hear nothing of it. Not wanting to lose the opportunity for a stunning gown, Jaime relented. Madame Yolande was also planning to commission a pair of matching slippers, new white gloves that promised to sparkle, and several new undergarments. When Jaime finally did leave the modiste, she felt more anxious than when she'd arrived.

Back at her flat, MacInnes announced, "Ye've a visitor, Miss, in the drawing room."

The first person she thought of was Lorne, but she knew that couldn't be as he'd made it clear he never wanted to see her again. She touched her hair, once more wet from the rain.

"Who is it? I need to refresh myself."

"Mr. Bell has arrived with news from Dunrobin."

"Oh." In that case, she didn't mind presenting herself slightly soggy. Jaime rushed toward the drawing room, finding Mr. Bell standing by her window, staring down at the street.

His face was somber, and her stomach did a flip already, knowing the news would be grim. Goodness, but she hoped it wasn't too grim. Her hand flew to her chest as she sucked in a worried breath.

"Miss Andrewson."

Jaime shook her head. "Please, there is no need for formalities. Just tell me what ye've learned."

"Your sister and her son did no' arrive at Dunrobin."

Jaime sank onto a chair. "Were they attacked on the road?" Oh, dear heavens, all this time was her sister lying in a shallow grave?

Mr. Bell shook his head. "She sent word ahead to the house that she was detained on a personal matter, and it would be some time before she arrived. I examined the letter, and it was in her hand. Did no' appear to be shaky strokes, but rather confident ones. We also found young Master Gordie's governess at an inn north of Edinburgh. Her rooms had been paid for the duration, and she'd expected them to return to fetch her but had no word when. I left a man with her in case your sister does return, but I have my doubts."

The investigator passed her the letter Shanna had written to those at Dunrobin, and Jaime stared at her sister's elegant scroll. Mr. Bell was right; the writing was languid and well thought. Not hurried or unsteady at all.

In her missive, she informed the household at Dunrobin that she'd gone abroad to settle some things of a personal nature, and that all employed and in residence were welcome to remain until she returned at which point they'd need to leave.

"What does this mean?" Where could she have gone? Shanna didn't have any errands to run abroad or scores to settle.

"I'm no' certain, miss. But I would suggest we hire several more men to find her."

"I agree."

Shanna would be livid when she found out that Jaime had hired men to hunt her down, but she'd never done anything so irresponsible in her life. Oh, poor Gordie! To be dragged who knew where with his mother, and his governess dropped off at an inn on the way.

"I want my nephew. If she refuses to return, please see that he is brought back to me."

Mr. Bell nodded. "And if she refuses to relinquish the child?"

Jaime thought about Shanna over all these years. How she'd been so happy to send her son off with tutors and governesses, of which there had been many, given Shanna's demands. Gordie had spent more time with Jaime at the wharf than he had with his mother in the nursery. "I do no' think she will disagree."

Bitterness burned in the back of Jaime's throat. With every day that ticked by, the pieces of a pedestal she'd placed her sister on were chipping away.

Had Shanna run away? It made no sense. Jaime had taken good care of them. Even bought her a bloody castle. She could not come up with even a single reasonable answer as to why her sister would abscond with her child to the continent or wherever it was that she'd gone.

Unless she'd had word that Lorne was alive and well. Perhaps Shanna didn't want to run into him at the castle. Maybe her sister was scared too, afraid of the humiliation of seeing the man who'd betrayed her. Or worse—afraid he might steal son, for as soon as he laid eyes on Gordie, he would know that the lad was his.

That made sense to Jaime. As much as Shanna had brushed aside her duties as a mother, she did love her son, and she wouldn't want him to be taken from her, especially by a man whom she'd trusted only to find his affection rescinded. If Jaime were a mother, she might have chosen the same path. It didn't make it right, though, and Gordie's place was home, not abroad.

"If that is all, miss, I best be on my way."

"Aye, please keep me informed, and tell Mr. MacInnes to please give ye the envelope I prepared."

"Of course." Mr. Bell tipped his head on his way out of the drawing room.

Jaime drifted to the window, watching a few moments later as her agent disappeared down the path.

"Where are ye, Shanna? What have ye done?" There were no answers in the empty drawing room. No magical resolutions from deep within her mind.

Jaime went upstairs to her sister's bedchamber, staring around the room, wondering if there would be any clues inside that would help her. A journal, a letter, something. Everything was in the same place Shanna had left it. Soft pink silk comforter on her four-poster bed. Her dressing table was cleared of her brushes and combs. The curtains were drawn back to let in daylight, illuminating the creams and pinks of the décor.

But Shanna's dressing table drawers were as empty as its surface, her wardrobe holding only the older gowns she'd not wanted and a few pairs of worn-out slippers. Nothing under the bed or mattress.

Sitting back on her heels on the floor, Jaime stared up at the ceiling, painted in delicate pink-and-gold scrolls. This was ridiculous. Shanna wasn't hiding anything. She must have been spooked by the news of the duke's return, just as Jaime had been. The careful world the two of them had built after the scandal and their parents disowning Shanna was crashing down around them.

It was up to Jaime to pick up the pieces.

8

Lorne loosened his cravat, feeling as though it were choking the life out of him. Or rather that the ball, and the dozens of carriages pulling up to his house with guests lavishly outfitted alighting, was suffocating him. The streetlamps outside shone brightly on them all, their jewels catching the light and twinkling.

He was fairly certain this had been a bad idea. One, because he abhorred most society functions, and two, because the whole reason he'd decided to have this ball in the first place was because he'd lost a wager to Alec. The added benefit was that he'd get to show the world he had no interest in Jaime Andrewson. To put the gossipmongers and their ridiculous rumors to rest.

Of course, since she wouldn't be in attendance, their disinterest in one another would be easily surmised. But he had hoped they could ignore each other, make a show of it. Though he wasn't certain why he'd agreed to the idea in the first place. It was clear the woman had no interest in saving her reputation, given she'd flat-out denied him.

Perhaps she was more like her sister than he'd thought.

Even as he thought it, he doubted it. There had always been differences between Jaime and Shanna, all the more so when Jaime was a young girl, not yet come out into society. There were, of course, the broader, more noticeable traits like intelligence, business acumen, and frivolousness. Both the former of which Jaime held copious amounts, and the latter was gifted to her sister.

There were also smaller, less noticeable qualities he'd taken note of as well. Years ago, when they'd had tea, Jaime had always made certain everyone was involved in the conversation, listening and recalling tidbits of personal anecdotes others told her in the past, while her sister was content to cut anyone off who she'd lost interest in. Jaime remembered he hated cucumbers, whereas Shanna always made certain there was an abundance of cucumber sandwiches on hand. He'd taken his betrothed's behavior for nerves and thought that since the pair were sisters, they were likely very similar, and it was taking Shanna a bit of time to warm up.

What a foolish idea that had been. And he should have known better, for he and Gille, were very different people.

A knock sounded at his door, and Mungo came through. "Your guests are arriving, Your Grace, and none can be announced or enter the ballroom without your presence. Or are ye forgoing the receiving line?"

Lorne groaned. How he hated the proper way of things. Why could they not just go and dance and mingle and gossip without him, then vacate the premises at a preferably tolerable hour, leaving him in peace?

"Do I have to?"

Mungo raised a single brow. "Ye do no' have to do anything, Your Grace, but the purpose of this function was to show your face, was it no'?"

"Somewhat."

Miraculously, Lorne's face had been unscathed by the cannon that laid him flat. He was lucky that way. But if he were to present himself naked before the ton below, they'd run screaming.

"I'm coming." He retightened his cravat and tried to remove the scowl from his face as he descended the stairs, but the latter was proving quite a feat.

The grand foyer of his ducal townhome was packed with aristocrats trying to show off their wealth and popularity. Mungo's voice belted out, silencing the crowd who turned as a collective to stare up at him, "His Grace, the Duke of Sutherland."

Lorne nodded to his old friend, and then with a forced smile, nodded at his guests as he descended, taking each stair deliberately and giving them ample time to ogle him. He cut a dashing figure in his kilt and doublet. The tartan socks and buckled shoes were a bit irritating considering he much preferred his riding boots, but at least they showed off the muscles in his legs. That was one thing he wanted—to show he was still the strongest fellow in the room.

At the base of the stairs with Mungo beside him, his guests were introduced and filed into the ballroom. One face after another in a blur. The only ones he was happy to recognize were Alec Hay, Euan Irvine, and his cousin Malcolm.

When at last he was set free from the tediousness of greeting every guest he wished had declined the invitation, he sought out his friends and cousin.

"Took ye long enough," Malcolm teased.

"If I have to smile and tell one more mother that her daughter is a vision, I'll hang myself." Lorne tugged at the collar of his shirt, wishing he could at least take off the cravat.

"Your ball is the talk of the town and will likely be the talk of London soon. Even my barber was talking about it," Alec murmured. "Nearly cut off my ear when I mentioned I was going."

Lorne chuckled. The four of them stood in the corner, observing the dance floor, as the small orchestra he'd hired for the occasion struck up a familiar song.

"Are ye no' dancing?" Euan asked, looking nervous as if he expected to be accosted by several of the mothers salivating on the sidelines.

"I've no interest." Lorne watched men gather ladies and pull them to the center of the floor.

"But it is your ball. Ye'll be expected to."

"And they'll be disappointed. I supposed I can no' interest any of ye in a fight instead?"

"Do ye think they'd notice if we went missing?" Malcolm asked.

Lorne let his gaze slide over the crowd. "Aye," he answered, disheartened. Nearly every eye was on him rather than the dancers, obviously assuming him to have chosen a partner for the first whirl.

"Why no' pick an older woman to be your dance partner," Euan suggested. "A widow, perhaps?"

"Or someone's granny?" Malcolm teased.

Lorne grinned. "That's no' a bad idea."

"My grandmother, the Dowager Countess of Errol, is here chaperoning my cousins," Alec offered. "I'll make the introductions."

Lorne nodded, following his friend to find an older woman sipping punch.

"My lady," Alec said. "Might I introduce ye to the Duke of Sutherland? He has requested your hand for this dance."

"Mine?" the dowager sputtered, flicking open her fan. "Och, but I'm too old to dance."

"A lady is never too old to dance. It would be my honor to have ye on my arm," Lorne said, bowing to Alec's granny.

"Well, if ye insist." The fan snapped closed.

"Oh, I do."

He took the older woman by the arm and led her out to the dance floor, joining the others. At the far end of the line, Euan had brought out his partner and Malcolm the same, both of them looking sour as hell. Alec, meanwhile, gloated on the side.

Well, here went nothing.

As much as Lorne thought he'd hate dancing, the dowager made it fun by whispering bits of gossip each time they were paired to turn and nodding in the direction of whoever she was speaking about as they broke apart.

"Ye're utterly charming," Lorne said, leading her off the floor when the dance ended.

"If only I were younger," she said with a mocking wistful sigh.

Lorne chuckled. "No one else would stand a chance. I thank ye for allowing me this dance, my lady. I simply could no' choose between all the twittering ninnies, and I much prefer the company of a mature woman."

Granny flashed open her fan and waved it in front of her face. "Ye're a charmer, Your Grace. And, I might add, it is good to have ye back alive."

Lorne pressed his hand over his heart and bowed. "Thank ye, my lady."

He retreated from the dowager, made his way back to the corner and stopped more times than he cared to be introduced to one debutante after another. He was nearly there when Mungo's voice boomed out of the crowd and stopped Lorne dead in his tracks.

"Miss Jaime Andrewson and the Viscountess Whittleburn."

JAIME STOOD AT THE ENTRANCE TO THE BALLROOM, ALL eyes on her and her aunt, who'd made a sneak attack visit that morning to inform her that she was not going to the ball alone. It was most unfortunate and rather irritating. Jaime was a grown woman and perfectly capable of taking care of herself.

But Jaime suspected the true reason her aunt had come up from London was that she wanted to be at the ball that was garnering all the talk of the Scottish ton, and even those in London who'd yet to step foot in Edinburgh.

It had been years since Jaime had been inside a ballroom, and nerves prickled every inch of her skin. The new gown fit like a glove, and when she twirled, the lights caught on the crystals, making it sparkle magically. It was the same when she walked, she noticed. She slowly made her way forward, smiling at familiar faces and trying not to look as frightened as she felt.

So many people looked astonished to see here there, and with little doubt as to why. It'd been years since she'd attended a ball, and now here she was, likely putting voice to all their rumors.

"Come, let us make our way to His Grace," her aunt whispered in her distinctly English aristocratic tones. "We are here to show that despite past fractures, our family ties are not destroyed."

"I'd rather no'," Jaime whispered. Oh, why had she decided to come?

"Which is why we should."

But they needn't have gone far, for the duke approached them, looking unbelievably confident and devastatingly handsome in his kilt and doublet. Had he always been so tall? His gray eyes were cool as they met hers. Jaime flicked her gaze up to the center of his forehead, when all she wanted to do was take him in. Even looking there at his head, her imagination conjured what she wasn't looking at. The turn of his muscled calf in his hose. The way his dark locks seemed to fall in all the right places, making him look as though he'd just come in from an exhilarating ride. The wide, full mouth that would undoubtedly demand she leave, but which she actually, for a fraction of a second, wondered what it would be like to kiss.

It was no wonder her sister had been obsessed with him. Lorne was too gorgeous for words. Unfairly good-looking. Damn him.

Aunt Beatrice tugged Jaime into a curtsy, which she did begrudgingly, hating the idea of groveling before the man who'd made it so clear the last time they'd spoken that she was not to be in his presence again. And yet, there was a thrum of excitement swirling in her belly, knowing his eyes were on her. Did he like her gown? Her hair?

"Lady Whittleburn and Miss Andrewson." Lorne's voice was smooth as silk, gliding over the silence of the ballroom as everyone—including Jaime—waited on bated breath for what he'd say next.

"Your Grace," Jaime murmured, while her aunt was a bit more enthusiastic.

"You have a lovely home, Your Grace, and what a magnificent fete you've put on. We are so very glad that you've returned."

"Thank ye, my lady." Lorne nodded his head, but his questioning gaze slid toward Jaime. From what she could tell peeking through her lashes, he was waiting for an explanation. And he'd be waiting a long time.

She was losing her nerve.

Beatrice grabbed Jaime's hand, starting to tug at the dance card tied around her wrist, but Jaime yanked back. "If you're not already full, which I'm certain you must be," her aunt said with a nervous laugh, "then I'm certain my niece would very much enjoy the honor of a dance. Two families coming together in peace, shall we say?"

Jaime sucked in a breath and held it, wishing she could run away. Oh, Aunt Beatrice, do shut up! Heat suffused her cheeks, and if the ballroom floor had opened up right then and there, she would have been the first to take a flying leap into a black hole. This was not at all what she'd had planned and it was embarrassing to boot. She was supposed to wait for an invitation to dance from any man, and she certainly didn't want one from Lorne. This was a far cry from pulling him aside and asking for a moment to speak about her sister in private, or not in private. They could have done it beside one of the palm plants near the window for all she cared. But not dancing. Not touching.

The silence was dragging on as Lorne studied her, making an already awkward moment seem a million times worse.

If someone threw flames upon her cheeks, Jaime might have felt better than with the raging inferno of her face right now. She peered through her lashes at Lorne, who was staring down at her, his expression blank. Oh, how she wished she could read behind the steel-gray of his eyes, see beyond the flatness of his full mouth.

"As it happens, I am free at this moment," he said at last. "Miss Andrewson." He held out his hand..

Jaime stared at his outstretched fingers— long, slim, capable fingers—aware that the entire room was staring at them. Aunt Beatrice nudged her in the small of her back, and Jaime was forced to take his offered appendage.

His palm was warm but not overly so. When his fingers

wound around her hand, she felt comforted—which she hated —and nervous all at once.

"Ye did no' have to offer," she murmured.

"On the contrary, Miss Andrewson, I had no choice. I thought ye were no' coming," he murmured so as not to be overheard by the other guests.

"I changed my mind." Now was her chance to tell him she wished to speak to him privately, but they'd reached the dance floor and taken their positions with the other dancers. And to leave would draw attention.

She faced him, and he studied her, seemingly not aware of anyone else there. Although knowing him, he didn't care about anyone else. He looked rather bored. And she tried not to take that personally.

With the various string instruments striking up their tune, she offered a curtsy, and Lorne bowed. She glided toward him, palms up, and they pressed together. Thank goodness for gloves because even with the thin layer of fabric between them, a spark seemed to ignite where her fingertips touched his. Their eyes met, and she boldly stared into his. She couldn't run away and hide, so she might as well be herself.

"Why did ye change your mind?" Lorne's voice was a low caress.

"I wanted to speak with ye about—" but she cut herself off as they exchanged partners for a turn. Back to Lorne, she said, "I needed to speak with ye."

"I am all ears for the rest of this dance, and then we will no' be seen again together tonight. That was the whole point of me issuing ye an invitation."

They parted once more. If he were only going to give her this dance, then she'd best make haste. Returning to him, she said quickly, "'Tis about my sister. I believe she might have run away."

"Why is that any of my concern?" Though outwardly he feigned indifference, she felt his body tense, and the slight twitch of his fingers on hers.

They drifted to their other partners, but Jaime kept her eyes on him. She found herself distracted by the intensity of his gaze, rather than the muted conversation of her other partner. The way he looked at her as if he could see every secret she tried to keep hidden. Though they danced apart, with their gazes locked, they could have been with each other.

Again, that spark when his hand touched hers.

"I need ye to tell me what happened between the both of ye." And I need to stop wanting ye to touch my hand.

"Ye already think ye know," he said.

"I want to hear it from ye. I need to know why ye abandoned Gordie."

He passed her off to another dancing partner without an answer, and when she came back to him, he was frowning down at her.

"This is no' an appropriate place for this conversation," he murmured.

"It was your choice to have our one conversation tonight on the dance floor."

"I was mistaken."

The dance ended, and Lorne took her by the arm, leading her away from the dance floor. "I shall return ye to your aunt, but in a quarter-hour, come to my gymnasium. There will be no one there. We'll be discreet, and I will tell ye what ye want to know."

"I can no' risk being found alone with ye. I could lose everything."

"Ye want answers?"

Of course, she did, more than anything. That was the

reason she'd risked coming to the ball in the first place. But one thing she couldn't risk was falling under his spell as Shanna had. Risking her company and future. Then again, what other choice did she have? If he promised to be discreet, could she trust him?

"Where is your gymnasium, Your Grace? I will be noticed nosing about."

"I'll have Mungo bring ye."

He handed her back to Aunt Beatrice. Jaime considered him while he attempted to melt into the crowd only to be pulled to the dance floor by an imploring mother and daughter. Even from her spot near the wall, punch now in hand, Lorne seemed to find her, watch her.

"How was it?" Aunt Beatrice asked, sipping her punch.

Jaime was grateful for the interruption, as she'd been finding it harder and harder to look away. "Awkward."

"I gathered. The both of you looked extremely pained to be in each other's company." Beatrice pursed her lips. "So much for showing that our family rift is healed."

"I most certainly was pained, and the rift is far from healed."

"A shame what happened between him and Shanna. He does not strike me as such a rogue, and yet he is."

"Aye." Or was he? From all outward appearances and the respect he seemed to garner from everyone in his presence, which couldn't be about his title alone, was he as bad as they'd been made to believe? "Auntie, I think I see Giselle over there. Would ye mind if I speak with her?"

"Oh, no, dear, go right ahead. I've a few friends I wish to catch up with as well."

There was a small sliver of Jaime that felt bad for lying to her aunt, but a larger part of herself that didn't. If Aunt Beatrice hadn't decided to come to Edinburgh, then she wouldn't have been aware of what Jaime was doing anyway. Besides, it wasn't as if the woman married to her father's brother had sought Jaime out in the past two years. She and Shanna were lucky for the shipping company because her uncle, who'd received her father's title, houses and fortune, had done little to see to their comfort. Shanna had been disowned, and Jaime's inheritance had been the company.

But bygones were bygones.

And Jaime wasn't going to wait for her aunt to realize she hadn't seen Giselle at all. She snuck out of the ballroom, pretending to look for the ladies' retiring room, and finally saw Mungo lurking in the shadows by a grandfather clock.

"This way," he murmured, leading her into the darkness past the winding staircase.

Jaime looked behind her once to make sure no roving eyes had followed them. The last thing she needed was for the morning's society papers to light the flames of an illicit affair with the duke. Goodness, but she'd never hear the end of that, and it would likely ruin some of her business too if they thought her suddenly falling away from her practical nature.

Mungo held open a door enough distance from the ballroom that the music was barely heard, and Jaime ducked inside. There was a candle lit in a lantern at the far side of the room. Looming shapes lurched from the shadows and Jaime tried to make sense of what they were. A large beam with a ladder on each end. A massive roped-off platform that looked like a pugilist ring. Was that how Lorne kept in shape? Balancing on a beam and beating up some poor sap? She nearly tripped over a hard, metal lump on the floor. Various heavy-looking objects littered the ground. What in blazes was this stuff?

"Let's no' dally," the duke said, drawing her eyes to his single lantern. She'd not seen him there, lurking in the dark.

Now he was visible, the outline of his body framed by the light.

"What is all this?" She was genuinely curious.

"My gymnasium."

"I suppose I was no' certain what that was. We've no' got one at our house, and I've not seen any elsewhere, either."

"Boxing ring, fencing planche, training dumbbells." He pointed to the ring, the beam and the lumpy metal things.

Jaime nodded, fascinated. There was a lot more to the duke than she would have guessed. And now she understood how he was so easily able to right the falling cargo box that two of her dockhands hadn't been able to get under control. He was strong. Very strong. And filled with many talents, it would seem.

"But ye did no' come here to admire my equipment."

Jaime's gaze settled on Lorne, and she stopped mid-stride, taking in the way the glow of the light made his gray eyes sparkle and how he appeared even bigger dressed in shadows. Why had his saying such made her want to admire him?

"Will ye tell me the truth?" Jaime picked her way over to him until they were only a few feet apart, the door to the massive gymnasium somewhere in the distance.

"Why?"

"Because everything seems so jumbled in my mind. Shanna's gone missing, and I'm fairly certain 'tis because she's... hiding from ye."

Lorne leaned against the wall, hooking one ankle over the other, crossing his arms. He looked so casual and yet so... intense at the very same time. "Why would she need to hide from me? It is ye who stole my castle."

Jaime straightened. She wasn't going to back down with her questions now that she had him alone, even if he were going to try to antagonize her. "I bought it fair and square."

"That's beside the point."

She found no issue with laying the truth at his feet. "I can only think she was afraid ye'd take her child."

"Why would I do that?" Lorne had the audacity to sound exasperated.

"It is your child. Most men would take responsibility for their offspring."

Lorne laughed and swiftly came forward until he was mere inches from her. She stared up into his eyes, feeling heat fill her body. She should back away. Leave this room immediately, but her feet remained rooted in place as she met his gaze and gave him as good as he got.

"I will tell ye this once, Jaime, and I hope ye listen well." His voice was low, holding authority and warning. But it didn't scare her. For some maddening reason, she felt... excited. "That child is no' mine. I never touched your sister. Never even kissed her." As he said the words, his gaze drifted over Jaime's mouth.

Suddenly, Jaime felt even more light-headed than she had upon entering this room that was so filled with Lorne. She licked her lips, attempting to breathe, but he was crowding the space around her. The scent of him enveloped her—spicy, woodsy...intoxicating.

"But..." She tried to make her throat and tongue work to form words. "How is that possible?"

Lorne raised a brow, a tiny quirk of his lips showing her he found her question amusing. "Did no one tell ye how bairns are made?"

Oh... Flames shot to her face once more. And the image he put into her mind of Lorne...naked. Corded muscles, long legs, tight chest, strong arms ready to—

Jaime shook her head in frustration, needing to clear the visualization.

"I do no' feel it is my place to explain such things, wee Jaime."

The way he said "wee Jaime" as if trying to make her feel infantile. "I know how bairns are made, thank ye verra much."

Lorne grinned, his gaze back on her lips, and dear heavens, he roved lower to her décolletage. Jaime whipped her hands up, covering her bosom, now quite certain Madame Yolande had cut the bodice lower than she'd agreed to. Air washed over her skin, causing gooseflesh to rise on her arms, and she realized it wasn't just air but his breath as he watched her.

"If ye know so much, lass"—his voice had taken on a softer tone, low and gravelly—"then I tell ye, if it was no' me who planted a bairn in your sister, then who did?"

"No one," Jaime said in a rush, still fighting all the sensations coursing through her. Coming here was a mistake. She should have written him a letter instead. Paper never elicited this kind of a reaction from her, not even her gothic romance novels.

"She is no' the Virgin Mary." Lorne huffed in exasperation. "I had no' planned to tell ye this, Jaime, but I am beyond frustrated with this situation, and I've grown weary of your accusations. Shanna had a lover. I caught the two of them together at our engagement ball. Because I'm a gentleman, I took the fall for her. And now ye know the truth."

Jaime gasped. "What? A lover? Who?"

She searched his face, looking for signs of deceit, but found his gaze steady, his face all too serious. Lorne telling the truth.

"I do no' know." With that admission, he backed away a step, taking with him his alluring scent and the warm rush of headiness his closeness had brought.

She was both relieved for the space put between them and disgruntled by it. Ridiculous. The strange and foreign feelings he'd spawned in her tonight were forbidden. Everything about Lorne was hazardous, and there was a great risk being here with him in the dark.

Jaime forced her hand away from her breasts, back down to her sides, and stood tall once more. She couldn't let him see how much he affected her. "But ye said ye caught the two of them together."

"He jumped out the window before I could see who it was."

"Out the window?" She laughed. "Ye're lying."

"Why would I lie? 'Twas a ground floor window; he'd only a couple of feet to drop and then he ran off into the night. I'm a lot of things, Jaime, but I'm no' a liar."

If she took her sister's situation out of the equation, she could believe him. Lorne had only ever been honorable. But the fact of the matter was, her sister's situation was a major part of both their lives and couldn't be negated. "Because ye do no' want to claim the child, or responsibility for the woman ye ruined."

Lorne let out a bitter, laugh. "Let me ask ye this, Jaime— why would I no' take responsibility for my wife and child? Why would I throw a woman I'd pledged to marry out if she were carrying my heir? My whole existence, the legacy of my line, is based on the act of reproduction. I would never take advantage of a woman, and I'd never leave my child behind. That makes absolutely no sense."

Jaime shook her head because everything he said seemed sensible. Even his voice was filled with reason. And now she was remembering small things that she didn't want to. Seeing Shanna writing a letter and then slipping it in her sleeve when no one was looking. Shanna, staring wistfully off in the distance and ignoring the duke. Shanna, forgetting again that the duke disliked cucumbers or that he'd arranged to take her for a ride in the park, and she'd gone out instead with a friend. All of these things, Jaime had taken as her sister being in love and distracted by Lorne—for who wouldn't be. Perhaps it had been that Shanna was thinking of another that entire time.

"Oh, no." Jaime fanned her face and took another step backward. How perspectives changed when looked at from different angles.

Now that Lorne had planted the idea of Shanna's lover in Jaime's mind, she could see that it wasn't the duke her sister dreamed about but someone else entirely. It had been Jaime back then who had kept encouraging her sister to do the things a bride-to-be would do. Inviting Lorne for tea, attending balls and picking out perfect dresses. Telling her sister the things that she'd noticed Lorne liked or disliked. Because Jaime had so badly wanted her sister to be happy, to be a duchess. Jaime's admiration for Lorne had so blinded her that she'd failed to see her sister didn't want him at all.

The question was, who had Shanna desired?

That was a question Lorne couldn't answer, and suddenly Jaime felt so overwhelmed because it wasn't just the truth of what happened between Lorne and Shanna that crashed into her like North Sea waves in a storm, but the other truth she'd denied for nearly a decade—Jaime had wanted Lorne.

Jaime turned, intending to flee the darkened room, the knowledge of her feelings, the intensity of his stare. Only as she ran, the lighting was terrible. The toe of her slipper caught on one of the heavy dumbbells, and she pitched head-first into the floor. Her hands slapped the wood, catching her before her face smacked into it.

The quick clip of Lorne's boots rushed behind her. As she was pushing herself up to sit, he knelt beside her, looking over her face and then the rest of her.

"Are ye all right?" He pressed a hand to her knee and then jerked away as if now realizing what he'd j done in that simple gesture.

Heat zinged up her thigh, settling somewhere in the middle, and she bit the inside of her cheek, her breathing uneven, which she hoped he'd conclude was because of her fall. Goodness, she needed to get out of here. The chill on her stockinged foot was warning enough she'd lost her shoe.

"My slipper." Jaime patted around, trying to find the shoe that had been caught and ripped off her foot. But it was Lorne who found it first, her hand brushing over his fingers.

Another zing of awareness rapidly shot up her arm.

"I've got it," he said slowly, reaching for her ankle. He smoothed his fingers over her foot, testing each toe. Nothing hurt, and his examination tickled. She bit the tip of her tongue to keep from laughing or gasping, really from reacting at all. Jaime was fairly certain the heat his touch caused would never go away. Her toes, foot and ankle would burn forever. "Nothing broken."

She wiggled her toes. Circled her ankle. Still, he held onto her. "No." The word came out in a rush of air. Jaime was surprised to find how much she liked the man she'd thought to be an arrogant fool. The impression she'd had of him since the incident with Shanna was being edged out by the man she used to know before that terrible moment—the man before her now.

Lorne eased her slipper gently back in place and placed her foot on the floor. Finally relinquishing her—regrettably. How could such a moment, the act of checking her for injury, of replacing her shoe feel so...intimate? So tender...

"Thank ye." Jaime stared at him, hoping the emotions she felt weren't screaming from her face. Normally one to wear a mask of placidity, she discovered it was incredibly hard to hide her thoughts at that moment. Perhaps the dim light was helpful enough.

Lorne stood and held out his hand, fingers stretching toward her. She took it, allowing him to lift her. But he didn't let go when she was on her feet again. Mere inches were between them. Warm fingers wrapped around hers. He was staring at her, searching her face, and she found herself doing the same thing. Words flew about her head, but nothing she could frame into a coherent thought except one—kiss me.

That was a shot of cold water to the face. Jaime backed up a step, slipping her hand from his.

"I need to go. My aunt is likely tearing the place apart looking for me."

Lorne grinned, some of that playful charm curling his lips, and she wanted to sigh at the sight of it. Her belly was full of butterflies. Oh, heavens, she had to remove herself from his presence at once.

"Should I carry ye out of here? I dinna want ye to fall again." The tone of his voice was teasing and endearing.

Lord, but she was in trouble. Go!

Jaime's voice, and her breath, abandoned her. All she could think about was how very close he was. How very dashing he was. How very charming.

"I can walk."

"As evidenced just now—by the time ye get back to the ballroom, ye'll be missing both shoes, and lucky no' to have a black eye."

Jaime couldn't help laughing and was glad for that little bit of sound because her brain refused to think of anything to say. Not when her heart was pounding so fast, and the anger and bitterness she'd held onto for all these years seemed to be melting away into a puddle of confusion and something else. A heated, tingling feeling that made her want to dance and escape at the same time.

"Perhaps we should start over," Lorne said softly, entreatingly.

Jaime cocked her head, the desire to flee dissipating as interest took the reins. "Start over?"

"Aye." The smile he gave her was enough to melt even the coldest ice, and Jaime was not immune to it. "I'm His Grace, the verra stuffy Duke of Sutherland, but my friends call me Lorne." He pressed a kiss to the back of her hand, and oh how she wished she weren't wearing gloves. Not that the slim fabric made a difference because she felt that press of his lips throughout her entire body.

9

Lorne wasn't certain if it was the way Jaime's eyes had widened, or the way she'd licked her lips as she stared at his mouth, how she'd trusted him with holding her foot. But at some point in the last quarter-hour, he'd realized two things.

One, he desired the fiery, irritating, beautiful pain in his arse. More than he'd ever desired another woman, and to the point that left a gorging ache in his groin. He should have seen to the need first thing when he'd returned from the continent, but alas, he'd had more urgent things on his mind. The more disagreeable she became, the more he wanted to needle her. The more she frowned, the more he wanted to laugh.

And two, he was fairly certain she felt the same way.

Bending over her hand, kissing her knuckles, flirting with her, was more instinctual than it had ever been with another female, including her sister, his ex-fiancée. His desire for her was crowding out his ultimate goal of regaining his castle and teaching the chit a valuable lesson, and yet the illogical side of him kept welcoming these feelings, ignoring the facts.

"Well, Your Stuffy Grace." Her voice had changed, sultry almost as she looked up at him, eyes all dewy and full of humor and something else—something with a sensual edge. She sounded hesitant as if she were trying on a new approach. "I'm Miss Jaime Hardheaded Andrewson. Lovely to make your acquaintance."

Lorne laughed. The lass had hit the nail right on the head. For she truly was hardheaded. She grinned at him, pleased with herself, causing his gaze to fall back to her mouth. A sudden swarm of desire hit him in the gut. The urge to kiss her was intense, stifling. But doing so would irrevocably change everything between them in that reckless moment, wouldn't it? And as much as he wanted to—as much as his desire for her had propelled them into this current situation —there was a part of him that held back. A part of him that shouted, "Stop this nonsense and leave this room immediately."

But Lorne ignored that cautious, likely smarter, part of himself. "Ye are lovely," he murmured.

Jaime's mouth fell open in surprise. "No. No. No. No. I can no' accept compliments, and you should no' be giving them. This is... This is too much." She pulled her hand from his grip and backed up a step. "We're supposed to hate each other."

"That is what everyone would expect."

"Then why do ye no'?"

Lorne shrugged. "What about ye?"

Jaime bit her lip, then said, "I...can no' say. I do no' know."

"Me either." Casting aside the warning ripping through him, he embraced that headier need. Lorne closed the distance between them, stroking his fingers over her warm cheek. Her skin was soft, the arch of her cheekbone delicate.

Nothing one would expect from a lass with an acid tongue. "I just know right now I want to kiss ye."

Jaime didn't retreat when he said it. Didn't shout no, or for him to go to the devil. Didn't wish him dead as she had on so many occasions since his return. Instead, she leaned into his fingers where they traced her face. Her eyes blinked up at him, inviting. But that wasn't enough, not where she was concerned. For over eight years, she'd believed him a scoundrel. A virtue-stealing rogue who'd defiled her sister and left her with a child to bear on her own.

If he were going to kiss Jaime, it would have to be with her explicit agreement. And good God, no one could find out. The papers would lap up every morsel like starved wolves, and all the wagers he'd burned in the hearth in his study would miraculously come back together.

This was a very stupid idea. He needed to leave.

"I want to kiss ye, too." There was no hesitation in her words this time.

Well, there it was—her permission, her desire. And Lorne found he was unable to fight against the impulse any longer. One taste, then he'd tell her to go back to her aunt before all of Edinburgh realized she'd been in the dark with him long enough to make her virtue a thing of the past.

Lorne came closer to her, his hands cupping her face. She tilted upward, her full lips beckoning. She was beautiful, tempting. A goddess who'd lured him in. Dipping low, he brushed his mouth tenderly over hers, felt her sigh on his skin. She was warm, soft, tasted of punch. Good God...

Jaime's fingers tentatively touched his chest as she returned his kiss, exploring him the way he wanted to explore her. But he restrained from slipping over her back down to her arse, keeping his hands to her face. But saints, he experienced the flutter of her fingers on his chest to his core, as if

ELIZA KNIGHT

she were reaching inside him and grabbing at the vulnerabilities he'd tried to hide.

He slanted his mouth over hers, deepening the kiss with a slide of his tongue between the seam of her lips. Jaime tightened her grip on his doublet, her tongue shyly coming into contact with his and then stroking with boldness. She might have been inexperienced with kissing, but the lass was quickly becoming an expert, taking the reins as she slid her mouth over his. And he let her, gave her this moment to discover, to savor.

The beast inside him wanted to crush his mouth to hers—to claim her, to show her what kissing was all about—but he also feared unleashing his passion would push her away. So, he held back. Gently stroking her tongue with his, discovering her mouth and letting her discover his in turn.

But there was only so much a man could handle, and when he reached the point where he wanted to tangle his fingers in her hair and rip out every pin that held it in place, he ended the kiss before he caused her any damage that couldn't be repaired.

"Ye need to go," he managed to croak through a tight throat.

Jaime looked up at him, stricken, and he studied the play of emotions skittering across her face. Disappointment, fear, anger, resolve. Lord, but she thought he was being an arse again.

"'Tis no' what ye think," he said, hoping to soften whatever answers she'd determined in her mind. "But if I kiss ye anymore, we're liable to end up on the floor, and...well... If we make it down there, I'm going to touch ye everywhere."

Jaime's mouth formed an O, and she let out a little gasp. Was that interest that flared in her gaze? No. He was imagining things, had to be.

"I see." She smoothed her hands down her skirt, which was only slightly rumpled from her fall.

"Aye." Lorne stepped back, trying to put space between them.

Regrettably, he watched her go, slipping out of the door to his gymnasium. And leaving him standing there, cock hard as stone and his mind filled with confusion. Jaime... He'd set out with the thought to seduce her, but now it seemed that she was the one doing the seducing. Or at the very least, he was tormenting himself by stealing heated kisses in the dark.

"What the hell?"

Lorne glanced up, surprised to see Alec coming through the door. All the desire pulsing in his veins was quick to vacate.

"Did ye come to box?" Lorne asked, nodding toward the ring.

"I might. What was Miss Andrewson doing in here?" Alec stomped forward, clearly out of sorts.

His friend must have thought Lorne had just finished ravishing the lass. Given another five seconds of kissing, he might have.

"It's no' what it looks like." Except that it partly was, though it hadn't started that way.

"She's got no father to protect her, no brothers. Her uncle could no' be bothered to leave London, and her silly aunt is half-sozzled with the other matrons in the ballroom and barely noticed she was gone. When I said marry her, I thought ye'd exchange vows before ye pulled her into a darkened room to ravish her. Good God, man, but ye can no' risk a scandal like this."

"Are ye taking up for the lass then?" Lorne asked, crossing his arms over his chest, more amused than anything else. Jaime need not worry about her virtue with him, even if he would have gladly taken it.

"Someone should if ye're going to be a rake about it."

Lorne chuckled. "She wanted to talk to me about Shanna. I kissed her, but I promise ye, I've no intention of bedding her." Well, not unless she agreed to wed him.

"Then why did ye kiss her?"

"Why does any man kiss a beautiful lass?" Lorne held his hands out, exasperated.

"Oh my God, man," Alec faltered. "Ye...love her?"

"Love" had not been the word Lorne would have used. It was a sentiment as foreign to him as losing a boxing match.

"Nay. I desire her." He cocked his head. "Does that mean ye've never kissed a woman ye did no' love?"

Alec ignored his question. "That is no' the type of woman ye simply desire and make your move on."

"I know." Lorne let out a long-suffering sigh, one which he felt a lot more than he'd realized.

"Listen, I know that your good name and reputation were smeared because of her sister, and I'll never understand why ye took the fall for her, but in this instance, ye actually are kissing the lass. And ye can no' risk it. Her uncle will come back from London and put a bullet between your eyes; he'll have no other choice."

"Aye." A bullet would spoil a lot of things.

"What the hell are ye thinking?"

Lorne shook his head. "I'm no' exactly sure what I'm thinking. Only that I...I like her. I find her amusing."

"I find my grandmother amusing, and I'm no' kissing her."

"That's foul."

Alec hooted. "It is rather, I know, but ye get the point. Jaime Andrewson is no' the type of lass ye have an assignation with. She's the type of lass ye marry."

"Aye. So ye think I should propose?"

"If ye're going to keep pulling her into darkened rooms for all to see, aye."

"No one saw."

"I did."

Lorne grunted. "Shite." He rubbed his hand through his hair. This was not at all what he'd had in mind for tonight. He'd wanted to show the world that he had no feelings for Jaime, and the exact opposite had occurred.

He had a whole lot of feelings for the lass, half of them pooling in his groin.

"Aye, shite is right." Alec snorted.

"She told me her sister had run away."

"That's odd."

"Said she thinks it's because Shanna did no' want to give me the lad."

Alec pulled a cigar from his pocket, holding it between two fingers, but made no move to light it. "But he's no' yours."

"Exactly. It's deuced confusing." He plucked the cigar from his friend's hand to smell it. "Did ye get this from my desk drawer?"

Alec grinned and waved away the query. "What do ye think it means, her running away?"

"I do no' know."

Alec took the cigar back and lit it with the lantern that Lorne had hung on the hook. "Odd that Gille and Shanna are both missing."

"What?" Lorne spat out the question, the thought having never entered his mind that the two of them were both missing—could it have been a coincidence?

Alec shrugged. "Seems strange, no?"

Lorne swallowed. Gille and Shanna—together? Nay. That would be almost a worse betrayal than selling the castle. "Impossible. Must be a coincidence, albeit a damned confounding one."

Alec blew out a perfect ring of smoke and then stabbed

the cigar into the center of it. "Has Malcolm found anything out yet about your wayward brother?"

"No' yet." Was it possible his brother had something to do with Shanna's disappearance?

JAIME WENT FIRST TO THE LADIES' RETIRING ROOM, HER face still in flames, her mouth feeling swollen from Lorne's kiss, and her mind racing so fast she was likely to trip over it. With a linen square, she dabbed water on her cheeks and neck, and sipped at cool cucumber water.

When at last her heart had ceased its pounding, and her cheeks wouldn't give away that she'd been thoroughly kissed, she went back to the ballroom, avoiding gazes, and imagining everyone knew what she'd been doing in the gymnasium. Lorne was not in sight, thank God, or else she was certain to be light-headed again.

Oh...but that kiss...

No! No, we will no' be thinking of that kiss! Even if it had made her toes curl, and she'd tossed aside every little thing she hated about him in order to feel the brush of his mouth on hers, the power of his body...And there it was, her face was flaming again.

When she finally located her aunt, the woman was in stitches with friends she'd likely not seen in a while. They were all dazzling in their silk gowns, white gloves, feathered and jeweled headpieces, sparkling gems at their necks. None of them spared Jaime a glance, much like when she'd come to these silly functions as a debutante.

"Auntie," Jaime murmured. "I have a headache. Shall I take the carriage and have him return for ye?"

Aunt Beatrice barely looked up from a friend who was

whispering in her ear. "Yes, dear, if you do not mind. I do hope you feel better by morning."

Jaime didn't mind at all. And in fact, Jaime gave her aunt a quick kiss before rushing from the room, afraid she'd change her mind. Fortunately, no one tried to stop her, though she did falter more than once when hands were raised to whisper as eyes focused on her. But she didn't have time to wonder what they were thinking, especially if it had anything to do with the duke.

Mungo stood by the front entrance, and when he looked at her, his expression softened only slightly. "Miss Andrewson," he said with all the formality expected of a butler.

"My carriage if ye could, please, sir."

Mungo studied her, and she had to wonder what he was thinking, knowing that he'd led her to the gymnasium to be alone with his master. "Are ye well? Ye look...flushed."

Well, if that comment didn't bring about more flames to her cheeks. What exactly did he think went on behind those doors? Oh, no, never mind, she didn't want to know the answer to that. "I'm perfectly fine, just a bit of a headache."

"Ah, well, the duke does have that effect on people."

Jaime was too shocked by the man's frankness even to answer, and she stopped herself short of laughing. To top it off, Mungo winked at her before going outside to summon her carriage. Perhaps he was not judging her, after all. When the butler returned, she was still flustered, so she thanked him and hurried down the stone steps, working hard to place one foot in front of the other before she tripped and fell on her face. Twice in one night would be entirely too much.

She nodded to her groom, who held open the carriage door and offered her his hand. Jaime practically dove into the carriage, sliding over the velvet seats, feeling some of the air return to her lungs at the prospect of soon being away from here. As she was about to shut the door, a large hand reached around to stop her.

"What..." she gasped, and then Lorne was there, climbing into the carriage with her and shutting the door. The small enclosure of her carriage shrank in size with him there, looming out of the darkness, a sinful angel coming to corrupt her some more. "Get out of my carriage." Her voice sounded as shocked as she felt.

"Marry me."

Had he said what she thought he said? "Pardon?"

"Marry me, Jaime Andrewson."

"Ye're mad. Or drunk. Get out of my carriage before someone sees ye." She tried to look around him to the front of the house.

"It will no' matter if they see me if ye agree to be my wife. We'll put all the questions and rumors to rest."

And she'd be able to kiss him whenever she wanted... Still, this was a terrible idea. A really bad idea. The man had been betrothed to her sister, and that had ended very badly on both sides. All of society thought he'd fathered her sister's bastard and abandoned her—not only because Shanna had said it, but because he'd never discredited her either. If Jaime agreed to marry him, goodness, she'd likely lose more than half her clientele. They would think her unreliable, disrespectful.

Not to mention what Shanna would think. Despite having lied about their situation, she had to have wanted to get even with the duke for something, right? Nay, Jaime could not marry him. Absolutely not. Marrying him was the very last thing on earth she should ever do. Even if kissing him had been glorious.

"Nay. I can no'. Now please, leave my carriage."

His mouth turned down in disappointment, and she

wanted so badly to tell him that she'd misspoken, that she would marry him, that her clients would understand, and so would Shanna, but that was nonsense and dangerous. Marrying him would be a betrayal to Shanna, to Gordie, to herself. Kissing him had been a step too far already. There was so much at risk for her to fall for a rogue's charm..

"Perhaps ye should think on it for a night before ye answer," he suggested, ever the stubborn duke used to getting what he wanted. Well, that wasn't fair either, because she was certain he hadn't wanted to be imprisoned for two years, nor have his family seat sold out from under him. Oh, but there she went again, going soft on him.

"I do no' need to think about it. My answer is no." She held her head high, hoping he would see that she, too, could be stubborn.

"Just as ye said no to coming to the ball."

He had a point there. "I came for answers, which ye gave me."

"Aye, I did. And now I'm giving ye something else—an offer of marriage."

"Not interested."

Lorne smiled. "Ah, aye, ye did mention ye were Jaime Hardheaded Andrewson. I'll find ye tomorrow." And then he was slipping out of her carriage and hurrying back into his house, leaving her speechless. Her mouth dry. Her body heavy.

She tapped the roof of the carriage, her gaze on the front of his house as he disappeared inside. The ride back to her flat was a blur. And when she stripped out of her clothes, took out the pins from her hair, all she could do was think of Lorne and the way he'd kissed her, the promise in the intensity of his stare, and his offer of marriage.

Marry me.

Even the splash of cold water on her face did nothing to dispel the desire he'd ignited or the questions lurching ceaselessly through her brain. It was not the proposal she'd dreamed of as a lass. Nothing romantic about it at all. He'd barged into her carriage and demanded she wed him. Taunted her with the fact that she'd already changed her mind once with him. Didn't he understand what a bad idea it was for the two of them to wed? The number of complications it would bring about was immeasurable. And one tiny little kiss couldn't erase all the headaches that would come with it.

Despite what Lorne had told Jaime, her sister's story had never changed. She'd always painted Lorne in a devious light as the seducer who had ruined her and left her with a child and a tattered reputation.

If Jaime were to announce that she was marrying him, her sister would be devastated. Heartbroken. Maybe not because her excuses had been true, but because Jaime had gone behind her back and would be publicly rebuking her sister's claims or casting them aside as their parents had done.

But Jaime believed Lorne. Trusting his word meant that all this time, Shanna had been deceiving the world. And more importantly, deceiving Jaime.

How could her sister be heartbroken over someone she'd destroyed? Because that was the truth of the matter, wasn't it? Shanna had been willing to destroy a man for her gain. And what gain that had been, Jaime couldn't figure out. Their parents had disowned her, and she'd lived exiled in Ireland until Jaime fetched her back to Scotland.

All of the information she'd found out tonight brought Jaime no closer to figuring out where her sister was now, for she'd not run away afraid that Lorne might take her child.

Jaime climbed into bed, sinking onto the soft linen sheets, curling her arm around a pillow, her body tired but her mind fully awake.

As she was sinking into sleep, her eyes popped open. The thing that had been tickling at the back of her mind all night but had yet to come to the surface, finally decided to peek its head out. If Lorne was telling the truth, and Gordie wasn't his son, then how did he look just like him?

🐜 10 🐝

Frigid water splashed on her face and two cups of tea did nothing to wake Jaime after a terrible night's sleep. So with eyes only marginally less puffy than when she'd finally given up and climbed out of bed to dress, she walked into her office at the wharf feeling very much worse for wear.

Emilia was already present and leapt to her feet, shoving her spectacles up the bridge of her nose. "Miss Andrewson, good morning."

Her clerk's eyes lit up behind the glassy spheres with questions, no doubt wanting to hear all about the night before, but Jaime's mind was still tied up in as many knots as it was when she'd lay down to sleep. Like a bunch of yarn, given to a kitten to play with. She was the yarn, and Lorne was the demon kitten.

His proposal. Well, if one could call that a proposal. It had been more like a demand. She didn't even ask for her tea the way he'd said, "Marry me." What would her household staff say if she started going around saying things like, "Tea me," and "Dress me," and "Carriage me." They'd think her a brute or neanderthal, not a lady or a respectable mistress.

Then, of course, also plaguing her was the other discovery she'd made—that if Gordie wasn't Lorne's son and yet looked like him, there was only one other alternative—a male relative. And she didn't think it had anything to do with the old Duke of Sutherland, long in his grave. But Gille, Lorne's younger half-brother, who'd been so eager to unload the castle on her, especially when she said she was going to gift it to her sister—he was a viable key.

Before leaving for the wharf, Jaime had sent out a hasty note to Mr. Bell. He needed to know what she'd learned from Lorne, as well as the questions she now had swirling about in her brain. Best for her investigator to be informed and get his men on the same page. Knowing such details might even change the direction they were headed with their search, and hopefully, they'd find Shanna and Gordie sooner. Jaime wanted answers, and she wanted them now.

Jaime snapped out of her head long enough to reply—relatively late—to her clerk. "Good morning, Emilia."

Emilia's brow wrinkled. "Ye look exhausted. Did ye dance all night?" The wistfulness on her clerk's face was too much to dismiss.

And it brought memories of Lorne, the way her fingers had tingled when their hands touched. His arms around her. The look in his eyes when he'd finished kissing her quite thoroughly. The way he'd slid into her carriage. Oh, the headiness of it all made her breath quicken even now. "I did dance, though no' all night."

"With the duke?"

"One dance with the duke." And one delicious, forbidden kiss.

"Oh, how I would have loved to be there. I've no' been to

a dance in months. No' since I visited my cousin in Dumfries. They had the most charming village dance."

"Perhaps I should arrange to have one, then," Jaime offered.

"Oh, but I do no' think I'd be allowed."

"Why no'? Ye could even help me plan it. We'd host it for our clients. A real Andrewson ball, would that no' be a delight?"

"But I'm no' a lady." Emilia worried her lower lip, and Jaime hated to see this smart and beautiful woman feeling incapable.

Jaime shrugged. "Oh, bother. Ye can see how much I care for such social norms, and besides, what better way for ye to find a handsome suitor? Aye, I think I should host a dance. We could even have it on one of the ships."

Before their conversation could go any further, the door to the office opened, and they both whirled to see the Duke of Sutherland standing in the entrance. His dark hair was a bit windblown, and he'd not shaved that morning, giving him a rugged sort of look that felt almost...dangerous. His clothes were rumpled, and parts of them might even have been what he'd worn the night before, though not all of them. The man was a handsome devil, to be sure. Not an altogether unwelcome sight, though he should have been.

Not only was Jaime surprised to see him there, but she was amazed he was even awake at such an hour. The guests wouldn't have left Sutherland Gate until the wee hours of the morning, which meant he'd likely gotten as much sleep as she had—equaling none. And judging from the look of him, he'd merely changed coats and freshened up enough not to be appalling—quite the opposite, much to her dismay.

"Your Grace," she drawled out, her gaze taking in his entire figure from head to toe. He was striking. How many times had she been stunned into silence when he'd entered their house as he courted her sister?

That was all in the past. She shook the daze away and focused on him once more. Oddly, he carried a basket just like the one she'd dragged around the gardens as a lass to pick flowers.

"Your butler said ye'd already left for the day." Lorne sauntered into the office, shutting the door behind him.

"Oh..." 'Had he gone to her flat?

Lorne held up the basket. "Coffee and scones. I'd have brought tea, but I needed something stronger."

And so did she. Oh, why did he have to bring her things and be so considerate? It made hating him harder. Made it harder for her to look at him as the rogue she wanted him to be. If he had come in appearing every bit the rake, that would have made it easier to not look at him at all. Of course, that was a lie. The more of a rakehell he appeared to be, the more she seemed to like him.

The duke settled the basket on Emilia's desk, who immediately went about setting out the food and drink. Jaime was stunned to see how thoughtful he'd been to include three cups instead of only two. As if he'd anticipated Jaime wouldn't be at her flat and had thought of Emilia here, not wanting to leave her out.

Drat ye, duke! He needed to stop being so nice.

"What are ye doing here?" Jaime asked, narrowing her gaze. There was an ulterior motive, she was certain, and she hoped it wasn't for him to demand she marry him again.

Lorne pointed to the items on Emilia's desk. "Coffee. Scones." His words were simple enough, but his eyes danced as if he waited for her to make him explain. He wanted her to ask; those eyes begged her to ask.

And she was going to. Devil take him. Och, but she was a

weak woman. "Besides that. Ye know verra well I've a cook that feeds me."

The corner of his mouth crooked in a grin. "A simple thank ye would suffice."

"Thank ye ever so much," Emilia gushed, scooping jam onto her scone.

"Thank ye," Jaime quipped and pursed her lips, not wanting to seem overly rude—not that she should care. The scent of the warm coffee being poured from the pot had her mouth salivating more than the fruity, buttery scones.

Lorne handed her a cup, his bare fingers brushing hers, sending a tingle racing up her arm and reminding her of the kiss they'd shared the night before. Where were her gloves? She never wore them in the office, as she didn't often have visitors, nor did she want to get any ink on them. Jaime yanked away before any more unwanted shivers could have their way with her.

"Do ye wish to speak in front of your witness?" he asked, a teasing lilt to his brogue.

Jaime nearly choked on the sip. Goodness, but was he about to demand marriage again? She couldn't risk it. "Nay."

Emilia perked up at that and set down her half-eaten scone. "I just realized I need to check on something. I'll be back in a few minutes."

Before Jaime could argue with her clerk, the woman had slipped from the office, closing the door behind her and leaving Jaime alone with Lorne. The silence between them pulsed with energy, likely supplied by both of them. If she was remembering the heated embrace, or even the gentle touch of his fingers on her ankle, was he?

Lorne's gaze swept over her, taking her in. And the way his lids lowered to half-mast, eliciting that heady, sensual look he'd given her in the gymnasium before he kissed her, was answer enough. He reached forward, his fingertips grazing her—thankfully woolen-sleeved—elbow. Jaime closed her eyes for a fraction longer than a blink, savoring the carress and wishing it away all at once.

In that split-second, Lorne closed the distance between them, the heat of his large body enveloping her. He touched her chin, lifting her face toward his. Gray eyes peered into her own, gauging her interest and seemingly finding it, for he leaned down and joined his mouth to hers.

With his lips fastened on hers, he removed her coffee cup, settling it somewhere, and then his hand pressed to the small of her back, urging her closer until their bodies were flush. The hardness and strength of him lined up to her softer curves. Everything with the duke was exaggerated. His size, his presence, his intensity. And his kiss.

She was melting into him. Losing the resolve she'd set for herself last night, and again this morning. Wanting him to kiss her, to fall into his enchanting, passionate embrace. There was no one here to see—no one to know, except for herself and him, she'd let her guard down. Allowed herself tumbled once more under the luscious spell of a man she'd been captivated by for years. Worshiped him, adored him, hated him...everything him.

Lorne captured her hands in his and placed them on his shoulders. And oh...the breadth of them. Corded muscles bunched beneath the fabric of his doublet. She flattened her palms against him, her fingers spread, and she felt him, studied the swells of hardness that made up his body. Ran her hands down his arms, stopping at his elbows and coursing back up again. As she touched, the feelings inside of her whirled and bucked. Fighting against one another.

Touch him more. Nay, run away. Oh, bother, touch him, kiss him more...

This was a bad idea, and she knew it. Had decided while rushing away from his house less than twelve hours ago that she would not, under any circumstances, allow him to kiss her again. Yet here she was. Thoroughly enjoying it. Life wasn't fair, she decided. If she'd been a man, she could have enjoyed his kiss for hours, days, again and again, and no one would be the wiser or care. But nay, she was a lass, and lassies weren't allowed to kiss whoever they wanted when they wanted.

And oh, how she wanted...

His tongue danced provocatively over hers, and she twirled her own inside his mouth, engaging in every bit of teasing and toying and tasting he provided. This naughty duke, full of vigor and deep wounds... His hand slipped down to her rear, tugging her tighter against him, and she gasped at the feel of him touching her in so intimate a place.

What could it hurt to allow herself a few more moments of wicked bliss? Perhaps that was the exhaustion talking. At any rate, it was what she'd blame her deranged thoughts and actions on.

Jaime leaned into him, her fingers threading in his hair.

And he groaned deep in his throat and whispered, "Marry me, please."

That woke Jaime up. She pulled away from him, her lips tingling, her body on fire. At least this time, he'd added "please." But no amount of manners—or fiery kisses—were going to change her mind. She was either incredibly intelligent or a great fool, and she didn't have the mental capacity at the moment to debate herself on that, only to set her foot down.

"I must decline, Your Grace. Ye know a union between us is out of the question. And this," she pointed between herself and him, "can no' happen again." She regretted it even as she declared it. Decided to back up a step for good measure and picked up her coffee as though it were a shield. She took a large gulp, nearly sputtering on the bitterness without cream and sugar.

"That bad, aye?" He chuckled. "Or was that from our kiss?"

Jaime rolled her eyes. "We will no' be talking about kissing. No' ever. Why did ye come here, Duke? Let's no' pretend it was simply to bring me breakfast."

"What if it was for the thing we're no' talking about?"

The kissing... Oh, to think he'd come all this way to lay his lips on hers. Nay! She couldn't romanticize this or him.

"Then, ye really ought to go now." She took another step away, hoping that it wasn't so obvious how thoroughly he'd kissed her. Her lips felt swollen from his kisses; her cheeks still flushed.

He set down his cup and stared at her seriously. "In truth, I came to repeat my offer."

"Which ye did. And I declined." She straightened, realizing too late that doing so pushed out her breasts, and his eyes fell to gaze at the swells. Thank goodness for her sturdy wool gown, practically buttoned up to the neck. Alas, he didn't seem to notice her sensible dress and instead appeared to be undressing her with his eyes. Curling her back now would only show she'd noticed the swift flit of his gaze, and she refused to give him that much, so she remained as she was, hating that her breath quickened.

"May I ask why?" he mused.

"We are no' suited. I'm a busy woman, and I've no' the time to think about romance."

His brow raised on that last word, and she was hasty to correct herself.

"And by romance, I mean courtship. Besides, many other things are plaguing me—one major obstacle that would bar me from ever standing at the altar with ye."

"Ah, are ye referring to your sister?"

Jaime licked her lips and nodded, trying to decipher how much to tell him about what she'd thought as she tossed and turned all night. He deserved to know that Gordie was his spitting image. That if Lorne wasn't the child's father, Gille might be. Unless Lorne had gotten blistering drunk one night and forgotten himself or what he'd done. But from what she understood of him, before and after the war, he was a man who rarely lost control, if ever. Even in kissing her, she felt the lion being held back by a chain, waiting to be unleashed.

He stepped closer to her, and she surprised herself by not retreating—at least not yet. The nearer he came, the more her body pulsed with a throttled craving. But thankfully, he stopped, leaving some space between them for her to breathe. "Do ye still believe me?"

Head titled up toward him, Jaime took him in. Lorne was so very tall and breathtaking. A gorgeous man, with a hint of something feral. She imagined when he did finally relinquish some of the control that he kept so wound up within himself, he'd be like a storm unleashing, destroying everything in its path. That made him a risk, didn't it? Or extremely desirable and exciting. To be on the end of that unrestrained passion. Her pulse skipped a beat. For a woman with a life was as rigid as hers, as regimented, as stalwart, he gave off the barest suggestion of unbridled enterprises that she would never dare to cross alone.

Jaime licked her lips, contemplating how she would answer. Because she did still believe him, and he deserved the truth. But he also deserved to know what troubled her mind. "Aye, but there is something ye should know."

"What is it?" Lorne's brows knitted together with concern.

It was incredibly hard to meet his gaze. She didn't want to see the pain that her revelation would no doubt cause him. How had her sister ever found him lacking? The very idea that Shanna had not been head over heels in love with the Duke of Sutherland was not only news to Jaime but shocking, too. For she had found him captivating from the moment he'd first come to their parent's townhome to call on her sister.

But this wasn't about Jaime or Shanna's desire for the duke, but rather the mutual subject Jaime and Lorne shared— her nephew's parentage.

"'Tis about the lad," she finally managed to say.

"Shanna's bairn?"

"He's no' so much a bairn anymore." Jaime held up her hand near her shoulder. "He's almost as tall as me now, even at barely eight years old."

The duke's face had hardened, and she couldn't read the thoughts that were hidden behind his stare. "What about him?"

"He..." Jaime swallowed. She needed to spit it out and be done with it. "He looks just like ye, Lorne. Everyone thinks so."

Lorne blanched, sucking his lips back against his teeth. He let out a curse under his breath. Hands fisted at his side, he whirled from her. Walked a few paces away before turning back around, eyes blazing with expected anger—and unexpected resignation. What did he know that he hadn't shared with her?

"Ye do no' seem as surprised as I thought ye'd be," she said. Jaime discarded her coffee cup onto the desk and walked a little closer to him, wanting to impart comfort, and not knowing how—or at least not in the way she suspected he would like.

Lorne exhaled loudly and ran his hand through his hair. "I did no' suspect anything between the two of them until last night."

"Last night?" Jaime's brows raised in question. "What happened last night?"

Lorne grinned at her, and she could tell he was making an

effort toss aside the major realizations they'd both had—and keep her from knowing what he'd discovered.

"I kissed ye." And his words were confirmation of what she'd thought.

"No' that, ye buffoon. Ye know what I mean."

"Buffoon or nay, I'd much rather talk about kissing."

Jaime crossed her arms over her chest and tapped her foot, trying to give him the look that made men leap to do her bidding on the docks. "Ye'd like to distract me."

He shrugged. "Beats the unpleasantness. And I've had about enough distasteful, obnoxious torments in the past decade to last me a lifetime."

She was about to beg him to explain it to her—all of it. His time away, the relationship he'd had with Shanna, the lies, the things he suspected, what he'd discovered last night. But there was a loud knock at her office door, followed by it bursting open, which stilled the words on her tongue.

Jaime leapt nearly six inches at the sudden intrusion, not understanding at first as three men bustled in that they weren't being attacked. She reached for the first thing she could grab, which was a coffee pot, ready to launch it at their heads. Lorne must have been striving to discover the same thing as he stood in a fighting stance, fists out, like a professional pugilist.

The lead man cleared his throat, and then Jaime recognized him as the magistrate for the wharf. He stood there, a frown on his face, his two deputies beside him.

Jaime lowered the coffee pot and told Lorne it was all right. While the duke lowered his fists, he did not look ready to give up the fight.

"Good morning, sir," Jaime said. "What can we do for ye?"

He handed her a folded piece of paper. "We've a need to search your ships, Miss Andrewson."

"By what requirement?" Lorne demanded with all the authority of a duke.

"And who are ye?" the magistrate asked, eyeing Lorne up and down, not recognizing him since he'd been away so long.

"I'm the Duke of Sutherland." The way he said it had both the deputies cringing and the magistrate shrinking a fraction of an inch.

"Apologies, Your Grace. I did no' mean to interrupt the business ye have with Miss Andrewson, but we've a need to search the ships," he explained. "There's been an anonymous tip—"

Jaime interrupted the magistrate. "Sir, ye may address me as they are my ships, and the duke is but my guest."

The magistrate looked shocked she would speak to him with such firmness, likely because she was a woman and also because she'd just discredited Lorne's position of authority. But this was her company and damned if she was going to let two men discuss it when neither had a vested interest.

Even if Lorne had asked her to marry him—that was a request she'd denied and would keep on denying.

"Aye, all right, Miss. We've received an anonymous tip that your ships contain contraband."

"Rubbish," Lorne said at the same time she said, "That's absurd."

"We must examine all accusations of such. Ye know the law," the magistrate said.

"Who made the accusation? If ye've a right to search, I've a right to know who would falsely accuse me and slander my company." Jaime stood her ground and wasn't going to be cowed by a man of the law, even if he was in the correct.

"I'm afraid that's confidential."

"That's shite," the duke said with a sneer at the magistrate. "Give me the name, or I'll have your job."

The magistrate swallowed hard, his cheeks turning a

ruddy color. "I do apologize, Your Grace, but it was anonymous. We're no' certain. It was a letter we received from an eyewitness."

"Who would want to destroy me like this?" Jaime asked, racking her brain. Certainly, plenty of other shipping companies would consider her a rival, but she was on good enough terms with the other companies that she believed they wouldn't sabotage her. None of them would stoop so low as to have her name and reputation dragged through the mud, for fear of retribution on their own business. Unless they felt certain that they'd not get caught. That was a possibility, she supposed, and she couldn't rule it out. Otherwise, she had no enemies. No one she could think of that would try to destroy her like this.

"Well, ye're welcome to go and have a look, but ye'll no' find whatever it is ye think ye're searching for. I run an upstanding enterprise, sir. My laborers are hard workers and good men. My books are clean, and our cargo is only top-notch—and legal."

"I believe ye, miss," the magistrate said. "We've never had trouble with ye before, but I have to take tips like this seriously, else I'll lose my job."

"Ye may yet," the duke warned.

"Please, Your Grace, I swear to ye, I know nothing of whoever made the claim. And I can promise when I find out, I'll come to ye straight away."

"Why no' come to me?" Jaime asked, exasperated. "'Tis my company."

"Right, miss. Right ye are. I will."

They followed the magistrate and his deputies outside and down to the docks, where Emilia was startled by their approach, as she was flirting with one of the sailors on the Shanna.

"What's happening?" her clerk asked, hurrying to comfort Jaime.

"A search for contraband," Jaime said. "A bogus claim and a waste of time."

The ships were searched one by one until finally, the magistrate and his men decided there was nothing to the accusation and apologized for having disrupted her day.

"Ye be sure to get me the information I want," Lorne warned the magistrate as he and his deputies departed.

"I will, Your Grace." The wharf official tipped his hat, then he and his men were off, fading from view but not from mind.

"This could ruin me," Jaime said. "Even a minor accusation like this is enough to set tongues wagging and make my clients wary."

Lorne shook his head. "They'll think it rubbish, lass. And I can promise ye I'll do everything in my power to find out who was behind it. Ye have my word."

⁂ I I ⁂

"**M**alcolm, I was just going to send ye a note." Lorne walked into his drawing room to find his cousin lounging in a chair reading the paper, an unlit cigar between his fingers.

Malcolm snapped the paper closed, tossed it on a side table, tucked the cigar into his pocket and stood. "Mungo said ye were out, but I did no' want to take the chance of missing ye."

"I hope ye were no' waiting long." Lorne embraced his cousin in a manly hug with plenty of mighty slaps to the back. It felt so good to be able to do something so normal again.

"No' at all."

"Can I get ye something? Tea? Whisky?"

Malcolm chuckled. "I'm fine, but ye might want a dram. I've come with news about Gille."

Lorne motioned for his cousin to sit back down while he went to the sideboard to pour himself three-fingers. "What did ye find out?"

"I met with the solicitor Gille hired for the sale of the castle. Matter of fact, do pour me one, too, cousin."

"Aye." Lorne filled another cup and then brought it over, too agitated to sit. They both took long sips, and finally, he said, "Do go on."

"The solicitor, a Mr. Corbett, did no' want to give me any information, but I stalked his office until he left and then broke in." When Lorne gaped at him, Malcolm grinned with satisfaction. "No' to worry, I did no' get caught. The information I'm giving ye is illegally obtained but seemed necessary."

"Ye took many risks to get me what I asked for."

"Worth it. Besides, I need to hone my skills continually."

Lorne chuckled. Though he wasn't privy to all his cousin's day-to-day activities, he knew that most of what he was employed to do by the War Office was of a secret nature.

After another sip of his whisky, Malcolm said, "Gille booked passage for himself to Ireland, along with his wife."

Lorne paused, drink halfway to his lips. "Wife? Who the hell did he marry? Did anyone know he'd wed? No one told me."

"No one knew. Trust me, all society would have exploded like Mt. Vesuvius if they'd known your brother eloped."

Lorne swirled the whisky around in his mouth. He'd been gone too long and knew next to nothing about his brother now. "Who is his bride?"

"I've got someone pulling the records, looking for the license."

"If there is one. Maybe it's a farce."

"Could be."

"Was his wife named on the ship's passenger list? What about the lad?"

Malcolm shook his head. "Nay, her name was not listed, and there is no mention of a child, irritating as that is."

Lorne walked to the sideboard, realizing he was going to need another splash of anti-lunacy. "What the bloody hell could he be doing in Ireland?" But the idea banged around in his skull louder than the bells in a church tower—if he were in said tower. "Shanna."

Malcolm stood up at that and joined Lorne at the sideboard, his face creased in worry. "What are ye thinking?"

"Shanna had a parcel of land in Ireland, a modest ten pounds castle on top." Back in the fifteenth century, Henry VI of England and Lord of Ireland at the time had granted his subjects ten pounds if they constructed tower keeps as a defensive measure to protect their lands. Passed down through the centuries, one of these small castles now belonged to the Andrewson family. "Since the two of them went missing at the same time, how likely is it they've gone there together? The only thing that boggles the mind is the child."

"Aye, I can no' imagine she would leave him behind. And would she have married Gille?"

Lorne set down his refreshed glass and rubbed his temples. "I do no' bloody know. It's all deuced aggravating."

"Aye. I plan on interviewing the crew of the ship today. Thought ye might want to join me."

"I'd love nothing more." And he hoped they'd get some answers.

The two of them headed out in Malcolm's waiting carriage for the docks at Leith. The Andrewson ships loomed larger than most but were farther down the wharf than the Dueling Brothers, a ship's name whose irony was not lost on Lorne in the least. It made him sick to his stomach. Gille had undoubtedly chosen this ship for his passage to Ireland for the moniker.

"Bastard," Malcolm muttered under his breath.

"He really is," Lorne agreed.

They alighted from the carriage and walked toward the ship. The crew was making repairs and cleaning, perhaps planning for the next passenger voyage.

"Ho, there," Malcolm called to a man who looked to be in charge, given he was just standing around pointing rather than doing any work.

The disgruntled man glanced down at them from his place on the deck, crossing his meaty arms over his even meatier chest. "What do ye want, guvnor?"

"We've some questions about two passengers." How Malcolm maintained his cool was beyond Lorne, who wanted to shake the captain for being difficult.

"I'm no' in the habit of answering questions," the captain replied with more than a touch of attitude.

Lorne pulled two coins from the hidden pocket in his doublet. "Does this help loosen your tongue?"

The man's eyes widened, and he nodded. "I just remembered that I've got a lot to say. Come on up."

They made their way up the gangplank, mindful to stay out of the crews' way. When they reached the resentful captain, he eyed them up and down with obvious disdain.

"Name's Miles. I'm the captain of the Dueling Brothers."

Lorne passed him one of the coins. "The other one's for ye when we get the answers we seek."

Miles frowned but nodded anyway, biting the coin to be sure it was real. "What can I help ye with?"

"We're looking for information on a passenger, Gille Gordon. Traveled aboard the ship to Ireland about two weeks ago."

"Oh, the young lord, aye. He was here. His wife was a pretty wee thing."

"What was her name?"

"Can no' recall." But the expression on his face said otherwise, as did his pointful look at the coin still waiting in Lorne's hand.

"Ye must no' want the other coin then." Lorne made a

move to tuck it into a pocket, which suddenly got the man speaking.

"Sherry? Shelly? Something like that?"

"Shanna?" Malcolm drawled out.

"Aye, that was it."

Lorne's gut tightened. "Did they have anyone else with them?"

"Aye, a wee porter."

"How wee?" Lorne narrowed his eyes.

"About yay high." The Captain held his hand mid-chest. "Looked a bit scared he did."

"Why was he no' listed on the passenger list?"

Miles shrugged. "No' a passenger."

"Did he set sail with them?" Malcolm asked.

"Aye."

Lorne frowned. "Then he was a passenger."

"We do no' count the help." Ballocks, but the captain was stubborn.

Lorne gritted his teeth in frustration. It was looking a lot like Shanna and Gille had taken the child with them. "What was the lad's name?"

"That I do no' know. They never addressed him, and he did no' speak. Once they had their cabin, the lad did no' come out of it."

"But he did debark with them in Ireland?" Malcolm clarified.

"Aye."

Thank goodness for Malcolm because Lorne was ready to wrap his fingers around the man's neck. It was like pulling teeth to get him to give them any information.

"Is there anything else ye can tell us about the three of them?" Malcolm's tone was steady.

"For newlyweds, they did no' seem all that happy with each other. Kept bickering, and barely a smile passed between them." Miles scratched his nose, perhaps thought about picking it, too.

"Anything else?" Malcolm urged.

"Aye. The man had a lot of coin. Paid us all to keep quiet."

"And yet here ye are, speaking to us." Lorne was surprised his voice came out jovial.

The captain grinned. "Got a family to feed. He did no' pay me enough."

Malcolm nodded. "We'll be back if we have more questions."

"Why do ye no' give me your names in case memory serves?"

"No." Lorne was adamant about it. There was no way he wanted the captain to be able to tell Gille about their questions. "We'll come back if we have need to speak to ye."

"Suit yourself."

Lorne handed the captain the other coin, and then he and Malcolm made their way off the ship. Down the gangway they went, with Lorne's gaze drifting down the wharf, wondering if Jaime had remained in her office or if she'd left already. He had half a mind to walk down there and find out. But she'd made it clear this morning she wanted distance, and besides, he didn't want to disappoint her with how little he knew. Aye, they'd discovered the direction in which Gille had run off with Shanna and the lad, but they didn't know anything else. It was best to wait and approach her when he could tell her something concrete.

There was also the fact that if he did see her, he would want to kiss her again. Badly.

Blimey...

"Care for a boxing match?" he asked Malcolm.

"I thought ye'd never ask."

J<small>AIME'S HEAD POUNDED AFTER VISITING THE VERY LAST</small>
shipping company to share that side of the quay with her. She
wasn't certain if her head ached from the worry of the accusation or the fact that she'd seen Lorne handing coins to one of
the captains, the Dueling Brothers.

She'd had her coachman stop long enough for her to
confirm it was him. Even if he were trying to be inconspicuous, the man could not hide. Along with his companion, the
duke descended from the ship, looking as if he owned every
vessel in the wharf, and then climbed into a carriage with a
crest slightly different than his own but also quite regal.

"Follow that carriage."

"Aye, miss."

They wove their way through the quickly crowding streets
of Edinburgh until they reached Sutherland Gate, where the
previously seen carriage had gone through the access to the
stable.

"Circle around. I'll be back," she said, alighting from the
carriage without waiting for her groom to put down the stool.

Acutely aware of what had happened the last time she
visited the duke at his place of residence, she still managed to
hold her head high as she approached the door, lifted the
unicorn and let it fall with a resounding thud.

Jaime didn't turn around, though she could feel eyes on
her, watching her. Waiting for her to be disgraced again.
Thank goodness she'd not gone home first, or else Aunt Beatrice would have made certain she didn't leave the house
without a proper chaperone, and the last place they would
have gone was to the Sutherland manse.

The door swung open, revealing Mungo there, looking at
her with something akin to amusement.

"Did ye come to fight?" he asked.

She cocked her head to the side to stare at the man.

"Well, I had hoped to have a civil conversation with His Grace for once."

"I've heard that before." Mungo beckoned her inside and then left her in the grand entrance, slipping into the shadows.

What the devil had he meant this time? The butler was full of riddles. But she didn't have time or the current brain capacity to decipher the puzzle of his words. Seconds later, Lorne appeared, sweat slicking his brown hair, his shirtsleeves rolled up to expose the strong, corded muscles of his arms. Was there anything more delicious than a man's forearms? She was certain right then and there that the answer was no.

"Oh," she breathed out, then clamped her mouth closed, embarrassed she'd said anything at all.

"Oh, indeed." He grinned with an air of mischief that made heat flood her cheeks. "What can I do for ye, Miss Andrewson?"

So many things... Naughty, wicked things. "I saw ye today. At the docks."

"Why did ye no' say hello?"

That was a good question. "Because it was more fun to spy on ye. What were ye doing there?"

"Questioning captains and crews."

"About?"

Lorne grinned and crossed his arms, emphasizing his muscular physique. "Am I under investigation, Miss Andrewson?"

"Maybe."

His grin widened, and his gaze roved over her from head to toe, heating her in all the places a man like him shouldn't be allowed to touch.

"I like it when ye investigate me." The duke's tone was not playful anymore but rather...sensual.

Jaime waved away his wicked insinuation in hopes of

fending off her desire. "Truly, Your Grace, ye are a pain in the—"

"Och, I can see we've been spending entirely too much time together. Ye've picked up my vulgar tongue." The way he drawled out the last word only had her remembering what he could do with that tongue.

"I'll ask again, what were ye doing?" she demanded, trying to be authoritative, but the way her gaze kept landing on his mouth, she was undermining herself.

"I'll fight ye for the challenge," he dared.

Fight? There was that word again. "Honestly, duke, I'm exhausted."

He frowned, disappointed, letting out a sigh. "And here I thought ye'd come all this way for a little fun."

"What's taking ye so long?" Another sweaty man came from the corridor behind the grand staircase and stopped when he saw her. "Ah, I see."

"Cousin, Miss Andrewson would like to challenge me."

"I would no'," she countered, crossing her arms over her chest, and backing toward the door.

"This, I'd like to see." His cousin grinned, looking nearly as handsome as Lorne. "I've never seen a female pugilist."

Ah, so they were discussing boxing. Goodness, but if he expected her to raise her fists? Nay. Just nay.

"I'm Malcolm Gordon, Earl of Dunlyon, by the way." The newcomer bowed. She thought she recognized him from the ball and today from the docks.

She affected a curtsey. "I'm Jaime Andrewson, daughter of the late Viscount Whittleburn."

"A pleasure to meet ye, miss, and my condolences on your father."

"Thank ye." She shook her head. "Now I confess I'm no' a pugilist, and so must be going."

Lorne made a dissatisfied noise. "Ye mean to tell me ye've no' learned a thing or two at the docks?"

She straightened her shoulders. "Well, as a matter of fact, I have learned some things."

"Show me, then. Come on, Miss Andrewson, I dare ye."

Jaime pursed her lips. "If I show ye, then ye'll tell me what ye were doing at the docks today?"

"Aye."

"Fine. Lead the way." She waved her arms forward, the same way she shooed away the birds who flocked the ship decks.

Lorne took her hand in his, and they followed Malcolm back to his gymnasium. It was much brighter inside than it had been the last time she'd been in there. But still, the sight of the pugilist ring, the fencing planche, and the various dumbbells scattered around had her face heating and her mind swinging back to the night of the ball when he'd kissed her. Hovered over her. Delicately touched her ankle. Oh, but she could swoon.

Lorne wrapped his hands around her waist, and she gasped at the contact as he lifted her until her feet touched the platform of the pugilist ring. She ducked beneath the rope, turning in a circle, mostly to get as far away from his touch as possible. Malcolm remained in place, arms crossed and a goofy grin on his face when Lorne leapt up to join her. The platform bounced with his weight, and she laughed in surprise.

"Hands up, Miss Andrewson, like this." Lorne showed her how to place her fists—thumb outside of her curled fingers—and her elbows bent.

"Are ye truly giving me permission to hit ye?" she asked. "And are ye going to hit me back?"

Lorne chuckled. "I'll no' hurt ye. And I doubt ye'll get in a lick."

Oh, that was a challenge worth taking. A decade's worth of pent-up frustration where this man was concerned, and here she was being given a chance to quell it? At the very least, it would keep her from kissing him. "Deal."

Lorne bobbed back and forth on his feet, a grin splitting his face that showed how eager he was for her to fight him. She watched his feet and imitated him, finding the surface flexed beneath their feet ever so slightly with their movements. She'd only ever been to a boxing match once, years ago, having snuck in with Giselle, dressed up like lads. But it was so long ago that she barely remembered it.

"Come on then, take your best shot," Lorne urged.

Jaime stepped forward, shot her fist out toward his belly, but he danced away, much quicker than she'd been able to punch. She tried again, still feeling her movements were constricted by her bodice and the thick layer of skirts she wore. But alas, she wasn't going to undress in front of them— as much as Lorne, and even his cousin might enjoy that.

As they circled one another, with her taking shots at him with her inadequate fists, she realized this was very much like a dance. And dancing, she was good at. She grew more confident, adding in a few of the dance steps she knew and was able to clip his elbow barely as he bounded away.

"I win," she said, dropping her fists. "I got ye."

Lorne laughed, a deep, hearty sound that made her smile. "Och, nay, lass, 'tis no' that easy. Ye have to take me down to win." He pointed at the base beneath their feet.

"Down, as in, to the ground?"

"Aye." The teasing glint in his eyes was almost too much for her.

Because when she thought about being down on the ground, she imagined them here not too long ago, in a similar situation, and her body tingled all over again.

"And yet, we both know who has had to catch whom

since we've met, aye?" She reminded him of how clumsy she was compared to him, and hopefully not of the kiss they shared.

"Indeed." But the wicked curl of his lips, the heated intensity of his stare told her she'd not succeeded.

"Ye have an unfair advantage with your inhuman ability to balance," she said stiffly in jest.

"All right, I'll give ye an advantage then. Malcolm, hand me one of the ties."

His cousin tossed him a length of fabric, and with a grin, Lorne put the fabric over his eyes and tied it at the back of his head.

"Blindfolded," Jaime said with a sigh of exasperation.

"Aye. Come at me again, lass. Let's see if ye can take down a blindfolded fellow."

Well, this ought to be easy and quite entertaining. As quietly as she could, Jaime tiptoed around Lorne, but he seemed to know where she was at all times. Even when she swung at him from behind, he whirled around and dodged. When she feinted right, then swung left, he still caught her.

"How about one hand behind my back?" he teased.

"Aye, I'll take that challenge," Jaime goaded, sweat marking her brow and her breath uneven from exertion. She was having a lot more fun than she would have guessed.

Lorne held one hand behind his back, seizing her flying fist with one hand and bearing a thwack to his ribs with her other.

"Aha!" she said with a laugh. "I finally landed a decent blow. And ye need not remind me it was to a blindfolded, one-armed man."

Lorne chuckled. "Again."

This time, she came at him with a similar move, but he snaked his free arm around her waist, whirled her around, and dipped her backward over his bent knee. All the breath left her, and her heart pounded so hard, she was certain Lorne could hear it. Maybe even Mungo, wherever he was.

Lorne's face came within an inch of hers, and he breathed her in, the move so elegant, so sensual, that she was rendered immobile by it. Wanted him to kiss her right then and there. Needed him to kiss her.

"I got ye," he whispered, his gaze moving to her mouth.

"Aye," she murmured back.

"Ye'll get better." He smiled.

But did she want to? If he were going to end each fight like this, why would she want to beat him? She would happily bungle every single time. Oh, what was she even thinking right now? There could be no next time, let alone more than once.

Lorne righted her, his fingers lingering a little longer on her waist as he pulled off his blindfold with the other hand.

"Well done, Miss Andrewson," Malcolm clapped. "Ye almost had him."

Jaime had nearly forgotten about his presence, and she swiveled her head toward him. "Thank ye, my lord, for your good cheer," she said with a laugh and then turned back to Lorne. "Ye won. I suppose ye're under no obligation to tell me why ye were at the docks."

"I had no' wanted to until I had more information to give ye, but alas, we are here, and there seems no point in keeping it from ye. Malcolm and I were interviewing the captains and crews because we discovered that my half-brother was on a ship that sailed for Ireland—with his wife—and a wee porter."

"His wife?" Jaime's hand flew to her chest, and her brows pinched so close together, she was nearly cross-eyed in shock. "Shanna?"

"Aye. And the wee porter sounds like her son, though I'm no' certain why they would make him dress in disguise."

Neither was she. "Perhaps to lead anyone astray who was looking for him. She has to have guessed I would. I did, in fact, send a man looking, and so did ye."

"Where would they go in Ireland?" Malcolm asked.

"I've a minor holding there."

Lorne cocked his head. "The holding in Shanna's dowry?"

"Used to be, but it was given to me when my parents disowned her. I never forced the issue, though I know it must have hurt her."

"And ye gave her Dunrobin, too."

Jaime smiled sadly and nodded. "'Tis beside the point. My guilt runs deep."

"And your sister cares no'." Lorne's words cut her to the quick, but she knew he was right.

"When did they sail?" she asked.

"About two weeks ago." Malcolm held out his hand to help her down from the ring.

"So what ye're saying is my sister was in the city all this time? Hiding?"

Lorne referred to Malcolm.

"At least before they left, miss, but I'm no' certain for how long."

Jaime bit her lip, straightening her gown and bodice as discreetly as she could. "Do ye think Shanna accused me and my ships? Perhaps in hopes of keeping me tied up with the business and unable to pursue her?"

Lorne shrugged. "I would no' put it past her or my brother, considering what we've been discovering."

"Och, poor, sweet Gordie." Jaime blew a loose lock from her face.

"Ye've no reason to believe he would come to harm, do ye?" Malcolm asked her.

Jaime shook her head. "Nay. She was a selfish mother, but no' cruel."

"That is good news, at least." Lorne ran a hand through his mussed hair.

"Aye." A clock chimed from somewhere within the house. "Oh, how I wish I could stay longer, but I must get going. My aunt will tear apart Edinburgh looking for me. She's decided that I need a chaperone, but only when it's convenient for her." Jaime gave a slight roll of her eyes. "Please let me know if ye find out anything more."

"Of course." Lorne led her toward the door but then paused. "Are ye all right leaving this way, or shall we arrange an escape?"

Jaime smiled and let out a short laugh. "I already came in this way. Better for them to see me leave than think me here all night."

"True." He lifted her hand to his lips, placing a kiss on her knuckles. "Until next time."

❧ 12 ❧

Jaime was preparing to play a game of cards with Aunt Beatrice after dinner when a loud knock sounded at her front door.

"Who could be visiting you at this hour?" Aunt Beatrice gave her a warning look that set Jaime's nerves on edge as if she'd spent the last two years entertaining gentleman callers or some such.

"I assure ye, I have no idea."

MacInnes appeared a moment later in the drawing room. "A Mr. Bell here to see ye, miss. I reminded him of the late hour, but he seems to think ye'll want to see him anyway."

Aunt Beatrice narrowed her gaze. "Mr. Bell? Who on earth is he?"

"An investigator," Jaime explained. "I sent him to find Shanna."

"Shanna? I thought she was at Dunrobin?"

"She never made it, Aunt." Jaime wasn't in the mood to tell her aunt the entire story of Shanna's duplicity, so instead asked MacInnes to show the man in.

Mr. Bell looked thoroughly dusty as if he'd ridden all the night through. He bowed before her and Aunt Beatrice.

"This is my aunt. Feel at ease to speak freely, as I would tell her what has happened anyway." Which she wouldn't normally, but since the woman was there, she might as well.

"Very well. It appears your sister has fled to Ireland aboard the Dueling Brothers."

Jaime nodded, not wanting to confess this was information she already knew, for then she'd have to explain how she came by such evidence, and well, that only made her think of Lorne's hands on her as he bent her backward, his grin wide and satisfied. And the great, cold dousing of Aunt Beatrice's chagrin, should she find out.

"I sent a man in that direction, miss, in hopes of finding her—and to be on the lookout for Master Gille, as it appears they were on the ship together."

Jaime pressed her hands together in front of her heart. "And Gordie, please tell me ye know something of him?"

"It appears he was acting as the couple's porter but did no' appear in distress."

"A porter," Aunt Beatrice exclaimed, clearly distraught as she whipped out a fan, waving it rapidly as she sank deeper into her chair.

"Are they married?" Jaime asked. This was the one thing Lorne had not yet been able to find out.

"That's where I've come from, miss. The traveling inn where I found the governess—

I checked the vicarage there and did find a marriage license for a Mr. Gille Gordon and his bride, Shanna Andrewson."

How much easier it was to marry in Scotland than it was in England. If they'd been across the border, the two of them would have had to wait for three weeks while the banns were read, for they'd not have been able to get a special license, or at the very least, it would have been difficult. But in any case, she would have heard of it, had that been the case. Not in this instance, however. They'd simply walked to the nearest priest they could find and exchanged vows.

Jaime let out a long sigh, trying to keep the frown from her face. Trying to ignore her aunt's increasing breaths.

"Married, my god." Beatrice seemed due for a fit of the vapors from all the tut-tutting she was doing.

Jaime rose and went to the cellarette, pouring her aunt a thimble of whisky and one for herself. "Can I get ye anything, Mr. Bell?"

She handed her aunt the whisky, and Beatrice drank with vigor.

"Nay, thank ye, miss. I need to be getting home. Ye were my first stop on the way, and I've my family waiting for me to return. As soon as I hear from my men, I'll be sure to let ye know what we've found."

Jaime nodded, and MacInnes escorted the man out.

"I suppose this was something that was a long time coming," Jaime mused, staring hard into the amber-colored spirits in her tiny cup. "And we can be glad he married her rather than abducting her."

"A long time coming?" Aunt Beatrice finished her dram but still had the wild look of a hunted deer in her eyes. Really, the dramatics were too much.

"Aye, I've a feeling Gordie is actually Gille's son." Jaime tipped the cup into her mouth, letting it burn a path down her throat, relishing that little bit of punishment.

"A feeling? What makes you say so? That's not true."

"We may need to open our minds to the possibility, Aunt."

Aunt Beatrice scrunched her nose in disapproval, and Jaime didn't have the patience now, despite the whisky, to give her aunt any further information. Instead, she rose and went to the writing desk, penning a quick note to Lorne.

"If ye'll excuse me but a moment, Aunt."

"No, no, I think I shall retire. I've had quite a shock." Aunt Beatrice rose. "It might be time for me to return to London, where I can quell some of the rumors before they run rampant."

In other words, she didn't want this news to reflect badly on her daughters, Jaime's cousins, who were starting in society. Jaime had not seen them in a decade—by choice of her aunt and uncle, who didn't want Shanna's reputation to influence their own three daughters. This had rubbed Jaime the wrong way.

"Oh, that is a shame ye feel the need to leave, and we've been having such a lovely visit," Jaime tried to keep her voice soft and sweet rather than elated. "But I understand. I will be sure to keep ye informed of all that happens."

"Yes, please do." Aunt Beatrice handed Jaime her empty whisky glass.

"Would ye like a glass to take up?"

Aunt Beatrice paused a moment, likely wanting that very thing, but shook her head. "I'll never sleep if I do."

Once her aunt was on her way up the stairs to the bedchambers, Jaime found MacInnes again.

"Please see this delivered to the duke." She pressed the note into her butler's hand.

"As ye wish, Miss, but might I remind ye of the time?"

"Nay, MacInnes, ye may no'." She smiled at him to soften her denial. "I am well aware, but this is a matter that can no' wait. Besides, I've already destroyed my reputation where the duke is concerned if ye read the papers."

"I never read such rubbish."

"Good, ye'll only want to burn them as I do."

MacInnes grinned. "Shall I wait for his reply, miss?"

"That will no' be necessary. Goodnight, MacInnes."

"And a goodnight to ye as well, miss."

Jaime watched her faithful servant leave, and then she wandered up to her room, her maid helping her undress and brush out her hair. Later, while she was sipping warm tea and curled on her chaise reading a novel, there came a tapping at her window. An erratic sound as if a branch hit the glass with every gust of wind. Except there wasn't a tree outside her bedroom—and hardly any gusts of wind.

Closing her book, Jaime rose and headed for the window, peeling back the curtain and lifting the sash. She inspected the large shape of a man looming in the shadow of her yard and a pebble hit her in the arm.

"OH, DAMN, SORRY!" LORNE CALLED UP.

Like an angel peering out over the land, Jaime's chestnut locks cascaded around her gorgeous face. The white of her nightgown looked ethereal in the moonlight. And all he could imagine was that beneath that gauzy film of fabric was her skin—naked. It was enough to make Lorne nearly lose his train of thought about why he'd made the late-night visit and pinged little stones from the gravel walk at her window like a rebellious lad.

"What are ye doing here?" she whispered loudly. "Ye'll wake my aunt."

"I got your missive."

"That did no' require a reply. It was merely informative."

"I disagree, and I think we ought to make a plan." How could he convince her to come down from where she perched... Preferably without changing?

"And this could no' wait until morning?" Jaime leaned farther out the window and gaze roving the building as if in search of anyone watching.

"Ye'll fall out. Get back in there," he warned.

"I'm seeing who's listening."

"Nobody."

"Go away. We'll meet in the morning. It's Sunday, and my dock crew has off. We can walk in the park."

"I'm coming up." He didn't want to wait until morning, not when he had something to tell her that neither of them had thought of before. Not when she looked delicious enough to eat. Och, what he wouldn't give at that moment for just one kiss.

"Nay! I'll no' open the door." She waved her hands, shooing him away.

"I'll scale the building."

"Ye'll break your neck."

"Then come down."

Jaime let out a disgruntled noise but then said, "Fine. I'll meet ye in the back garden."

Lorne grinned, watching as she shut the window and drew her drapes. A short time later, he heard soft footsteps in the grass, and then there she was, wrapped in a dressing gown, hiding that filmy nightgown from view. But he could still see the outline of her body. Her womanly curves were making him want to reach forward and explore every inch of her.

"Ye could have come without this," he teased, plucking at the sleeve and giving her a brazen wink.

"Do no' be ridiculous."

"I'm quite serious."

She wrapped her arms around herself. But rather than cover the lushness of her breasts, it only emphasized their tempting shape. She rolled her eyes, a gesture he was coming to find quite endearing. "What could no' wait?"

"I think I know what's happened."

"And that is?"

He beckoned her to follow him out of the center of the garden, where they were easily seen, and under an arbor of vegetation. "I think what they've done goes deeper than either of us has considered. They sold ye the castle, which ye then gifted to your sister. So, ye handed my brother a large sum of money and your sister a veritable fortune in my seat."

"Aye," Jaime drawled, a little frown wrinkling her adorable nose.

"If they are married, the castle returns to Gille's hands."

Jaime's hand flew to her mouth. "Oh my god. It was a ploy to gain funds?"

"Aye. And as soon as they learned I'd returned from the dead, they were quick to run. They knew they'd lose the castle, but they did no' want the fortune ye gave them to be taken too." It all made perfectly horrible sense.

"Do ye think my sister could have known about this? Why would she do it, and why would Gille?" She rubbed at her arms, either from the evening chill or the news he'd just relayed.

And if he looked well enough, he could make out the shape of her hardened nipples. Dear God, help me...

Lorne cleared his throat and hoped to do the same to his mind, which had gone straight to the gutter. "I can no' answer for why your sister would do anything, other than they must have been attached for a very long time. And love makes men do odd things." He frowned. Like show up at a lass's house and throw rocks at her window.

Jaime stared at him for a several beats, the air crackling between them. She licked her lips and shivered, which almost had him groaning. "My investigator has sent a man to Ireland to find them."

"As has my cousin. Let me give ye my jacket." He started to unbutton, but she stilled his hand with hers, surprisingly warm for the shivering she was doing.

"Keep it. We'll no' be much longer." She let out a sigh. "I

feel helpless staying in the city, waiting to find out what's happening."

"Shall we go to Ireland, then?" Please say aye. Let me take ye away from here. To be alone with ye...for hours.

Her eyes widened at that suggestion. "I can no' do that."

"And why no'?" But he knew exactly why not. He knew a hundred reasons why not.

"I've a business to run."

That was only one. "Emilia could manage in the meantime."

Jaime shook her head. "That is too much to ask of her."

"Is it? She seems capable." And he was being truthful.

Jaime pursed her lips. "Likely, she is very capable. But I've no chaperone. My aunt is returning to London, and I can no' pick up and leave Scotland on a whim."

"But ye've property in Ireland and ships. Perhaps it is part of your business, and no one else's, for that matter."

Jaime chuckled sofly. "And that does no' explain why ye're there with me."

Lorne shrugged. "Considering I've been contemplating expanding my wool distribution to Ireland and using your ships to do so, I say it is perfectly explained."

"I'll think about it."

"We'll need to leave sooner rather than later." Tonight. Let's run away right now.

Jaime shivered again, and he took her hands in his, her fingertips chilled from the night air, drawing her closer. He rubbed life back into her hands. "Ye're cold."

"Only mildly. But I should get back inside. We're lucky no' to have been seen yet."

"One more thing," Lorne hedged. "A kiss before I leave."

He thought she would pull away, that she would shake her head at him, and rail at his impropriety, but she didn't. Jaime surprised him by tipping her head up.

"Just one."

Lorne thought he'd died and gone to heaven as he dipped his face to hers. She was glorious. Soft lips, quickly warmed by his breath. He tugged her hands toward his chest, wanting to feel her touch him, wanting to hold her in his arms. She was so supple and curvy beneath the thin layers. Before in her thick skirts and bodice, he'd let his imagination run wild with thoughts of what she'd feel like, but now, oh now, he knew. Rounded hips, a flat belly, and breasts... Och, but her breasts were full, and he desired nothing more than to cup them, massage them, kiss them. To savor the jutting points tempting him.

Sliding his mouth from hers, he trailed kisses down her neck, tasting the faint salt of her skin, the subtle floral scent of her. Jaime leaned her head to the side, giving him better access, a soft sigh on her mouth, and he went lower, his lips gliding over the length of her collarbone. This was wrong. He should stop. It was one thing to fantasize about her, but to make good on it...

Lorne ignored the good-intentioned side of himself. His hands went over her back, following the curve of her spine until he reached her bottom. There, he gripped the round-ness of her. Groaned softly at the way she felt. Bloody hell... Her fingers clutched at his shoulders, her body bowing toward him, sinking against his frame, instead of relenting, instead of running.

Lorne dragged them deeper into the shadows of her garden, finding a bench where he settled with her on his lap.

"I know ye said only one kiss, but I beg of ye, Jaime, do no' make me stop at one."

"Fine, two," she said on a sigh. "But only two."

Then he was going to make it a good one.

THIS WAS MADNESS. LIKE EVERY MOMENT SHE SPENT IN Lorne's presence, Jaime seemed to lose a little bit of her mind each time. And now here she was, sitting on his lap in a darkened garden, lucky that the shade of the arbor hid them from moonlight. But if anyone should come walking out and happened to duck beneath, they'd be caught. And the scandal sheets would have no end of fun with their silly cartoons and riffs on her person.

Lorne shifted her so that her bottom hit the cold stone, warmed slightly from the heat of his body, and then he knelt before her, wrapping his coat around her shoulders. From his kneeling position, he stared up at her. The toes of her night slippers, wet from the grass, were pressed to the fronts of his knees.

"What are ye doing?" she asked.

"I'm going to give ye that second kiss."

"Kneeling on the ground?" She raised a questioning brow.

He grinned, looking as roguish as ever. "'Tis the perfect spot, lass." He placed his hands on her knees, the heat of his palms searing through her muslin nightgown.

She should shove his hands away. Jump up and run inside. But she didn't.

Instead, she eyed him with curiosity. And felt the cold night air touch her ankles and then her calves, as he slowly slid her nightgown upward. The tips of his fingers stroked over her ever-growing bared flesh, and she sucked in a breath, frozen still. Her gaze locked on his. Every inch of her sang with...what? Desire. Passion. Anticipation.

With her legs, exposed...that should have made her stop. But nay...

In her haze of lunacy, she didn't care about being caught or how extremely wicked this was. Jaime's interest was most certainly piqued. And then he was bending down and pressing his lips to her exposed knee.

"Oh," she gasped. "That was your second kiss."

"Och, nay, lass. This is one long kiss. A special kiss." He lifted her leg by the ankle, touching his mouth to the delicate point of her bone. "I'm still no' done."

She nodded, licking her lips and watching him trail his lips up the length of her leg, pausing at her knee. Who was she to say no to him giving her this long, special kiss? It felt so good... She admitted she was incapable of asking him to stop. Because she wanted more... More of whatever it was that his eyes were promising.

"That is, this is..." But she couldn't find the words to describe how she felt or what she wanted.

Lorne's hands slipped higher on her bare legs to the tops of her thighs. He paused. Looking up at her, waiting, she guessed, for permission. She nodded. The grin that covered his lips right then and there sent a shiver of delicious antici-pation through her. He kissed higher, his hot mouth climbing the inside of her thigh. Oh, this was fantastically wicked. Ruination was hers. It was almost a certainty. This would get her banned from society. But even knowing that didn't make her say "No more," didn't make her snap her legs closed as he kissed higher, his head disappearing beneath her nightgown.

Hot breath fanned over her sex, and Jaime gasped, then sucked her lower lip into her mouth to keep from making any more noise. But it was hard not to when he kissed her right there.

The warmth of his hands on her knees pressed gently outward, opening her to him. And then slick, wicked velvet stroked along her folds—his tongue!

Her hands curled around the edge of the stone bench, gripping tight to keep herself from falling over in pleasure. Her grip anchored her to this spot when what he was doing to her made her want to float higher and higher until she disappeared into the clouds. Lorne's grasp on her thighs, his tongue moving in maddening, delicious circles over the very heat of her, ignited a passion, a hunger inside her that demanded to be fed.

She bit her lip hard, breathing in erratic puffs through her nose as he increased his speed, as he lashed her with that naughty tongue. Oh, but this special kiss... Her legs were shaking, her palms damp on the stone. It was difficult to remain quiet. Little whimpers escaped her unbidden, and she was powerless to pull them back.

Every stroke, nudge, lick had her falling deeper and deeper into rapture. Was it possible to fly and fall at the same time? Because that was what this felt like. Never in her life would she have guessed a man could kiss a woman like this. And never again would she be the same. Even the thought of kissing was ruined for her.

Ruined by this devilishly handsome and infuriating duke.

Her hips rolled forward, searching for more of what he was giving, more of the pleasure, more of the... And then it was there, the thing she'd been unwittingly craving and reaching for, breaking her apart inside. Everything came alive then. Every nerve ending on fire and pulsing as her body shook against his kiss.

Lorne slid his mouth along her trembling thigh, coming out from beneath her nightdress, looking extremely pleased with himself.

"How did ye like that kiss?" he asked with a languid wink.

Jaime swallowed, sucked in air, tried to find her voice, and at last said, "In case ye could no' tell, I liked it verra much."

He laughed softly, then kissed her. "Ye have no idea how much I want ye right now. Ye'd better get inside before I have my way with ye."

If his having his way with her was anything like what she'd just experienced, Jaime was half-tempted to let him. He smoothed the skirt of her nightgown back into place and stood, holding out his hand. She took his offered hand and stood, wanting to curl into his body. But they'd dallied long enough, and if her aunt came looking for her, and subsequently found Jaime missing, she'd send out an alarm that woke the whole city.

"I shall come by tomorrow to escort ye for a promenade through the park, Miss Andrewson."

She snickered at the way he used her formal name after where his mouth had just been.

"And I trust ye'll be more gentlemanly in broad daylight." She lifted off his jacket, grateful for the warmth it had provided her, though she suspected with what had just happened, she wouldn't be cold for a very long time.

"I can no' make any promises."

Jaime laughed and then sprinted for the back door. What had she allowed to happen? Goodness, she'd practically made love to Lorne in the garden. And she'd enjoyed every minute of it. Somehow, he'd had more control than she did, stopping before they'd gone any further. And she realized at that moment, that she could trust him. Trust him with her whole life. And she definitely could not trust herself, at least when it came to his kisses.

What would she have done this past week without Lorne here to lean on? They were both victims of their siblings' nefarious plot. But they were more than partners in unfolding the layers of treachery. They were something deeper.

Being with him brought out all sorts of memories and feelings from before the war, before Shanna had made up the lies about him. Made her remember that she...loved him.

Jaime stilled, a lump in her throat. Her breath was completely gone. Loved him. Aye. That was the rub, wasn't it? The tragic truth. Knowing her own heart, and even after experiencing what they just had, Jaime still didn't see how to make this work between them.

Which meant traveling to Ireland together was probably —nay, most definitely—a bad idea. Since they'd been unable to keep their hands off each other every time they'd met the last few days, there was no telling what tempting mischief they'd get up to on a ship in the middle of the ocean.

As she got into her bedchamber, a crack of thunder shuddered the window. And then just as suddenly, rain pelted down, pinging wildly against the glass. Jaime refused to take it as a bad omen, however. For if it were bad, then they would have been rained on in the yard, right?

✨ 13 ✨

An emergency with one of her ships delayed Jaime from deciding about traveling to Ireland the following day.

She was there working alongside her men to transfer cargo from one ship to another after a mast had been struck by lightning in the storm the night before. The needed repairs threatened to delay the shipping, and that could not happen.

With most of the Andrewson ships commissioned for work, it took some finagling, but Jaime was able' to configure a different route and schedule with Emilia's help. Barring any further calamities, it would enable them to be about their business in a timely fashion, with none of her clients dissatisfied.

Jaime's lady's maid, Alison, had roused her before dawn to tell her the news of the mast. In a flash, she'd been out of bed, ready to take on the misfortune within a quarter-hour. Her hair was tied up in an untidy knot, and she was wearing the least fashionable of her working gowns and her sturdy boots. Physical labor nixed the need for fashion.

It was a good thing Aunt Beatrice had left that morning, for she might have truly lost consciousness if she saw Jaime working so well alongside the men, slickened with sweat and muck.

Dawn had barely broken when Jaime's work was interrupted by a slow rise in the chatter, and her men pointing toward the docks. She followed their gazes. Standing there in breeches and linen shirts with their sleeves rolled up was the Duke of Sutherland, his cousin Malcolm, and his friends Alec and Euan, the latter two whom she briefly recalled from the ball.

"Oh God, what's happened?" she murmured, straightening. She could only think a major disaster had happened to bring the men here to her ship.

"Pardon?" Emilia said.

"Nothing. I'll be right back." Jaime hurried down the gangplank, her boots thundering against the wood, to the four waiting aristocrats. All larger than life and dressed considerably down for their stations. Below the elbows of Lorne's shirtsleeves, his skin was exposed. Well-muscled forearms they were, but his left arm bore the brunt of a massive scar. She didn't want to stare and quickly averted her gaze. "Good morning, sirs, how can I help ye? Has something happened?"

"We heard about the ship," Lorne said, nodding. "We came to help."

Jaime wrinkled her nose at him. She could not have been more surprised if the mast had reassembled itself. "What?"

He glanced behind her and pointed. "Is that no' your ship?"

Jaime didn't look. "Aye."

"With the broken mast?" He slowly spoke as if trying to color a picture for her.

"Aye."

He waited perhaps for her to say more, and when she didn't, he continued, "Thought ye could use a few extra hands. We were all meeting today for a bit of exercise, and well, this will do nicely—as well as help ye out."

She stood in stunned silence for a moment, trying to comprehend. But her tired brain couldn't put two and two together. "Why would ye want to help me?"

The three men with Lorne raised eyebrows in his direction and then excused themselves toward the ship to get to work.

"Nay, do no' go up there," Jaime said.

The men pivoted around, puzzled expressions on their faces. However, on the ship deck, Emilia saw the men coming and called them to her, embracing the extra help as Jaime should have. The men looked to her for confirmation, and Jaime gave a resigned nod.

She turned back to Lorne. It was hard to meet his gaze after last night. She'd let herself fall under his spell once more, succumbed to pleasure, and now he was here, attempting to help her. The last thing he should be doing. They should be far from each other. And most certainly, not helping each other. "What's this all about?"

Lorne let out a short, exasperated sigh. "Exactly as I said. We came to help."

"I do no' need ye."

"I know. Ye're a verra capable woman. If these men were no' in your employ, I believe ye'd try to take on the whole bloody task yourself." He sounded irritated, and she couldn't blame him.

He was not wrong. She did like being in control. And she was at present acting like more than her usual stubborn self. "How did ye find out about it?"

"The missive ye sent with your butler."

"I sent no such missive..." But her voice trailed off, and

she frowned. MacInnes. The old fool was meddling. Had he seen them the night before? Her face heated at the thought.

"Well, someone did. And now, here I am. Point me in the direction of where ye'd like me to help first." He leaned closer, his clean scent surrounding her. The heat of his breath fanned over her cheek as he whispered near her ear, "And stop trying to push me away, lass. I'm no' going anywhere."

Especially after last night... She could have finished that sentence for him.

"I'm no' going to Ireland today." She felt it necessary to say so, even if it was obvious.

"I had surmised as much."

After several minutes of wrestling with herself to find her voice, Jaime relented. "Fine, ye can help. Come on."

Lorne followed her up the gangplank, her skin prickling with need at his nearness. She led him down into the dimly lit underbelly of the ship where men were lifting barrels and crates.

"All of this has to go," she said.

"All right." Lorne lifted a barrel that would ordinarily be hefted by two men, as if it weighed nothing at all, and then climbed the ladder with it, all while Jaime watched.

His strong legs carried him up the ladder, the muscles of his arse bunching in his breeches, and she had to look away, as the sight of him made all sorts of naughty thoughts tumble about in her lunatic brain.

"Are ye all right?" Emilia asked.

"Perfectly." But Jaime's voice was high and tight, giving away she was exactly the opposite of perfect. "Let's get back to work."

Emilia tried to hide her grin and pointed to one of the smaller crates. The two of them maneuvered it up the ladder and handed it on to the men.

"I'm impressed," Lorne said softly, winking at her as she

came back down the ladder. "No' only do ye have a lot of strength, but ye did no' fall in the process."

"Ye're a jackarse." She grinned at his surprised expression. "When on a ship, talk like a sailor." This time, she winked at him, grabbed the closest, small crate, and climbed back up.

He maneuvered behind her, another barrel balanced in his grasp and delivered it to a man who beckoned on the deck. They worked side by side for hours, passing glances, and at one moment, he accidentally slid against her—though she was fairly certain it was on purpose. His chest skimming against her arm made her entire body tingle, and the fact that he gave her a roguish grin showed her he knew exactly what he was doing. Another touch like that, and she was going to drag him deeper into the ship where they'd be covered in darkness, press him up against the ship's wall and...

Jaime cleared her throat and put herself back to work, hoping the physical exhaustion would help banish the carnal thoughts from her mind.

With the four strapping noblemen adding to the help, they emptied the ship's cargo by mid-afternoon rather than evening as she'd estimated they'd be completed.

With plenty of daylight still left, the crew boarded the transferred ship and worked to set sail.

Emilia and Jaime stood on the dock with Lorne and his companions, staring with satisfaction at the ships. Her arms were on fire, her back ached, and her legs felt heavier than the crates and barrels they'd moved. A hot bath sounded like heaven about then.

"Well done, Miss Andrewson," Lorne said. "Though I'm certain ye need no compliments from me."

Jaime smiled at him, grateful. "We were able to get everything done much quicker than anticipated. I do verra much appreciate the added assistance. And in fact, I should like to invite the four of ye to a ball I'll be hosting upon the ship soon."

Emilia let out a little gasp but outwardly did not show any other signs of surprise or excitement.

"I've no' yet had the invitations made. But I think it will be a lovely boon to our clients and any potential merchants who wish to use us for their wares."

"I canna speak for my friends here, but can tell ye I would be delighted," Lorne said.

"I would as well," and "same here" was heard from the other men.

Good, she had several people on the invitation list already then. She just needed to plan the fete. After she got Shanna and Gordie back, of course.

Tired and covered in sweat that had started to dry and further stiffened her already stiff working gown, Jaime decided it was time to call it a day. "I bid ye farewell."

"Or we could get some ice cream," Lorne suggested.

"What?" She stared at him, surprised by the invitation for something so...not him and because she was thoroughly disgusting at the moment.

"There's a delectable place between here and your flat."

"I am no' at all suitable for such an outing in my present condition." Jaime smiled to soften her rejection. "But I do thank ye for the invitation."

"Tomorrow, then?"

"Perhaps." Two rejections in a matter of minutes would have his friends talking.

"I'll pick ye up at noon."

"Have ye no' got anything better to do than follow me about, Your Grace?" she teased.

Lorne's companions chuckled at that, and one of them shook their head.

"Ye wound me," Lorne said.

"Ye lie."

His grin widened. "I'll see ye tomorrow." And with that, he disappeared with his friends down the dock toward a waiting carriage.

"YE'VE GOT IT BAD," MALCOLM SAID WITH A HORRIFIED expression on his face. "I thought ye did when I watched the two of ye box, but this?" Malcolm shook his head.

"Box? Do tell." Alec leaned forward in the already cramped carriage. "Did she kick your arse?"

Euan chuckled. "In every way, I'd say, from how his eyes never left her backside today."

Lorne punched his friend in the shoulder. "I'll no' have ye talk about my future wife's backside."

"So she agreed to marry ye?" Alec asked, his brow winged in surprise. "I would have bet money she'd refuse again."

"No' yet. But she will." Lorne ran his hands through his hair. "A little more convincing, and then I've no doubt she'll say aye."

"How much convincing does it take for a lass to forget the past?" Malcolm, always the sober one in the group, raised the pressing question.

"We've both been victims of our siblings. Give me one good reason we should no' join forces." Lorne crossed his arms over his chest, feeling irritated, mostly because he knew it was true. Jaime herself had said as much.

"Well, the fact that your siblings joined forces to sabotage both of ye?" Alec said with a face that screamed obviously.

"The question is why," Euan offered. "What did they have to gain?"

Lorne disclosed what Malcolm and Jaime's investigator had unearthed, as well as their own theories.

"That's mad." Euan shook his head in disbelief. "Hard to fathom that the two of them would seek to harm both of ye. To rob ye both."

"Aye," Lorne agreed.

"How has it been working out with the lass?" Alec asked.

"When I'm away from her, all I do is think about being near her again. I never felt that way about anyone—save my horse, maybe."

The men chuckled and bumped elbows at that.

"Have ye told her yet?" Malcolm asked.

"I've asked her to marry me. More than once."

"But have ye told her how ye feel?"

Lorne thought back to the kisses, the way he'd worshipped her in the garden. "No' in so many words, but I'm fairly certain my actions have."

"Sometimes females want to hear the exact words. As if those utterances are the key that unlocks their brains," Euan said.

"How would ye know? Ye've yet to marry," Lorne pointed out. "Or come close to it."

"I've enough sisters to manage. And they make their feelings quite clear."

"That is true. I'm no' sure how he survived," Alec said, giving their friend a concerned look. "Six sisters are quite a force."

"Ye have no idea." Euan rolled his eyes and gave a loud groan.

"Well, I suppose it can no' hurt my case," Lorne said skeptically. "I've already shown her in many ways, today included, that I care for her and her future. And by letting her boss me around, I think I've made it clear I'm no' there to take away her business or her fortune."

"Aye, but ye did set out to woo her just to get the castle back, did ye no'?" Alec reminded him.

Lorne nodded. Why did this have to be so complicated? If only it had been her he'd wooed before the war. But alas, he was a different man now, and back then, he might not have wanted the same things or respected her for who she was.

"She's a bright lass. Probably figured out a while ago what ye were after. I think it best ye explain to her that ye want her whether or no' ye get the castle back." Why did Alec have to make sense?

Still, it seemed a task heavier when enacted than pondered. "I'll have to think on what would be best said. Dinner at the club?"

"Aye," the three of them agreed.

No sooner had they arrived at the club than Malcolm was pulled aside by one of the footmen.

"I'll be back soon," he said, without telling them where he was headed.

Was it about Gille? Lorne hoped so. They'd been waiting long enough to put that matter to rest.

He hadn't even considered what he would do with his brother once he finally found him. Accuse him of selling the castle out from under him? But Gille had thought his brother dead, so really, he'd only been selling it out from under himself. However, if his scheme had been to gain the castle and the money for it by marrying Shanna, what more could he want? Lorne felt like shouting from the confusion and ridiculousness of it all.

He could have his brother thrown in debtor's prison, which would likely be what happened when it was eventually found out that he didn't have the money to pay Miss Andrewson back.

A sick feeling came into his stomach then, curdling around the steak and ale pie he'd consumed. Jaime had said she'd gifted Dunrobin to her sister. Did that mean she'd signed over the deed? If that were the case, then their legal matters became more difficult.

"Let's wager on billiards," Lorne said. He needed a distraction from his brother and Jaime. And while he would have rather taken his friends back to Sutherland Gate for a round in the ring or on the planche, they had to wait for Malcolm to return. Because part of that churning in his stomach was a hunch that something had been discovered, and he didn't want to miss out on whatever that was.

Just as Alec was pocketing yet another sovereign of Lorne's money, Malcolm returned and nodded for him to join him in a private corner of the club.

"Well, 'tis a good thing the two of ye did no' go to Ireland."

"I'm listening."

"Word has come to me that our subjects were intending to leave Ireland on a ship bound for Scotland. My man was able to delay that ship's leaving to return here first—and he partnered with Miss Andrewson's investigator, who remained behind to follow them on the ship and the road. He overheard them saying they planned to go to Dunrobin and hole up there. No' allow anyone in. They're planning to hold the lad for ransom."

"What? Their own child."

"Gille was saying he would no' be going to prison over it. But my man wondered if they maybe meant something else. It sounded more dramatic than the scam they put on."

Lorne shook his head. This was not the truth he wanted to hear. Somewhere deep inside, he'd been hoping all this time that his brother hadn't betrayed him. That this was all a misunderstanding. "So they are going to be at Dunrobin?"

"Aye. If I were ye, I'd make haste to leave tonight and get there well ahead of them."

14

J aime stared at Lorne, who sat across from her in his carriage on their way to the wharf. They were alone inside. Alison—her maid, tasked with keeping her reputation intact per MacInnes—rode perch outside with Mungo at the rear of the carriage, while their coachman took the front.

Lorne had an elbow propped by the window, a finger on his cheek, while his chin rested in his hand. That had been his position since they'd climbed in and sat down. He considered the outside as he likely considered what would happen once they boarded the ship, and if luck were on their side, when they arrived at Dunrobin later tonight. Jaime had tried her best not to look at him, to stare out the window as well, but it was a task she found most grueling, and he a subject far more interesting.

Earlier this morning, at an incredibly indecent hour, Lorne had knocked on the door of her residence and told her the news of Gille and Shanna's movements and that they had to travel north as quickly as possible to beat the two criminals at their own game.

One of her ships required a good scrubbing and happened to be free for the next two days, so they decided to take it north—an expensive way to travel but much faster than taking a carriage. Even if they rode at a fast clip by coach, it would be a week before they arrived, considering the terrain and given they'd need to change the horses and drivers frequently. Her ship could see them there in as little as a day since it was able to travel at a top speed of nearly 20-knots an hour, and then be returned to Edinburgh ready for business. And so it had been decided.

Emilia had been more than happy to take on her duties at Andrewson Shipping while Jaime was away, and MacInnes had nearly climbed inside her trunk upon learning she was traveling. It had only been with an explicit promise from Lorne that he would allow the older man to slit his throat if any harm befell Jaime that allowed her to leave without the butler at all.

And once more, she was glad her aunt had returned to London to look after the interests of her daughters rather than remain behind to meddle in hers, as she would never have allowed Jaime to take this long trip north with Lorne alone. It was unsuitable. Of course, Jaime didn't care.

For a woman she was already the quintessential example of all things unsuitable.

"What is our plan?" she asked Lorne, breaking the silence.

Lorne turned toward her, his hand falling into his lap, and she tried to avoid following the path but her eyes disobeyed her. Long, capable fingers. The shape of his thighs. She was quick to snap her glance back up to his.

There was the barest hint of a smile on his lips. "We do no' want Gille and Shanna to know we are there or that we're aware of their return or their schemes. Although, they must have guessed as much with their plan for the poor lad."

Sweet Gordie was falling victim to those who should care about him most. The notion was disturbing on so many levels and made Jaime furious. "How much lead time do ye think we have on them?"

"Sounded as if Malcolm's man was able to stall their ship for a day. So, at least a week. As soon as they arrive in Scotland, they'll most likely be riding north for Dunrobin. I can't imagine they'd commission a ship. But if they do, then we'll have two days or so. It is my understanding that as soon as a time can be established, your investigator will ride ahead to give us the warning."

"Aye. Thank goodness for Mr. Bell, who will be watching over the wee lad as they go." Jaime shook her head, still thoroughly confused as to how Shanna could go along with a plan like that. It was her son. Flesh and blood. A child she'd grown and nurtured in the womb. Didn't that mean anything to her? Was her greed so great that she'd be willing to put her son up for ransom?

Jaime had never believed the things her parents said about Shanna, thinking them harsh in their judgment. But from where she sat now, looking back and looking forward, it felt as though her sister had pulled the wool over Jaime's eyes in more ways than one.

"So we'll be waiting on bated breath for two days to a week." Jaime's stomach had already twisted itself into knots.

"Aye." Lorne sounded as disappointed as she was. Both of them wanted to get this over with.

Jaime glanced out the window, taking note that they were very close to the wharf. She jumped when Lorne touched her knee and jerked her gaze up from where she'd been focusing on her hands.

"Wring your fingers any tighter, lass, and ye'll have nothing left to mark up your ledgers."

She grinned. "I'm just so worried."

"All will be well, sweetling. I promise."

Jaime's chest warmed at the endearment and at his confidence. She wished she had the same assurance, but it felt as if everything were falling apart, and imminent disaster awaited them. "I want to save Gordie. It'll be a bonus if I get some of my money back. And of course, I'll sign the castle back over to ye." This was not what she'd told him originally. But money or not, it was a mistake to have bought the place. It didn't belong to her. An expensive lesson to learn, but one she wasn't going to ignore.

Lorne shook his head, a small smile on his lips. "If ye still want Dunrobin, it is yours to keep."

"What?" She flattened her spine against the carriage seat.

"I've made it clear I want to marry ye, Jaime. I...care for ye, lass. I enjoy your company. Marry me, and the castle is yours. Do no' marry me, and it is still yours. But if ye agree to be my wife, I'll draw up papers to see that the land is entailed to females only if it makes ye feel better."

At her shocked silence, he continued, "There's something I've realized, and I may no' have been clear in the telling of it, but for me, life is no' worth living unless ye've got someone to share it with. I rotted away in that prison for two years, wishing I'd had someone at home thinking about me. And when I realized that ye were the only one doing so—even in death exacting your revenge on me—I knew ye were the woman for me."

Jaime gaped at him. "Ye do realize what ye just said, aye?"

He grinned and leaned forward, taking her hands in his. "Aye. That even in death, ye could no' stop obsessing over me."

Jaime swatted him playfully. "I hated ye."

Lorne tugged her over to his lap, and she settled on the

solidness of him, wishing they weren't about to be interrupted by their servants.

"But ye only hated me so much because your feelings beforehand were already strong."

Her face flamed. "Ye knew?"

"No' until I started to think about it." He nuzzled her neck, pressing a kiss to her flaming skin. "And truth be told, lass, more often than no' back then I thought, 'well, Jaime's a darling, Shanna must be, too.' Night and day, the two of ye were."

"I'm so sorry she disappointed ye."

"Och, lass. Do no' be feeling sorry for me. 'Tis I who is feeling that way for ye. Ye've been a victim this whole time, and I can no' figure out why they'd abuse ye so. Me, I can understand. Gille was always jealous." Lorne shook his head.

"I think Shanna blames me for what happened with my parents. They disowned her because they did no' want her reputation to tarnish mine. That was a harsh punishment for a young lass who had nothing and no one. She was no more than a child. Her anger must have festered while she was away. I tried to write to her and sneak the letters out of the house, but my parents confiscated them, and I never heard from her either. It wasn't until they had passed that I brought her back, but by then, I think she already hated me."

"Ah, makes sense, even if it is unfair. It would seem our siblings have taken normal rivalries between relations to a whole new level."

"Aye."

The carriage pulled up to the docks, and Jaime scrambled off of Lorne's lap to sit across from him, smoothing her hands over her rumpled skirt as a groom opened the door for their descent. Their luggage was carried onto the smaller frigate with a minimal crew that they'd be using. Mungo and Alison waited behind them like stalwart bodyguards. As if their presence alone could keep the two of them from acting on their impulses.

Emilia met them at the docks and wished them luck. All of it was happening so fast as the sun rose on the horizon.

"Do take care," Jaime started. "The whisky—"

"Sails tomorrow. Do no' worry." Emilia smiled confidently. "I have it all under control. I will no' let ye down."

"Ye are a gem," Jaime crowed. "I think ye're due a raise."

"I will no' turn ye down."

"Well, ye know where to find me should ye need anything."

"With all due respect as my employer—go. We will be fine."

Jaime laughed, thanked Emilia again, and then hurried up the gangway with Lorne and their faithful servants.

The sails were let out, a brisk morning wind making their departure quick. No time to turn back. She would be alone with Lorne for possibly a week before her sister arrived. An entire week to get up to mischief.

Jaime shook her head. She should not be thinking about it that way at all. In fact, she should watch the seagulls that circled overhead as the ship moved away from the quay. And this time, she wouldn't shoo them because she needed them as a distraction from the man who stood beside her.

"Are ye tired? Would ye like to nap?"

Jaime glanced up at Lorne and gave him a derisive look, all the easier to forget she wanted to kiss him. "Do ye think because I'm a female, I'm no' used to waking before dawn? I'll have ye know the reason I was ready so quickly was that I'd already been up for hours and dressed. I run a shipping company, duke, no' a salon."

Lorne held up his hands and backed away slowly, shaking

his head with a laugh. "Ye need no' bite my head off, lass. I was no' suggesting the like at all. Only trying to see to your comfort."

Jaime pressed her lips together. She wasn't used to someone seeing to her comfort besides the people she paid to do it. The experience was foreign to her but pleasant.

Jaime leaned against the rail, gazing out over the ocean as the distance between them and the shore grew. "I'm sorry," she said. "I...I'm just used to people thinking that because I'm a woman I'm no' capable."

Lorne joined her at the rail, his large hands flattened on the wood, but she could feel his eyes on her rather than the diminishing wharf. "Anyone who would think that does no' know ye verra well."

She cocked her head at him. "And ye do?"

"I think I do, lass."

Jaime turned to look at him, studying his strong jaw, the line of his nose with the bump on the bridge from where it had been broken. His wide, full mouth that could do all sorts of things to her body, and then finally his eyes. A steel-gray, they were fathomless. Sturdy. Dependable.

Not at all the eyes that she'd imagined she'd see while she spent so much time hating him. But as she gazed into his eyes now, she saw the young duke she'd from nearly a decade before still lingering there. Only now, he was wiser, a little harder. And more serious. But the warmth of him, the confidence, the wit. Those things that she'd fallen in love with him for were all still there. Combined with the man he was now, they made him all the more appealing.

What a disaster.

"Ye might," she offered. "But only time will tell."

"Does that mean ye plan to give me the time?"

"Just that I'm considering it."

But she was doing a lot more than considering it. There were parts of her she'd hidden away. Told herself that she would never be able to open those boxes and give voice to the hopes she'd had for a husband, a family. When she'd taken over the company, the business had been her main goal—her only goal besides the revenge against Lorne and seeing to her sister's comfort. She'd tossed away any idea of a future family of her own.

And now Lorne had stormed back into her life, vibrantly alive, and offered the things she'd never dreamed she'd have. Had told herself not to even think about wanting.

Drat the tiny boxes she'd kept locked in her heart, for they were starting to peek open. Little whispers that try as she might, she couldn't ignore. The more she listened, the more the bolted boxes wrenched open. Now, here she was, standing before him, wishing he would kiss her and that no one would care.

"What are ye thinking?" he asked. "Ye've a faraway look. And I'll be honest, I'm intrigued because ye're no longer frowning at me."

Heat rushed to her face. "I was only thinking about how much has changed since ye came back from France."

It was the first time she'd not said, "come back from the dead," and the little tug at the corner of Lorne's lip told her he'd noticed.

"Ye mean more than my brother selling ye my castle and then eloping with your sister?"

Jaime laughed and pressed her hand to her hot face. "I can no' believe all of this is happening. It is almost too wild for the truth."

Lorne chuckled. "If it were in a book, I doubt I'd believe it."

"Me either. Although I've read some pretty fantastical tales."

"Ye like to read?"

"Ah-ha! Something ye did no' know about me," she teased.

"Now that I think of it, I do recall seeing ye in the drawing room of your parents' manse with your nose in a book."

"Ye would be right."

"I also enjoy books. It was one of the things I missed the most when I was imprisoned."

"Will ye tell me about it? Your imprisonment."

A dark cloud fell over his face, and she thought he would shut down, but he smiled. "A somber discussion should be done over tea, or whisky perhaps."

"Why no' both? We're on a ship, after all. No one can tell us we're behaving improperly by imbibing in spirits so early in the morning." She glanced to where Mungo and Alison lurked nearby. "Except maybe those two. But we can tell them to leave us alone for a little bit, aye?"

"My kind of lass." He grinned, and she led him into the captain's quarters, which her captain had graciously given up during this particular journey. "Besides, the fact that we're traveling together is liable to stir up enough trouble that morning whisky will be the least of our problems."

"True."

They sent Mungo and Alison to get tea, whisky, and sandwiches from the ship's kitchen. While they waited, they made themselves comfortable in the cabin. She sank onto a well-cushioned alcove with wide windows staring out at the view, and Lorne sat in a wing-backed chair, his long, muscled legs spread out before him. She endeavored not to look at him, even though her wayward gaze kept roving over.

Goodness, but he was handsome and alluring. Unfairly so, to be sure.

She was amazed at how comfortable they could be together in silence, especially given a fortnight ago, she might have pulled a pistol on him if he dared get cozy in her presence. Even though she tried to hide her feelings from herself, it was hard not to feel warmer when he was around—even charged with an extra dose of energy that was as foreign to her as being timid.

Happiness.

❧ 15 ❧

The lass was so incredibly arresting.

Perched on the pillows, her legs curled beneath her, he could almost envision they were having a relaxing day in each other's company rather than trying to head two idiots off at the pass.

As she stared out at the water, she looked peaceful. As though she belonged on the sea. From what he knew of the Andrewson Shipping Company, her father had inherited the business from his sire but had more interest in being in London than Scotland and even less interest in running a company. Before Lorne had left for war, it seemed the shipping company was on the verge of bankruptcy. Lorne could only credit its current success to the woman sitting before him.

What couldn't she do when she put her mind to it?

Alison and Mungo did not knock as they entered. Lorne kept his face sober, rather than breaking out into a smile at the volatile expression on her face as the maid passed his way and how Mungo glowered at her. The two of them were getting along splendidly.

It was obvious the woman didn't like that her mistress was alone with him—a concern Mungo didn't have—and the persnickety lady's maid was going to let Lorne know that she wasn't going to make his life easy, or give them privacy. And that was fine by him. Whatever Alison needed to see that he was truly a decent man for her mistress. At Mungo had his back should the maidservant try to carve his heart out with a teaspoon.

With the tea service placed on the small table before them, Alison and Mungo took up guard by the door. Jaime poured out for the two of them, topping each cup of tea with a splash of whisky and a wink. The light sway of the ship barely registered with the liquid in their cups. She passed him his spiked tea and then raised her cup to clink gently against his.

"To resolutions."

"Resolutions?" Lorne asked.

"Aye, we've a number of quandaries. And we're going to need the fortitude to get through them."

"Ah, aye, I see. To resolutions." He sipped the liquor with lay a soothing path down his throat.

She picked up one of the small sandwiches and nibbled.

"Elegant fare for a ship." Lorne lifted one of the sandwiches, taking note that not one of them held a cucumber. He didn't bother to nibble but popped the whole square into his mouth.

Jaime laughed. "Only when I'm aboard. I think they like to remind me I'm a lady and not a coarse buccaneer."

"Why can ye no' be both?" He wiggled his brows.

She cocked her head at him, a soft laugh falling from her delicate throat. "Ye'd be the first man to suggest it."

He grinned and raised his cup again. "Resolutions, remember? I like to be a trailblazer. After all, I did come back from the dead."

Jaime flicked her gaze toward her maid and Mungo. "Ye may leave us. Both of ye."

The maid narrowed her gaze, not wanting to exit at all, and Mungo appeared ready to throttle her.

"Alison, I will be perfectly fine, I can assure ye. The duke is a gentleman, and I am more than capable of handling myself. Why no' go and have a cup, both of ye. We've some matters to discuss."

Alison did not look happy at all about the prospect and flashed Lorne a glower that promised she'd slit his throat as fast as MacInnes would.

"I promise to take good care of Miss Andrewson. Ye have my word. And I'm as good as my word, am I no', Mungo?"

Mungo nodded. "Aye, Your Grace."

Alison bowed her head and exited, hesitating in shutting the door and then finally disappearing when Mungo yanked it closed for her.

"What are the odds she stands outside listening?" Lorne asked with a raised brow.

Jaime grinned at him over the rim of her cup. "We'd be fools to believe otherwise."

"Mungo," he called. "To tea, both of ye!"

A small scuffle sounded on the other side of the door that had Lorne thinking Mungo may have had to carry Alison off like a sack of wool.

"Ah, where were we?" Lorne said, pouring a healthy splash of whisky into his cup. "I believe ye wanted to know about my journey overseas."

"I feel compelled to remind ye that ye're under no obligation to talk to me about your time in prison."

Lorne took a fortifying sip of his whisky. "I've no' spoken to anyone about it. I gave the War Office the basic facts, but I've kept the rest to myself."

"I will no' pry if ye do no' want to share. But as a friend—"

He interrupted her. "A friend, ye say? Is it true? Are ye feeling well?"

Jaime chuckled and popped the rest of her sandwich into her mouth. "I'll deny it should anyone ask."

"There she is." He plucked another tea sandwich and ate it in one bite. "I want to tell ye, lass."

Jaime settled back against the cushions with her feet tucked under her, teacup in her lap. She watched him—patient, no judgment—and he realized then, he wanted nothing more than share his story with this woman and this woman alone.

"We were close to defeat, but my men and I soldiered on. Fighting the demandable French, knowing that death was soon to be our sentence." He paused a moment, feeling himself sink back onto that smoke-covered field, where bodies littered the blood-soaked earth. "I ordered my men to retreat. We needed to get away from the blasted cannon fire. And as we made haste, the ground around me exploded. I was knocked unconscious."

Jaime was silent, but her expression said everything she felt—horror, fear, trepidation.

"When I woke, I was no longer on the field but in a dark cell. A dungeon in a French bastard's fortress." Her soft gasp was enough to make him want to leap up and pull her into his arms. To change the subject. Perhaps back to kissing. "Shall I stop?"

"Nay," she whispered.

"All right, but ye must tell me if this is too much."

Her wide brown eyes never left his. "I will. Please, continue."

"All right." Lorne washed the bitter memory down with the last dregs of his tea. "I did not know if my men had made it to safety or no'. No idea how long they planned to keep me." He held out his cup for a refill. "For days, they questioned me. Tortured me. The only thing that made me think they did no' mean to kill me was the fact that my wounds from the battlefield were treated, as were the wounds they inflicted through torture."

"Lorne," she murmured. "I had no idea."

"No one did, sweetling. Else I imagine I'd have come home a lot sooner. They got inventive with their torment, pitting one prisoner against the other. Whenever I got close enough to one of the guards, I would fight him too in hopes of escaping or at least allowing one of the other men to leave."

"Did ye know any of them?"

He shook his head. "Never met any of them in my life. But I never forgot their faces and if I came across them today, I'd recognize them. I didn't realize how much time had elapsed. One day, the men and I devised a plan. When they unlocked the cell and we passed through, one of us stuck a slim piece of rock in the side slot, so they'd think they'd locked it, but truly the rock would block the bolt. We prayed it would work. And it did. When the guards settled down for the evening, which often meant drinking and gambling, we slipped right past them and into the night."

"That easily?" She looked surprised, as she should be, because it wasn't.

He shook his head but didn't want to tell her that they'd overpowered and killed the guards. Stole their clothes and coin to book passage. But as he gazed into her eyes, he knew he could trust her with his dark secrets. "We did some things..."

Jaime nodded, a slight smile on her lips. "Good. They deserved it."

And that was that—full and utter acceptance.

Lorne set down his cup, took off his doublet, and rolled up the sleeve of his linen shirt. He'd seen her glance at the scars poking out when he'd come to help her on her ship. Seen the curiosity that lingered in her gaze. And he wasn't afraid to share his wounds with her.

"What are ye doing?" she asked, eyes on his movements.

"I want to show ye my scars."

"All of them?" She glanced at the door.

"No' all of them, lass—we have to save something for the wedding night." He was teasing, though he did hope a marriage between them would happen.

"Alison may have a fit of apoplexy."

"She might." He winked. "I hope ye will no'."

"I'm no' scared, Lorne. No scar ye show me would change how I feel about ye."

He paused, unable to not tease her. "Are ye admitting to having feelings for me?"

"Aye, I'm just no' going to tell ye what they are."

He laughed at that and stood, walking to where she sat. He held out his left arm, so she could see the wicked scar that ran from below his elbow on his forearm all the way up to his shoulder, though he'd not pushed his sleeve up more than his bicep.

Jaime set down her tea and reached tentatively for his arm, her brown eyes gazing at him for permission. She untucked her legs from beneath her and stood.

Lorne nodded and felt the jolt of lightning through his skin when she traced his scar with her finger from the bottom to where his shirt sleeve stopped. She slipped her fingers beneath his sleeve, moving upward toward his shoulder, tracing the puckered skin.

"Is this from the cannon or their treatment of ye?"

Was it him, or did her eyes seem wetter than before? "The cannon."

"Ye're lucky no' to have lost your arm." Her face was grim, worried, and perhaps even a little relieved.

"I am."

"I want to see the rest."

Lorne stiffened, feeling the shock of her words down to his toes. Show her the rest... Lord help him, he wouldn't do that. Not without an "I do" before a priest. He wanted her, both body and soul. Had been willing to give her the most delicious pleasure in the garden of her flat. But to show himself... It was a terrifying thought. Would make a woman run, he was certain. However, wouldn't he want to know now if that was going to be her reaction, rather than find out on the wedding night that he was a battered and scarred monster?

"I can no' show them all to ye, lass. It would no' be proper, and I did promise Alison." He reached for his cravat and paused, realizing that by removing this particular piece, Alison would think he'd removed them all. "If I undo this, I'll never be able to get it back in place, and your maid will slit my throat for certain."

Jaime laughed. "I can help."

"Then I'll show ye the scars on my chest, but nothing more." He tugged at his cravat in earnest this time, irritated by the damnable garment anyway, always feeling a little bit as if he were being choked.

When at last he was free, Lorne discarded the fabric on the chair he'd vacated and then started with the buttons of his shirt. Three buttons total revealed half his chest, where the skin near his left collarbone puckered and twisted, a continuation of the wound from his arm. That was as much as he was willing to remove. It was only that side of him that had been ruined; the other remained untouched as if to mock him for the rest of his life. It was only the warmth of the whisky that kept him from shuddering.

Jaime reached forward, the light stroke of her fingertips tracing the scars from his shoulder over his collarbone to the dip in his neck. He sucked in a breath at her touch, how gentle it was, how much it lit his skin aflame. The expression on her face was not of disgust at all. Nothing like what he imagined when she gazed at his broken body.

"Does it still hurt?" she asked, flicking her gaze up toward his.

He started to shake his head and then decided to be honest. "Every once in a while, there's a twinge of something unpleasant, but then it is quickly gone, or else whisky helps."

She smiled up at him softly as her hand flattened right over the place where his heart battered his ribcage. He was captivated by her brown eyes, the delicate fringe of black lashes, and the deep emotion that seemed to emanate from her. Lorne placed his hand over hers where she touched him.

"The scars do no' bother ye?"

"Bother me?" She wrinkled her nose, appearing truly confused. "Ye were fighting for your country. Wounded by the enemy. How could I ever think that your scars were anything other than marks of valor? A visible, palpable sign of your bravery and your victory. They tried to kill ye, but ye survived. If anything..." She licked her lower lip as she glanced down at their joined hands. "If anything, I think they make ye more of a man, Lorne."

More of a man...

Good God. He wanted to kiss her. Her servants, and his promises, be damned.

Lorne bent forward and captured her mouth with his. She gasped, staggering a little at his sudden embrace, but then she wrapped her other arm around his shoulders, her fingers curling against the back of his neck. Tasting of whisky and desire, Jaime kissed him back. Hard, passionate. Her tongue dueled with his as if neither of them could control themselves any longer. Two lost souls who'd been dying of thirst and finally found an oasis in which to quench their tireless craving.

Where one part of him had been aflame, now all of him was. Desire thrummed in his veins and pooled in his groin. The need for this woman to be his. To claim her utterly and forever.

He enfolded his arm around her waist and tugged her flush against him. Heated breath fanned across his face. And then there was a jolt, and they stumbled as the ship rocked from one side to the other—the only thing that kept him from lifting her and carrying her to the captain's bed that was through the double doors at their rear. Their kiss broke as they both staggered, tumbling backward. Lorne lost his balance, falling with Jaime on top of him. Splayed fully over him, her soft breasts pressed to his chest, her hips on his hardened arousal...

She stared down at him, eyes full of passion, her lips a rosy red. She felt good, delicious and ripe. It was entirely too tempting to have her like this. So close, and yet not be able to claim her.

Her breasts pushed against the confines of her gown and tested the limits of his control. Supple, creamy globes. Only inches from his mouth and he wanted so badly to taste her.

Again, why hadn't he slaked his need with some willing widow or courtesan? But he knew the answer to that, and it was because the only woman he truly wanted was currently lying on top of him. Tormenting him.

Jaime stared down where their hands were still joined on his chest, and then she bent and kissed his scarred collarbone, the heat of her lips pressing to his skin almost too much. Lorne groaned, and then...he felt something in his eyes as foreign to him as weakness—tears.

He blinked rapidly to dispel the emotion, the potent reaction. And then he closed his eyes, his head leaning back against the floor, his breaths heavy. Because the alternative was to roll her over and lift her skirts.

"Why did ye do that?" he asked, his voice tight, his throat closing.

"I may own this ship, but I'll have ye know I do no' own the ocean, and I can no' make it rock us onto our arses simply by wishing it so."

Lorne opened his eyes to stare at her, face full of teasing mirth. He chuckled. "Ye're a hoyden."

"Perhaps. But I would no' change who I am."

"And neither would I."

"I used to be scared of who I was. Scared of being alone. Of relinquishing control if I did ever..." The column of her throat bobbed. "If I ever found someone."

"I would never take away your control, lass. Well, perhaps only when I had ye naked and pinned beneath me."

"Ye're a rogue."

"Aye, but I'm a rogue who wants ye, lass. A rogue who would never expect ye to give up the things ye love, what ye've worked for. I would give ye anything ye asked."

"Even the thing ye prized the most," she mused, referring back to his statement in the carriage that he would give her Dunrobin.

"Even that. I'll ask ye once more if ye'd be my wife, Jaime." Lorne was certain he could no longer live without her. She fascinated him absolutely. She was grounded, determined, independent. Someone he could lean on and confide in without judgment. Having grown up in an undependable world lasting into adulthood, she was what he needed most. No secrets. No games.

Exactly what he needed.

Jaime's lips parted. However, nothing came out but a sigh. He thought she would pull away. Stand up and cross the room to put as much distance between them as she possibly could, as she had done every other time. But she didn't. It felt as though she might have been sinking closer to him.

"Aye," she whispered.

Lorne's breath left him in a whoosh, and he hadn't the power to suck it back in. Had he heard her correctly? Aye.

"I know 'tis wrong," Jaime was saying. "To have wanted ye and loved ye for as long as I have, but I can no' fight it any longer. Society be damned."

Loved...

Lorne couldn't breathe. Perhaps he'd fallen and hit his head when the ship jerked. That was it. He was hearing things all wrong.

"Say something," Jaime said, her brow furrowing in that way he liked.

"I love ye, too." Those were not the words he'd expected to come out of his mouth. Not by a long shot. He'd been thinking more along the lines of "What? What did ye say?"

But there they were. Devotional words that captured the depth of his feelings, the truth of his heart.

Jaime grinned. "How?"

"How could I no'?"

"I'm a hoyden. I stole your castle, and I wished ye dead."

"And ye loved me, lass."

Lorne rolled with her until she was pinned under him. Her lush body felt so right, and his hard places sank against all her softer ones. Leaning upon his elbow, he stared down into her gorgeous face. Creamy cheeks flushed. Her eyes searched his for answers he'd happily give her for the rest of their days. He settled his pelvis against hers, a lithe leg bent at the knee pressed to his hip.

"How could it be wrong?" he asked. "It should have been ye from the beginning."

"My father would have never allowed it, nor my mother."

"Neither would ye," he said with a smile, kissing her briefly. "No' if it meant taking something from your sister."

"Even when she did no' want it."

"Ye're too generous."

"And yet I took your castle."

He chuckled softly. "Maybe ye acquired it because ye wanted a piece of me."

"But I gifted it to my sister."

"No' really. If ye'd truly given it to her, ye would have had the deed put in her name and not kept it for yourself."

He could see the surprised look on her face, almost as if she'd realized at that moment what she'd done.

"Ye're right. I wanted it for myself." She stroked the side of his face. "I wanted a piece of ye."

"And I freely give it to ye, my love. All of the pieces of me." Lorne kissed her again, and she wrapped her arms around him, deepening their kiss with a slide of her tongue over his.

It was then the door to their cabin banged open, and a shocked Alison gasped loudly enough to crack the spell.

"Ye promised, Your Grace," Alison said, her matronly eyes boring into him. It was only Mungo holding the maidservant back that kept her from charging forward.

Lorne smiled widely. "She has agreed to be my wife."

Alison waved away that statement. "Then ye'll have to wait until after the wedding to take such liberties."

Jaime pressed her lips together, clearly trying not to laugh as Lorne stood and pulled her to her feet.

"Miss Andrewson asked me to chaperone her, and I made a promise to MacInnes. He'll have my head if he finds out..." She paused a minute. "Is it true? Have ye agreed to marry?"

"Aye, Alison. I have."

"Well, 'tis a good thing then. Perhaps we can do so when we arrive at Dunrobin. Indeed, I'll arrange it with your housekeeper as soon as we arrive. And then ye can..." She waved her hand in their general vicinity. "Until then, Your Grace, Mungo will help ye redress, and Miss Andrewson, let us go back into the captain's bedchamber to fix ye up. No sense in anyone else guessing what might have happened when I left the two of ye alone for a second."

"I assure ye, Alison, nothing untoward has occurred, other than a little kiss," Jaime was saying.

Alison rolled her eyes and muttered, "Every little kiss like that is why the world is populated."

Mungo snorted at that and then quickly schooled his face in all seriousness.

Lorne laughed hard, though, finding the woman's humor too much to admonish her for speaking so out of turn to a duke.

"I can see why my fiancée has kept ye on, Alison. Ye're most loyal."

Alison gave him one last glower before shutting the door and taking his view of Jaime with her.

"Had your hands full, Mungo?"

"No' as full as ye, Your Grace."

Lorne narrowed his gaze. "I think ye're being impertinent, but I'll let it slide on account of my happiness."

Mungo grinned. "Glad to have ye back, Your Grace."

16

With their two stubborn heads put together, Mungo and Alison were able to keep Jaime and Lorne from any further physical contact for the rest of the day's journey. Of course, this only made Jaime want to be nearer to Lorne, especially now that she'd agreed to marry him. Now that he'd trusted her enough to open up about what had happened to him in captivity.

Besides, hadn't the curmudgeons ever heard about the lure of the forbidden? Still, they made excellent gatekeepers. Though, she suspected it was more likely Mungo was holding Alison back from tossing Lorne overboard.

At last, they reached the shores of Dunrobin, with the castle looming toward the sky as if some merry fortress out of a fairytale. "It's lovely." Jaime stood beside Lorne at the ship's helm, the closest they'd been in hours, now that Alison and Mungo saw they were ending their journey.

"There's nothing quite like the feeling of coming home." There was a great depth of emotion in his words.

That feeling he spoke of—a sensation she was certain he

must sense more acutely after having been gone from it for so long. She slipped her hand in his, entwining their fingers.

"I have to apologize," she said. "Before we get off this ship." Jaime turned to face him.

"For what?" He looked puzzled.

"For the first thing ye realized when ye got home to Dunrobin was that ye'd been robbed—and I the thief."

He smiled down at her, affectionately squeezed her hand and tucked an errant hair behind her ear. "That was no' the first thing I realized, lass," he teased.

"The second, then."

"Something like that." He winked.

"I know ye jest, but I am serious. It is inexcusable, and I am sorry from the bottom of my heart that I placed such hurt on ye. I..."

He stroked her cheek, ignoring the clearing throat of her maid a few feet away. "If ye had no', would we be where we are today?"

"I'm no' certain."

"Me either. Why would I have had a reason to ride to Edinburgh, to burst in on ye at your flat or your place of business? I would no'. So I'd no' change it. No more feeling guilty, soon-to-be Duchess of Sutherland. I will no' allow it."

Duchess... When he'd asked her to marry him over the last couple of weeks, and even when she'd agreed hours ago, never had it crossed her mind that she'd be a duchess. It had only been that she was going to be Lorne's wife, his lover. The protector of his heart, and he hers. But duchess... The word was grand. The responsibility, grander.

"I can see your face is paling. What is it?" Lorne looked down at her, concern etched between his brows.

"Only that I had no' thought much of being a duchess."

"There's nothing to it. I promise." He raised her hand to his mouth, kissing her knuckles.

"Says a man born and bred to be a duke."

He grinned. "To a woman who runs a thriving empire. Being a duchess is much the same, only ye have more servants."

Jaime laughed. "I'll take your word for it."

"I would never steer ye wrong."

She felt his promise all the way to her marrow. Oh, how she wanted to shoo away her maid and plant her lips on his. To kiss him hard as they weighed anchor at the single dock on his shores.

Soon, the crew was ready for them to debark.

"After ye, Miss Andrewson," Lorne said.

"'Tis only fitting that ye should be first on the dock," she said.

Lorne shrugged. "Why? It is your castle."

"And I'm giving it back to ye." She planted her leather boots right where they were and was not going to budge.

"And I'm giving it to ye. So ye see, ye first." Lorne held out his arm, indicating she should go before him.

"Seems I'm not the only hardheaded person on the ship," she muttered. "If ye insist."

"If ye do no' go quick, I'm liable to toss ye over my shoulder and take ye down myself. But I think doing that would scandalize Alison even more than we already have."

Jaime laughed. "She's going to need a strong cup of tea when we get inside."

"I'll make certain Mrs. Blair takes care of her."

"Your housekeeper?"

"Aye, she's like MacInnes to me."

Jaime knew exactly what he meant by that. MacInnes was like a father or grandfather to her. There since she'd been a lass and with only her best interests at heart.

"I can no' wait to meet her, then. She sounds divine." With that, Jaime climbed the few steps to the rail and balanced herself on the gangplank all the way to the dock, with Lorne following behind her. They walked over the beach to the grand gate that led into a massive walled garden with so many different encompassing parts that Jaime thought for certain it would take her days to explore it all.

That was one thing she'd not done after purchasing Dunrobin—visit it. Some part of her simply couldn't do it. The guilty part, she was sure. That little voice inside her said she'd done the wrong thing. Even if she'd thought Lorne dead, it had felt dishonest to steal his family seat.

Lorne took her hand as their boots crunched on the gravel toward stone stairs. She paused a moment at the base, staring up at the turrets and shining glass windows that bespoke of Sutherland wealth.

"My goodness," she breathed out.

"Aye, it only gets better the closer ye get, does it no'?"

"Infinitely."

"I can no' wait for us to make it our home."

Their home... She smiled at him, wistful. Why did it feel like everything was bound to go amiss at some point? She wanted this so badly, and it felt as if it would be snatched away before she could truly grasp it all as a reality. As though it were too good to be true.

They climbed the stairs, greeted at the top by a line of servants and guards.

"Your Grace," an elderly woman said. "Welcome back." She slid her glance toward Jaime, a brow winging in question.

"Miss Andrewson, might I introduce ye to Mrs. Blair?"

The housekeeper's mouth dropped open at Jaime's identification, and for a moment, she felt her face heat, and she sank into herself. All of these people knew what she had done. Hated her for it. Would they pick up the closest thing to a weapon and shoo her out?

"My fiancée," Lorne added. "We're to be married as soon as we can get to the kirk."

"So soon?" Mrs. Blair blurted out and then pressed her hands over her mouth as if she wanted to keep the words that she'd already let out from being expressed.

Lorne only laughed. "A long enough time has passed since Dunrobin had a mistress."

"What about the ownership of the castle?" Mrs. Blair asked, staring accusingly at Jaime. "J. Andrewson?"

"This," Lorne put his arm around her shoulders, "is the mysterious J."

A cloud fell over the older woman's face, and Jaime had the extreme desire to run away—and quickly.

"Oh, Mrs. Blair, no need to fash." Lorne gave the housekeeper the same smile he'd used on her a time or two in hope of swaying her to his cause. "There has been a misunderstanding. And my fiancée has given me back the castle, and I, in turn, will bequeath it to her and any daughters born of our union."

Mungo came around the duke and put his arm comfortingly around Mrs. Blair's shoulders. "The lad is quite infatuated, and if I may be plain, the sentiment seems to be mutual."

"Indeed it is," Alison muttered behind them.

Jaime needed to make amends with the servants here at Dunrobin if she didn't want to be hiding in her wardrobe for the rest of her life. Shanna's letter dismissing them all in Jaime's name had marked her as a tyrant, and she couldn't let that be the way they saw her.

Out from under Lorne's arm, she stepped forward and walked toward the housekeeper and other castle servants. Though it was difficult, she forced a smile on her face that she prayed held no trace of her nerves.

"I must apologize for what has transpired. Of course, I

never knew the duke would come back, as I suspect none of ye did. And it was never my intention to cast anyone out. The letter ye received giving warning of such was no' sent by me at all—ye're all as welcome as ye've been for generations. I want nothing more than to make your duke happy."

She thought it too soon to tell them that she was also a shipping magnate. They wouldn't understand it, just as most people didn't when they realized that it was her in charge of the business, hence the reason she often signed initial correspondence J. Andrewson. No one ever suspected she was a woman.

"And I want nothing but my future duchess's happiness." Lorne was beside her again, his hand slipping into hers. He glanced down at her. "And we need your help. All of ye. There's been a lot of trickery afoot, which is why we came from Edinburgh by ship to arrive as fast as we could. If ye could all assemble in the great hall, I want to tell ye of what's to come."

"Aye, Your Grace." The servants bowed and nodded, spreading into two lines that he led Jaime through, with the others taking up the rear.

Inside the castle, Jaime stilled at the grandeur. If she'd thought his house in Edinburgh was exquisite, this castle made Sutherland Gate look like a simple croft.

And now it was her home—nay, their home.

HUSBAND.

Jaime stared in wonder at the man who was not but a few feet away from her, undoing the ties of his cravat and then the buttons of his shirt. Only this afternoon, they'd found themselves in a similar position, unmarried.

And a swift exchange of vows on the Sutherland kirk steps several hours ago had changed that.

It was all a whirl now. Saying "I do," the chaste kiss, sweeping into the dining hall where a feast was served, the divine wine. And now, here they were in the chamber they'd share as husband and wife.

And Lorne was undressing.

He'd shooed away Mungo and Alison, who'd both wanted to help prepare the bride and groom for bed. Lorne had said he wanted to do it himself.

Undress her.

In the flickering candlelight, his skin glowed golden as inch by inch was revealed. Butterflies danced in her belly as she watched. He tugged the unbuttoned shirt over his head, revealing a sprinkling of dark hair that traveled in an arrow pattern down into his breeches.

Lorne didn't move to unbutton his breeches, which was quite disappointing. But she didn't have long to think about it as he came forward, his hands fanning the sides of her face. His touch was warm, a little coarse, but positively heaven-sent.

"Ye have to stop looking at me like this, or all I've got planned will be tossed out the window," he said.

"What have ye planned? And how am I looking?" Her face heated, and she licked her lips, nervous and excited all at once. Flashes of their amatory encounter in her garden had her nipples puckering and the place between her legs tingling in anticipation. The way he'd felt lying on top of her on the ship... All the delicious sensations that coursed through her.

"Ye look like ye want to lick me from head to toe."

"Oh..." And she did want to, now that he'd put that thought into her head. It sounded like a very good idea.

"And, the things I have planned... I'll start with a kiss." He brushed his mouth on hers, his hands smoothing down her back as he did so to clasp her bottom.

She loved the solid feel of him, the possessive way he touched her. How every part of her was jealous of wherever his hands happened to be. Jaime put her arms around his shoulders, playing with his hair for only a moment, before sliding over the wide, muscular expanse of his bare back. There were scars on the left side, a continuation of those on his arm and chest. But the rest was smooth and rippling with strength.

He deepened the kiss, his tongue caressing over hers, and she clutched on to him, acutely aware that she could kiss him like this for the rest of her days, and no one could say anything about it.

A moment later, chilled air touched her back, replaced by warm hands she wished were on her skin; alas, her chemise was still in the way. While she'd been distracted by the feel of his spine, his kiss, Lorne had undone every button of her gown. He'd plucked at the ribbons that Alison had fussed over putting in place. He smoothed the fabric down her arms, her hips, her thighs until every bit pooled at her feet, and all the while his mouth never left hers. Teasing little licks and strokes. A nibble of her lips, a soft groan from deep in his throat when she mimicked him. She was becoming quite adept at this kissing thing, she was certain. And, did she enjoy it.

"Ye do no' wear a corset?" he whispered.

"I hate them." Instead, her chemise had a ribbon tied beneath her bosom for enhancement, which she reached for now.

"Nay, let me." His fingers swept hers as he pinched the ribbon and pulled it until it loosened. He cupped her breasts through the fabric, his thumbs brushing over her nipples which peaked in response. With a satisfied grin, he leaned down and nuzzled her breasts until she squirmed, wanting more, but he only teased her. Then he was grazing his mouth over the swells of her bare breasts where they peeked from the top of the fabric, and her neck, then her mouth again. His hands rounded over her bottom, tugging her close. With her gown gone, the hardness of his arousal pressed more noticeably to her belly, and she inched closer, wanting to feel more.

Lorne's fingers bunched her chemise up around her thighs, and then he broke the kiss to tug it overhead, leaving her standing in her stockings and garters.

"Ye are exquisite," he murmured, his gaze raking down the length of her and the look of pure hunger on his face sending shivers through her.

Lorne knelt before her, untying her garters one at a time and fluttering little kisses to her thighs and knees as he did it. He unrolled her stockings and tossed them aside. She watched the deft way his fingers worked in utter fascination, and then he glanced up at her, stopping her breath altogether.

"I do no' know how anyone did no' scoop ye up before I came back, but I am a man truly blessed."

Jaime smiled. "Fate, I suppose. Or my stubbornness."

"I've never been more grateful." He chuckled, then reached his hands behind her and drew her nearer until his face was buried between her thighs, and he was breathing her in, placing small butterfly kisses on the very heat of her.

Jaime's legs trembled, her knees threatening to buckle. She grasped his shoulders for balance, a whimper escaping her. How could she be expected to concentrate on standing when he was doing that?

Lorne stood then, taking away the worry she had for her stability, and lifted her by her bottom. As he did so, her legs instinctively circled his waist. She gasped at the feel of rough breeches against her sex, then felt her insides flutter at the hardness encased beneath as it rubbed against her most sensitive place.

"Oh, Lorne," she murmured, kissing his neck, feeling the quickened pulse beneath her tongue as she mimicked what he'd done to her.

"Naughty lass," he groaned. Lorne laid her out on the bed, then knelt on the floor, his hands pressing her thighs wider as he looked at her.

"Please," she murmured.

He grinned. "Ye need no' beg, lass, for I have no plans to waylay this decadent treat." And then he placed his lips there, his wicked tongue stroking along her folds until he reached that tight knot of euphoria.

Jaime's fingers curled into the coverlet, her head thrown back in pleasure as he swirled and licked and sucked. He took his time tormenting her. Fast then slow, and then he'd pull away until she begged him to come back. Over and over, until at last, that blessed peak descended upon her, shattering her insides. Her legs shook violently as her body exploded in pleasure. Back bowed, hips thrust forward. Oh, it was heaven.

When she was finally able to open her eyes, it was to watch Lorne take off his breeches, his male organ springing free of the confines. She had thought she'd be frightened of it when she finally did see it, having only felt it before when he rubbed it against her. However, Lorne's body did nothing but make her want more. She beckoned for him, and he didn't hesitate climbing over her, between her thighs. He rested on an elbow, his face near hers, his warm, thick shaft probed with scorching delight at her center.

"Are ye ready?" he asked.

His fingers danced over her thigh, to her pulsing core, and he slipped one inside of her. She lifted her hips, arched her back and moaned. Another finger dipped inside, stretching her most deliciously.

"Aye," she whimpered.

There was that wicked grin again. "Ye are, my love." Lorne took hold of his length and slid it along her wet folds until he lodged at her entrance. "This may hurt, but only a little, I hope."

He kissed her then, stroking his tongue along hers, a soft moan on his lips as he surged forward, breaking the barrier of her entrance, claiming her body as he seized her mouth. She cried out at the sudden intrusion, at the small pinch of pain. While his body stilled on top of hers, inside of her, his mouth continued to work, kissing her with such passion she soon forgot the discomfort of their joining.

"Are ye all right?" He hovered over her, eyes locked on hers.

"Verra," Jaime said with a smile.

"Good." He kissed her again, then trailed his lips down her neck as he started to move. He swirled his tongue over her nipple, sucked, licked. His hips pulled back, then pushed forward again and again while his mouth and hands seemed to be everywhere.

Jaime spread her legs wider, her eyes open in surprise at the pleasant sensations rippling from within. She'd not expected it to feel so good...so different than his mouth on her. It was an altered, deeper pleasure.

With her arms and legs wrapped around her husband, Jaime let him take her to unknown lands. His body was magic. Every second heightened her pleasure. She gasped, moaned, and he did the same, sharing in the heady sensations. The way her pleasure had intensified with his mouth on her started all over again.

She clung to him, her hips rising to meet his thrusts. Lorne's pace increased, his breath on her neck coming faster and faster, sparking even newer heights inside her. She could barely catch her breath before another gasp of bliss was pushing all the air in her lungs back out again.

Just when she thought it couldn't get any better, she reached her climax. A cry of pleasure echoed from her throat. Everything tightened within her and out of her, and Lorne groaned loudly as her body spasmed around him. He thrust harder, faster, and then he too was crying out her name.

"Oh, Jaime, my love."

They rode the waves of ecstasy together, their breaths coming in pants, their bodies slick from exertion, until he collapsed, rolling to his side and pulling her with him.

Lorne kissed to her tenderly on the forehead, and his arm tucked protectively around her. "I hope I did no' hurt ye."

"Oh, no, ye did the exact opposite." She stroked the side of his face and smiled. "So far ye've proved me wrong about my thoughts on marriage, although to be fair I had no' taken into account this side of things. And though I've no experience, I must imagine ye are quite good at what ye're doing."

Lorne chuckled. "I love ye, Jaime Hardheaded Andrewson Gordon."

"Oh, goodness, I'd no' realized my new name yet. 'Tis a good, strong name."

"And goes perfectly with a good, strong woman."

Jaime sighed and snuggled closer. "I love ye, my husband."

🙊 17 🙈

Lorne woke before dawn, a habit he'd embraced well before he'd had to dodge bombs and his captors. However, what surprised him this morning was waking to an empty bed the day after getting married.

He bolted upright, afraid that it had all been a dream.

"Jaime?" he called, but there was no answer from the adjoining dressing room.

Lorne shoved aside the coverlet and rose. Splashed some water on his face and dressed in breeches and a shirt. No doublet, as he didn't often dress formally when at Dunrobin since he spent much of his day working with his people in the fields, farms or stables. He would have preferred his kilt, but that required more time to assemble than the breeches at the moment.

In the great hall, he found his wife sitting at the far end of the table, though not at the head, sipping a cup of tea and reading. There was a low fire in the hearth, crackling and popping. The thick walls muffled distant sounds of the servants working. Mungo stood by the door leading to the kitchens and nodded at Lorne's greeting.

Jaime glanced up when she saw him and smiled. "Good morning." She held up the book. "I hope ye do no' mind I borrowed this from your library. I've always loved The Iliad."

"One of my favorites. May I join ye?"

"Aye. Of course." She set down her book to pour him some tea.

"Ye did no' need to stop reading on my account." He pressed a kiss to her lips when she turned to look up at him, and his body stirred with renewed desire. They'd made love several times during the night, and each time was better and better. And he would have liked very much to swipe away the tea things, dismiss Mungo, and make love to her right then and there.

Reluctantly, he pulled away to slide into a chair beside her. "Ye're up early."

She grinned over her teacup. "I've always been so."

Lorne was pleasantly surprised to find that they had that in common. "Would ye like to ride with me? I tend to do so first thing, before attending other business."

"I would love to. It's been so long since I've been atop a horse."

"Then ye're in luck. We have one of the best stables in the Highlands."

Mrs. Blair arrived moments later with their breakfast. Eggs, bacon and freshly baked bread, toasted and smothered in butter. They both ate with gusto, and when they finished, he led her out to the stable.

Lorne's favorite horse was still in Edinburgh, as he'd not wanted to torment the poor beast with a trip on the high seas, but he had plenty of other stock to choose from.

"Were the horses a part of your deal?" he asked. It didn't look like there'd been any depletion of the stable.

"Nay, only the furnishings."

Lorne had been hoping she'd say the opposite. "I suppose

it only gives credence to our hypothesis that my brother planned to maintain control of the castle all along. Otherwise, he'd have made certain to take the horses. They're worth a fortune."

"I would say so."

Lorne chose a large, black steed, while Jaime acquainted herself with several mares until she found the right one. A dappled gray who gingerly tasted the apple Jaime held out. They waited for the stable lads to get their mounts saddled, which didn't take long. Then they were off, riding over the grounds and toward the village so he might greet his people properly, something he'd not been able to do on his previous journey.

Lorne watched the way her arse rose deliberately up and down, her thighs clutching the sides of the horse. She might not have been on a horse lately, but she'd not lost her skill. Hell, he wouldn't mind if she rode him that way, and his body responded hotly to the idea. Blood pooling in his groin and pressing uncomfortably against his breeches. Again, he was annoyed he'd not taken the time to put on his kilt. He cleared his throat, trying to gain back a measure of control before he stopped their ride and pulled her onto his lap. "Ye're a verra good rider. Where did ye learn?"

"Thank ye." Jaime glanced behind at him, her brown eyes sparkling with joy. "In Ireland, actually. I'm afraid my parents never let me ride in London or Edinburgh, where we spent most of our time. But when we went to Ireland, I took great pleasure in the moors."

"Do ye miss Ireland?"

"I've been too busy to miss it. But now that I'm here, I think so, a little bit."

"Understandable."

"And ye, did ye miss riding?" She slowed so that they were riding beside each other.

"Verra much. The exercises I do in my gymnasium keep my upper body in shape and hone my balance, but riding, there is something different about how it works the legs. The arse." He chuckled when she made a pretense of peering behind him at his rear.

"Indeed. My bottom will likely be sore later."

"I'm more than happy to help ye with that."

"I bet ye are." She passed him a wicked grin he couldn't help returning. "My mother often said that men did no' like a woman with a round bottom and that riding horses would give me one."

"Your mother is wrong on both accounts," Lorne said.

"I agree. She had a lot of...ideas." Jaime rolled her eyes. "I miss her though and should no' talk ill of the dead. But she and I...we had a troublesome relationship, to say the least. After Shanna's great disappointment, Mother was ten times harsher and more critical in my debut and subsequent seasons. Her ideas of what the perfect wife and debutante should be did no' exactly align with mine."

"They sound more like criticisms than ideas if ye do no' mind me saying."

"They often were, aye."

"But ye survived."

"Oh." Her face blanched, then quickly colored red. She reached over, her delicate fingers stroking his arm. "How can I ever think what happened to me was a hardship when ye have been through infinitely more."

Lorne shifted his reins to one hand, captured her hand where she touched him, and brought it to his lips. "Och, love, we all experience hardships in our way, and I would never compare myself to ye, nor take away the validity of any pain ye might have felt. I'm only sorry I could no' have been there to spare your feelings. I, for one, adore your independence, cleverness and mind for business."

She grinned, squeezing his hand before returning to her reins. "Thank ye. And that is why I agreed to marry ye." She cocked her head to the side, thoughtful. "I wonder if my mother's way of parading us and berating us was one of the reasons Shanna felt the need to...find love elsewhere?"

"Ye mean to say it was no' because of me?" He winged a doubtful brow.

"Oh, it was no' your doing, Lorne. Else I would no' have fallen in love with ye all those years ago. Ye possess many qualities that are attractive to a young lass, as well as a more mature one."

Lorne slowed his horse, and Jaime followed suit, looking at him with a puzzled expression.

"What is it?" she asked.

But his throat was tight with need, with emotion, and he didn't know precisely how to convey himself in words. So Lorne seized her reins and eased their mounts closer until her knee brushed his, their thighs pressed together, and then he touched her chin and drew her in for a kiss. This was a much better way to express what he felt. Adoration, infatuation, happiness, desire. Saints, but he relished kissing her, the feel of her lips on his. The way she eagerly kissed him back. The little whimpers she made in the back of her throat reminded him of how she enthusiastically made love.

They broke apart when he was reaching for her hip to drag her on top of him, both of them panting, wanting. He couldn't wait. Didn't want to go back to the castle when they'd yet to reach the village. He needed her. Now. His wife —his love.

"Come here." Lorne led her into a copse of trees and practically leapt off his horse. He lifted Jaime from her mount, holding her steady against him as he kissed her hard.

"What are we doing?" she murmured against his lips.

"I'm going to make love to my wife."

"Here? In broad daylight?" Jaime pulled away to stare up at the sky and then around them as if assessing who might see.

"Damn right." Lorne didn't wait for her to ask any more questions; instead, he captured her mouth in another searing kiss. His blood fired with the enthusiasm in which she kissed him back. He was hard, hot, and utterly consumed by her.

Lorne laid out the plaid blanket he always kept rolled on his horse and settled his wife upon it, hovering over her, staring at the way the light that broke through the trees made little gold flecks sparkle in the brown irises of her eyes.

Jaime surprised him, however, when she pushed against his chest until he lifted and then promptly shoved him onto his back.

"I want to try it like this," she said. "With me on top. It can be done, right?"

"Och, aye, lass." How could he deny her? Or himself?

She lifted her skirts until they were bunched around her thighs and hips, the heat of her sex searing through his breeches. Lorne groaned and hurried to undo the front of his breeches. At last he was free, his engorged shaft pressing hotly to her slick heat.

"God, ye feel good," he groaned.

With a hand on her hip and another on her breasts, Lorne thrust upward. Their bodies fit together as if they were made for each other. They both cried out, Jaime's head falling back.

"Show me what to do," she said.

"Ye already know." He gripped her hips and encouraged her to ride him.

And oh, was his wife a quick learner. Jaime rolled her hips, undulating back and forth, driving him wild. Over and over. Her breasts bounced within the confines of her gown but free from the corsets she refused to wear. Lorne gripped her breast, tugged her bodice down enough to free her nipple, a beautiful pink in the sunlight. He lifted enough to take her nipple into his mouth, sucking the hardened, sweet flesh.

Jaime gasped and cried out, riding him faster. He was going to finish before she even got close at this rate. All the years of pent-up desire was to blame. Or else it was this beautiful nymph he'd married.

Lorne reached between their bodies, finding her nub of pleasure and stroking as she rocked back and forth, up and down. She gasped, her thighs clamping hard against his hips, making him increase not only the pace of his fingers but the thrusts of his hips. Her cries of release were muffled as she bit her lip to keep from alerting all of the forest to their deeds. Watching her climax was one of the most stunning things he'd ever witnessed. The way her lips parted, how her cheeks were flushed, her eyes blinking open in surprise and then slamming closed as she release. He could watch her all day—wanted to watch her all the more—but already he'd held on longer than was humanly possible. Once he felt her body spasming around his, Lorne let go, flooding his seed inside her.

He collapsed back onto the blanket with a long, satisfied sigh.

"That was fun," Jaime said, staring down at him with a wide grin.

"Ye are fun, lass." He reached up and gave her nipple a light pinch before tucking her breast back into her bodice.

She laughed. "Now that is the first time I've ever heard someone say that." And with that, she bent over him, her hair cocooning their kiss.

The only problem was they could not be cocooned forever, nor could they remain in the woods. Soon their traitorous siblings would descend upon Dunrobin, and Lorne was certain the bliss they'd found would be shattered. He hoped not forever.

JAIME HAD LAIN AWAKE FOR WHAT FELT LIKE HOURS BEFORE she finally climbed out of bed and headed down to the kitchens. Those in the village had been so excited to have their chief return and been nothing but kind to her. They seemed genuinely excited to have a mistress back at the castle and for Dunrobin to once again be in Sutherland hands. But there had still not been any word of Shanna or Gordie, and Jaime was growing more concerned by the day for her nephew's welfare. She and Lorne had put plans in place, had a man following them, but still, she worried it wasn't enough.

And so, rather than toss around in bed, she did what she often did when she couldn't sleep. Jaime made a habit of baking. At midnight. Not only did it help to alleviate some of the nerves that barred her from sleeping, but it was often a surprise treat for the household to learn that she'd made them scones or biscuits, and they had one less chore to do in the morning.

A lady shouldn't bake—at least that was what her mother told her. After all, a lady had servants to do such mundane tasks. But what if a lady enjoyed baking? Her mother had always waved off her words as if that were the silliest thing she'd ever heard. Fortunately, the staff had often indulged Jaime when her mother wasn't around, and so at an early age, she'd gotten used to commandeering the kitchen in the middle of the night.

It took her some time to acquaint herself with the Dunrobin kitchens, which were much larger than any she'd ever been in before. The cook ran the kitchen in quite an orderly fashion, but eventually, she located the butter, flour, sugar and salt. The bowls and spoons. The rollers, the baking pans.

Jaime had dropped the last dollop of butter into a mixing

bowl when she heard a noise outside the kitchen. She paused. As it was the middle of the night, she was in her nightgown and wrapper. She'd not expected any of the servants to wake, not at this hour. Nor to find her basically undressed.

But there it was again, the sound. And then the door to the kitchen whooshed open, and Lorne stood on the threshold, taking her in. She sighed in relief and then in delight. He looked wickedly disheveled in the soft candlelight, hair tousled, no shirt, and his breeches barely done up. Jaime couldn't help licking her lips as she took him in. A slow grin curled one side of his mouth as he watched her.

"Found ye. What are ye doing?" he asked.

Jaime cocked a nonchalant shoulder as if this were totally normal. "Making shortbread."

"An interesting hour for such a task." He stepped into the kitchen, letting the door shut behind him.

"Ye'll get used to it."

He grinned. "I wonder, do ye ever sleep?"

"Sometimes." She laughed and then poured in the sugar and salt. "Want to stir?"

"Aye."

He came around the wide preparation table and pressed a kiss on her mouth. His fingers spread over hers as he took the large wooden spoon and then effortlessly mixed the sugar and butter—a task that required a lot more exertion and time for her.

"You make a verra good scullion," Jaime teased, poking him in the ribs and then thinking better of that gesture in favor of running her hands over his naked skin.

"I never knew baking was done in so…sensual a way," he teased as she trailed her fingers down his ribs, sliding over to his hip.

"Aye." Baking, she was certain, was never going to be the same again. Jaime circled to her husband's back and pressed her lips to his spine. A little shiver made his body tremble beneath her touch. She wrapped her arms around his middle and splayed on his taut abdomen. "And even better when ye are making sweets."

"Och, lass, if ye keep this up, I'll no' finish the task. Tell me what is next, I beg of ye."

"Now the flour." She reluctantly moved away from him to measure the exact amounts and then poured them into the sweetened butter mixture. "And stir again, duke, while I continue my exploration."

Suddenly, Jaime felt extremely adventurous—not to mention wicked. She sank to her knees and nudged Lorne back from the table enough that she could edge in front of him, her mouth level with his quickly expanding breeches. She glanced up at him, finding his gaze hungry for what she wanted.

"Och, lass, this is no' how Cook does it." He was trying to jest, but his voice was heavy with desire.

"Thank God," she teased, then tugged open the front of his breeches. She took his rigid shaft in hand, and kissed the very tip, lapping at him the way he liked, a trick she'd learned on their wedding night when he'd taught her how to pleasure him with her mouth.

She tormented him, growing bolder, swirling her tongue around the salty crown. Licking him from base to tip, and she then took him into her mouth, sliding her lips down. Lorne groaned, stiffening in pleasure.

Jaime stopped. "Do no' halt your stirring, duke, else I can no' continue."

"Och, nay, do no' stop." He stirred with renewed vigor.

She smiled around his eager erection and then took him deeper into her mouth. There was no way she was going to stop now. Not when the fun was just beginning. Up and down, slowly, she worked him into a frenzy until pieces of dough flicked onto her head as he stirred faster, in rhythm with the way his hips rocked into her mouth.

But before he found release, Lorne leapt backward and hauled her to her feet, then higher still as he sat her in a pile of flour on the preparation table, spread her thighs wide and thrust home.

She clung to him, a gasp of pleasure and a little laugh at his eagerness.

"Ye're a naughty duchess," he murmured against her ear.

"And this is how ye'll punish me."

"Aye, over and over."

And if by sending her body into one rollicking spasm after another was what he meant by punishment, Jaime took it with relish.

18

Lorne held Jaime's hand as they walked along the beach, their bare toes sinking into the sand, and the gentle laps of the North Sea washing over their feet. The day had been uneventful, to which they'd both been grateful as they'd spent the majority of it in pleasant company with each other, basking in newlywed bliss. Knowing that the peace of it was going to come crashing down on them soon seemed to make them both eager to soak it up.

Jaime let go of his hand as she bent to pick up a shell.

"As a wedding present, I think I shall build ye a bigger pier, my duchess. Perhaps even a dozen, so ye can bring every one of your ships to Dunrobin if ye choose." Lorne paused, looking out at the ocean, then turned back to his wife. "What say ye, sweetling?"

Jaime smiled up at him, lips parting to speak when above her head he saw the flag waving frantically from the top of the garden steps. The very one he'd asked Mungo to use as a signal if riders were approaching.

"We need to go. Now." Lorne gripped Jaime's hand and started to run, with her keeping stride beside him.

The delirious bubble of newly wedded bliss was effectively popped.

They hurried through the garden, both of their boots forgotten at the beach as they rushed to the castle before they were seen. Everyone knew the plan was to make it seem as though the castle was nearly deserted. They rushed up the stairs and through the door of the kitchens. The staff was in an uproar over the approach of a single rider.

That was interesting. Not a carriage or a trio. But a single. Had to be Jaime's investigator.

As they made their way to the great hall at the moment the single rider came through the gate, they learned it was indeed Mr. Bell. Jaime rushed to greet him, tugging him inside. There was a measure of relief at the wayward siblings not yet arriving, yet a heightened level of nerves.

"They will be here within a few hours, maybe less," the man said. "I passed them on the road to get here to warn ye."

"Thank ye, Mr. Bell. We are grateful for your devoted service," Jaime said. "We've had a room made up for ye and will send up a plate. Ye must be exhausted."

"I am grateful to Your Graces for your hospitality."

"'Tis us who are grateful," Lorne said. "Ye've been extremely instrumental in this whole affair."

"I am glad to be of service."

Mrs. Blair ushered the investigator up the stairs toward his guestroom.

When they were alone in Lorne's study, Jaime said, "There was a part of me that hoped none of this was true. That we'd find out we were wrong."

Lorne nodded grimly, pouring them each a small glass of whisky. "I know, lass, 'twas the same for me. I still can no' believe that my brother would do this. After all that I gave him, did for him."

Jaime linked her hand around his when he handed her the cup. "I verra much feel the same way."

The minutes ticked by like hours. They tried a game of chess, reading aloud from The Iliad, and when those distractions didn't take, they made love on his desk. At last, they were warned of an approaching carriage.

"He'd better have our ancestor's sword with him," Lorne muttered.

"What?"

Lorne glanced down at his beautiful bride. "He stole it when he left. A sword used by our ancestor, who fought alongside William Wallace in the War of Independence."

"My goodness. Why would he take that?" She wrinkled her nose.

"I have no idea."

Less than a minute later, voices were heard in the entryway as Mungo and Mrs. Blair greeted the newcomers. The voices of Gille and Shanna were distinctive, pinging painfully in his memory. He had a sudden realization that he'd heard the two of them talking, recognizing their voices before he'd entered that study to find them all those years ago. His mind had blocked out Gille's voice even then. But hearing them muffled together now, rather than seeing them, brought the memory swiftly and painfully back. Lorne gritted his teeth, and Jaime squeezed his hand.

"'Tis lucky for us that they chose betrayal," she said. "Else that would be your wife, and ye and I could never have been together."

"I'd never thought of it that way." He glanced down at her and smiled. "What a relief it is no' so. This is why I love ye. But I still will no' be easy to forgive."

As planned, the trio was ushered into the great hall, the main door blocked, and upon entry, they did not see Lorne and Jaime by the hearth, but the young lad did.

Gordie shrieked, "Aunt Jaime!" and rushed toward her, arms outstretched and a massive smile on his face.

Jaime knelt to catch him while Lorne stared, stunned at seeing a mirror image of himself. He did a double take, raking his memory for any moment he could have fathered the child. But he never made love to Shanna. Never so much as kissed the ungrateful, conniving wench. So how was it possible that the lad could bear such a resemblance?

Lorne returned his gaze to the couple by the door who stood equally stunned, faces pale at the sight of them, not having expected to find them there. At least their ruse had worked. The lad favored Gille. Before now, Lorne had not realized how much he and his half-brother were alike, always believing his brother to favor his stepmother rather than their shared father.

"Glad ye could finally join us," Lorne drawled out.

"Ye're alive." Gille's words sounded like an accusation. "And here."

"Clearly," Lorne said dryly. "And the two of ye have been scheming, it seems, for quite a long time." He glanced down pointedly at the child, then back up at them, the expression on his face as blank as he could make it, though he felt fire in his chest. A rage that wanted to be expressed through pounding fists.

"Well, ye can no' have it all, brother," Gille said. "Prodigal heir, favorite of the clan. I was tired of playing second fiddle, and so I fiddled with what was yours."

Shanna had the good sense to look appalled at that statement, but Lorne didn't react at all, even though his first instinct was to pummel Gille into the ground. Even now, the thorny blackguard showed no remorse for his actions.

"Och, do no' kid yourself," Lorne said. "That woman was never mine."

Shanna's mouth dropped open, an unladylike snort

popping out of it. "Jaime, are ye going to let him speak about me that way?"

Jaime, who'd been silent up to this point, let out a short, bitter laugh. "Ye can no' be serious."

Shanna's jaw dropped lower, her shock palpable.

"I'd close your mouth, else risk a bat flying in." Jaime pursed her lips, looking as ready for a fight as Lorne felt.

Lorne had never heard that kind of statement before, but it seemed to work as Shanna did close her mouth. The woman crossed her arms over her chest and glared at his duchess. Not that her misdirected anger made a difference. Jaime did not back down.

Lorne turned to Mungo. "Search their belongings for the Magnus sword."

Mungo nodded and left the room with Gille protesting loudly, "Do no' touch my things, ye mewling lapdog! Ye have no right—"

"Oh, brother," Lorne said, "do shut up. Ye're in no position to argue or negotiate. Ye're lucky I've no' had ye arrested."

Gille whipped back around, his cheeks ruddy with anger. "Arrested? For what crime?"

Lorne ticked off the reasons casually on his fingers. "Breach of contract, theft, embezzlement—the list goes on."

"Breach of contract?" Gille's arms flung about wildly, in danger of knocking into Shanna or the marble bust of King Robert the Bruce. "I've no contract with ye. Lies!"

Och, but this was going to be exhausting. Lorne wished it were already over. "Aye, but I had a contract with your wife, Shanna, and ye aided her in breaking it."

"All right, that is true. But nothing else. Not the castle. How can I be blamed for the theft of something that was my own?" This time the back of Gille's hand did come into contact with Robert the Bruce's nose, and his brother yanked his hand back, glaring at the bust as if it had bitten him on purpose.

"It was never yours." Lorne held out his arms. "I'm no' dead."

"This is preposterous." Gille rubbed his hand, a little bit of spittle flying from his mouth to land on his knuckle.

"As is your behavior," Lorne said, trying to keep his tone bored. "Some things never change, I suppose. Were ye no' given everything ye wanted?"

"No. I was no' and I resent ye for that," Gille had the audacity to say. "Even when ye had gone to war, and I was left in charge, the blasted people of this medieval clan would no' defer to me. It was always 'What would Lorne do? What would Lorne say? That's no' how Lorne does it.'" He quoted these queries in a singsong, nasally voice that made Lorne want to knock him out. "One grows rather tired of such idiotic statements."

"Or perhaps ye were the idiot, as is evidenced now." Lorne tried to convey his disinterest, which was an effort in willpower. Every inch of him wanted to break out into a furious diatribe. But his brother was a stubborn fool and a self-righteous one at that. Anything Lorne said, Gille would not accept. His brother only wanted to hear what he had in his own mind, and men like that could not be contended with. Best to let it lie where it was and state only the facts.

Lorne glanced down at Jaime, who had a protective arm around her nephew, and the lad looked back and forth between them all, something vulnerable in his eyes.

Mungo returned then with the sword, and without Lorne having to tell him, placed it back where it belonged.

"My duchess still holds the deed to the castle," Lorne said. "So even as ye hoped to gain the cash and the lands, ye were gravely mistaken in that step, beyond the blatant reality that ye could no' have legally sold my property."

"Duchess?" Gille sputtered. "Ye married her?"

"Ye little thief," Shanna hissed at Jaime.

This time it was Jaime who answered, sounding rather wearied herself. "Oh, Shanna, do no' be ridiculous. I know the truth of what ye did, how ye spurned him for half a man. What was there to steal when ye'd already run off with your lover? Lorne came to me willingly. And as he stated, he was never yours."

"Half a man?" Gille was practically purple at that insult. "I should have paid those bastards twice as much to make ye disappear," Gille shouted, stabbing his finger toward Lorne.

Paid to make him disappear... That was a surprise. "Pardon?" Lorne blinked in shock.

Shanna's head whipped toward her lover, and she slapped his arm. Gille blanched, clearly regretting saying those words aloud.

"What he means is, he would have paid for ye to disappear," Shanna said. "But of course, he would never do that because it would be wrong. Right?"

"He did it," Gordie said, his small voice steady. "I heard him say he did on the ship."

"Ye little bastard," Gille shouted toward the lad. Fists bunched, he marched forward.

However, Lorne need not have punched his brother in the mouth because Mungo did it for him, knocking Gille to the ground with Shanna screaming in frantic panic beside him.

"Sorry, Your Grace, but it could no' be helped."

"Completely understand. He deserved it. And if ye'd no' have done it, I would," Lorne said. "Ye have my permission to do so again should the situation require it."

"My pleasure, Your Grace." Mungo bowed his head, then stepped back to his spot by the door.

Shanna glanced to Lorne, to Jaime and her son. "How could ye allow him to be beaten?"

"How could ye see nothing wrong with him paying for Lorne to be imprisoned? For him being about to beat your child for telling the truth? Shanna, ye are astounding in your selfishness."

"My selfishness?" Shanna screeched, turning as purple and ugly as her husband. How had Lorne ever found her pretty? "What about ye? Ye stole everything from me."

"I did no such thing." Jaime sounded exasperated now. This stupid argument was taking a toll on her.

"Our parents, the inheritance, the business, my husband. My child." This time, her pointed glare landed on the lad who sank deeper against Jaime. "There, you have it." Shanna pointed accusingly at Jaime. "He prefers ye, always has. I want to wipe that pitying look off your face."

"I see," Jaime said, without even a spark of the anger her sister had just spewed at her. "Well, that's unfortunate, Shanna, for all I can do is pity ye. Legions of women were jealous of ye. Daughter of a lord, a castle in Ireland as your dowry, the attentions of a duke. London and Edinburgh seasons. The best gowns and slippers. And even when ye fell from grace, our parents allowed ye to stay at their Irish castle anyway. Your exile was the same as someone else's fantasy. Yet, it was no' good enough. Even when I, feeling awful that ye had been ill-used, believed your lies, and brought ye back to Edinburgh. Fed ye, clothed ye, spoiled ye all over again. And to what purpose—all so ye could go behind my back. Ye might as well have stabbed me with the Sutherland sword."

Jaime shook her head as if the things she said were the saddest in the world. Then, her gaze directed at her sister—the pity gone, replaced by strength and by authority. "But hear this now—ye will return to Ireland. Ye and your lover. And ye will no' set foot in Scotland again. Gordie is going to remain here with Lorne and me. We will raise him as our own —as the son ye proclaimed belonged to Lorne."

"Ye canna do that! He is no' the father of my son. I never touched him." Shanna looked ready to attack them all, snarling like a rabid dog.

"Pity ye should have claimed such for the last decade then. All of society believes he is the duke's son. It is only proper for a duke to claim his son and take him from the mother."

"Gille, say something," Shanna begged her lover, who was now rousing on the floor.

"Oh, do let the little welp go already, Shanna. Ye told me yourself ye loathed being a mother and I can no' abide to look at his judging eyes another minute. He's more Lorne's son than anyone else's, sharing that same disdainful expression. Who cares if I was the one to plant the seed?"

Lorne wanted to pummel Gille into unconsciousness again. He didn't even recognize the man as his brother, so foul and cruel as he was.

"I want to stay here," Gordie said, his voice even as he blinked up at Jaime and then at Lorne. "Does no' anyone care to ask me? Aunt Jaime, please, I want to stay."

Lorne was surprised at how much the lad did remind him of himself. Even at the tender age of eight, he was not afraid to make his desires known.

"And so ye shall," Jaime said, then glanced at Lorne. "Right?"

"Aye, of course," Lorne said, keeping his eyes on the lad. He ruffled his dark hair, eliciting a tentative smile from the child. "Mrs. Blair, would ye please escort Lord Gille and his wife to their chamber? Mungo will accompany ye to make certain everything goes well. We wish ye a good rest, since you're going to need it for your journey back to Ireland tomorrow. And thank ye ever so much for returning the sword and the lad."

"That's all I'll be returning to ye, ye bastard," Gille

shouted. "Son of a whore..." He continued spewing vulgarity that Lorne only blinked at.

"Pardon me, Your Grace," Mungo interjected. "But I do believe there is a large chest in your study that also belongs to ye. Found it in the carriage. And if I may beat the man once more?"

"Ye stole my money!" Gille screeched.

Lorne wanted to shout, "Aye, please shut him up," but Gille was so loud, it took all his calm not to start bellowing himself.

"I've heard quite enough of this," Lorne muttered. "Thank ye, Mungo. That will no' be necessary this time. Gille, if ye do no' want to spend the night in the dungeon, I suggest ye either leave or go with Mrs. Blair to your chamber."

"We are leaving." Gille grabbed Shanna by the hand. "Now. And ye'll pay for this."

"I highly doubt that. For if ye come after me, my wife, or the lad, I will have ye tossed into the closest jail cell and make certain ye rot in it forever."

Shanna, for her part, did not argue at all. She sniffed the air as some of the more snobbish ladies at court and whirled on her heel, marching out of Dunrobin much as she'd marched around society—high-and-mighty, even when brought low.

Jaime took Lorne's hand in hers, glancing up at him, and mouthed, "Thank ye."

He winked down at her, certain that they'd done the right thing. As the big door to the castle slammed closed, he was not the only one to breathe a sigh of relief. Wee Gordie looked ready to collapse at his liberation.

"Ye promise never to let me go again?" Gordie asked Jaime.

"I swear on my life, sweet lad." She pulled him in for a hug and kissed his forehead.

Lorne gathered them both up in his arms, holding them until Mungo returned to signal that Gille and Shanna had gone.

"Gordie, how do ye feel about boxing?" he asked.

The lad's face lit up, and he leapt away from Jaime, holding up his hands in the perfect stance. "I learned a lot at the docks."

Lorne grinned. "I think we're going to get along fine then." He ruffled the lad's hair. "Now run along with Mrs. Blair. She'll see ye set up in a room of your own."

Gordie ran off as if he had not a care in the world, and Lorne wished adults could bounce back so readily. When he was gone, Lorne put his arms around Jaime, and she sagged against his chest.

"Ye showed great restraint," she said.

"Only for your sake, my love. I would have very much liked to teach him a lesson. As it is, he will never understand the gift we've given him."

"They do no' deserve our kindness."

"Nay, they do no'." He tilted her chin up, pressed his mouth to hers. "But as I often reminded myself when I was imprisoned—the best way to beat your enemy is to succeed. And, my darling wife, we have done that in spades."

Jaime wrapped her arms around his shoulders, her fingers threading into his hair as she tugged him down for another kiss. "I love ye."

EPILOGUE

Edinburgh, Scotland
Several weeks later

The gymnasium at Sutherland Gate was alive with shouts and laughter. In the ring, Jaime circled her husband, while on the ground, surrounding them, stood their onlookers.

Gordie cheered them on, along with Malcolm, Alec, Euan, Mungo, MacInnes and even Mrs. Blair and Alison, who fretted in unison.

This was one of Lorne and Jaime's very favorite pastimes —besides the other activities they liked to enjoy in private, which were also as stimulating and vigorous. And tonight would be the icing on the cake—for they were going to have their ball on the ship and give the Shanna a new name—the Emilia.

"Ye've been practicing," Lorne accused with a wide grin.

"Gordie makes an excellent sparring partner." She feinted left and then gave Lorne a swift punch on the right.

Lorne laughed and jumped back, as he always did when she hit him. He claimed they didn't hurt, but she'd never tell him she didn't hit as hard as she could, just like he never connected at all. The only thing he did to take her down was wrap his arms around her and pin her either upright against him or down on the ring mat. And when in private, all he had to do was kiss her, and she lost all sense of time and place, sinking into pleasure.

They'd been back in Edinburgh for the last two weeks, after having stayed at Dunrobin an extra week getting Gordie settled and enjoying a bit of privacy themselves before their new lives would begin. It had also given their households time to move her belongings into Sutherland Gate. But rather than sell her flat, she kept it as an inheritance for her nephew.

Emilia had been a wonderful asset for Andrewson Shipping while Jaime was away. Jaime was so impressed that she added another woman to her staff, Emilia's sister. Anastasia was doing splendidly, and Jaime was glad for the extra help now that she had Gordie to take care of. And one day, she'd have children of her own.

But that didn't keep her from coming into the office each day, often with the young lad in tow. After all, Jaime had decided that one day, the company would be his. Lorne had even taken an interest in helping, and she'd been glad to show him the ropes too. It made talking about her plans much easier if he actually knew what she was referring to. And besides, Andrewson Shipping had always been a family company. Lorne and Gordie were her family now. And by extension, so were Emilia and Anastasia.

The thump of Lorne's feet on the boxing mat brought her back to reality. He came barreling toward her, arms outstretched, ready to wrap her up. But Jaime bounced and twirled out of his way, a fake kick on his rear as she managed to get behind him. Their onlookers cheered and laughed at that. Taking a second too long to smile at her audience was her downfall, however.

Always quick on his feet, Lorne spun and enfolded an arm around her waist, lifting her into the air.

"Got ye," he said triumphantly, spinning with her held against him.

"And so ye did." She planted a kiss on his lips, all too swift with the company present.

"Who is next?" Lorne said to the crowd as he set her down on her feet. "They get to go against me, as I've won."

Alec raised his hand. "I would have much rather gone against your wife, but I suppose ye'll do."

Jaime laughed. "Perhaps the duke will go easy on ye and simply hoist ye into the air rather than land a blow."

Alec snickered, climbing up through the rings. "Do ye think he'll expect me to kiss him too?"

"He might."

"Try it and die," Lorne threatened with a mock growl.

Jaime gave Lorne one last kiss and then scrambled out of the ring to stand with her nephew.

"I call winner," Gordie shouted with glee.

Jaime smiled on with love at her new family, her new friends. In the grand scheme of things, she was the winner in the room. Before Lorne had come bursting back into her life, she'd not realized how truly miserable she was. Living only for work, for the comfort of an ungrateful sister, not partaking in the simple pleasures of life. Or boxing, for that matter, a sport she'd not even known she liked until Lorne.

Now her eyes were open, and she was filled with love and joy. With a bit of planning and some help, she intended to live every day the way she wanted—to the fullest. And with her heart bursting.

Jaime's gaze settled on her husband as he bounced around the ring, dodging, blocking, passing blows. He was more handsome to her now than he'd been a decade ago. And she couldn't help smiling, a soft sigh on her lips as the crowd let out a whoop.

This was her dream come true.

❧

If you enjoyed **RETURN OF THE SCOT***, please spread the word by leaving a review on the site where you purchased your copy, or a reader site such as Goodreads! I love to hear from readers! Visit me on Facebook:* https://www.facebook.com/elizaknightfiction. I'm also on Instagram @ElizaKnightFiction and Twitter: @ElizaKnight *Many thanks!*

Stay tuned for more of Eliza's brand new Scottish Regency series — *SCOTS OF HONOR!*

HIGHLAND WAR HEROES REBUILDING THEIR LIVES GRAPPLE with ladies forging their own paths—who will win?

Regency Scotland comes alive in the vibrant and sexy new SCOTS OF HONOR series by USA Today bestselling author Eliza Knight. Scottish military heroes, who want nothing more than to lay low after the ravages of war in 19th century France, find their Highland homecomings vastly contradict their simple desires. Especially when they meet the feisty lasses who are tenacious enough to take them on, and show them just what they've been missing out of life. In battle they can't be beaten, but in love, they all find the ultimate surrender.

Return of the Scot
The Scot is Hers

Taming the Scot

Want to read more Scottish romance novels by Eliza?

Check out her Stolen Bride Series!

The Highlander's Temptation
The Highlander's Reward
The Highlander's Conquest
The Highlander's Lady
The Highlander's Warrior Bride
The Highlander's Triumph
The Highlander's Sin
Wild Highland Mistletoe (a Stolen Bride winter novella)
The Highlander's Charm (a Stolen Bride novella)
A Kilted Christmas Wish – a contemporary Holiday spin-off

How about some fierce Highland rebels? Check out Eliz'as Prince Charlie's Angels series!

The Rebel Wears Plaid
Truly Madly Plaid
You've Got Plaid

ABOUT THE AUTHOR

Eliza Knight is a *USA Today* bestselling author of many historical adventures. Escape to Scotland for irresistible heroes, courageous heroines and daring escapades. Join Eliza (sometimes as E.) on riveting journeys that cross landscapes around the world. While not reading, writing or researching for her latest book, she chases after her three children. In her spare time (if there is such a thing...) she likes daydreaming, wine-tasting, traveling, hiking, staring at the stars, watching movies, shopping and visiting with family and friends. She lives atop a small mountain with her own knight in shining armor, three princesses and two very naughty puppies.

Visit Eliza at http://www.elizaknight.com or her historical blog History Undressed: www.historyundressed.com. Sign up for her newsletter to get news about books, events, contests and sneak peaks! http://eepurl.com/CSFFD

- facebook.com/elizaknightfiction
- twitter.com/elizaknight
- instagram.com/elizaknightfiction
- bookbub.com/authors/eliza-knight
- goodreads.com/elizaknight

Printed in Great Britain
by Amazon